PLAYING
IT SAFE

ALSO BY ASHLEY WEAVER

PLAYING IT SAFE

An Electra McDonnell Novel

A S H L E Y   W E A V E R

MINOTAUR
BOOKS
NEW YORK

First published in the United States by Minotaur Books, an imprint of St. Martin's Publishing Group

www.minotaurbooks.com

Designed by Omar Chapa

Library of Congress Cataloging-in-Publication Data

Names: Weaver, Ashley, author.
Title: Playing it safe / Ashley Weaver.
Description: First edition. | New York : Minotaur Books, 2023. | Series: An Electra McDonnell novel ; [3]
Identifiers: LCCN 2022056022 | ISBN 9781250885876 (hardcover) | ISBN 9781250885883 (ebook)
Subjects: LCSH: World War, 1939–1945—Fiction. | LCGFT: Detective and mystery fiction. | War fiction. | Spy fiction. | Novels.
Classification: LCC PS3623.E3828 P57 2023 | DDC 813/.6—dc23/ eng/20221212
LC record available at https://lccn.loc.gov/2022056022

First Edition: 2023

10 9 8 7 6 5 4 3 2 1

For my aunt Darlene Baskin,
who shares my love of mysteries and makes the best bundt cake.

And in memory of Angela Lansbury,
who gave us our favorite fictional mystery writer, J. B. Fletcher.

PLAYING IT SAFE

CHAPTER ONE

LONDON
4 OCTOBER 1940

It's a strange thing living with the sensation that the world might at any moment fall down around your ears.

I'd done a lot of dangerous—to say nothing of illegal—things in my lifetime, but residing in London during the German Blitz was in an altogether different class.

The bombs had fallen every night for nearly a month straight, and it didn't appear there was any end in sight. Every night, I wondered how we could possibly manage to make it through, and every morning, we got up and waded through the rubble, put things together as best we could, and did our best to carry on. Would there be anything of London left after all of this? Sometimes I wondered.

There had started to be a horrible sort of routine to it: knowing what to expect, knowing that nightfall would bring death and destruction, but being powerless to stop it. Our dread grew as the twilight faded, and then, sure as clockwork, the sound of the air-raid sirens.

It was enough to try the steadiest of nerves.

On this particular afternoon, a bit at loose ends, I was glad I had plans to fill the hours until the dreaded dusk descended. I was meeting Felix, my sort-of beau, at the cinema. I hoped Felix's pleasant company and the comfort of a familiar picture would do something to draw my thoughts away from the grimness of the world we were living in.

I pulled on my favorite blue jumper over my white blouse and tweed skirt and left my flat, walking along the path past the large kitchen garden—thinner now that autumn was upon us—to the big house that sat in front of it. That was where my Uncle Mick lived, where I had grown up with my cousins, Colm and Toby.

Looking over all of us had been Nacy Dean, the housekeeper who had been more like a mother to us, as three motherless young children. It was she who I sought out as I entered the house.

"Nacy?"

"In the kitchen, love!"

Nacy could almost always be found in the kitchen, and the house always smelled wonderful as a result. Even rationing couldn't beat Nacy Dean. She was a wizard in the kitchen.

"What are you cooking?" I asked.

"Just a bit of stew," she said, stirring the bubbling pot on the hob. "Something I threw together from what I found at the shops today."

"Wonderful. I can't wait to eat later," I said. "I just popped in to let you know I'm going to the cinema."

"Alone?"

"Felix is meeting me there when he's finished at the hospital." Felix had just taken a job doing office work at the hospital. He was working long hours, and we'd had very little time to spend together recently.

"You will be back before dark, won't you?" Nacy asked.

"Of course."

"Do take care, Ellie."

"I will," I promised. Nacy had always fussed over us when we were little, and it hadn't stopped now that we were grown. The war had made it worse, of course, but she'd done it well before the Germans started making trouble.

I left the house and set out for the Odeon on Church Road. Ever since this cinema had opened the previous year, it had been one of my favorite places for an evening's entertainment. It was usually less crowded than the cinema near the Tube station, and, besides that, I liked the way the Odeon looked. A brick building with a rounded, turret-like entrance, it had always looked a bit like a castle in a fairy tale to me. I blamed my Irish blood for these flights of fancy.

Like the rest of the city, the Odeon was doing its best to soldier on. That meant that shows were still running, though they generally closed in time for us to get home before the nightly air raids.

We'd had several bombs dropped in Hendon, but thus far the Odeon stood unscathed. I was learning—as we all were, I suspected—that it was important to enjoy things while we could and not think too much about the future.

I reached the cinema, purchased a ticket, and slipped into my favorite seat near the back. It seemed I wasn't the only one who'd decided on an hour or two of escape; there was a decent-sized audience this afternoon. I noticed several uniformed young men with their girls.

Felix wouldn't be here until halfway through the film, but that was all right. We'd seen it before. They were showing an older film: *Bachelor Mother,* starring Ginger Rogers making a go of it without Fred Astaire. It was lighthearted and amusing, just the sort of thing I was in the mood for.

Of course, there were the newsreels to watch first. If the movie to come would be a distraction, the newsreel was a grim reminder of what I was trying to be distracted from.

It was hard to see scenes of torpedoes exploding near battle-ships in the Channel, or the destruction caused by battle, or soldiers marching away from home to do their bit. It always made me think of my cousin Toby, who'd been missing since the Battle of Dunkirk. With each passing day with no word from the army that he'd been listed as a prisoner, it became more likely that he was dead.

As I usually did when thinking melancholy thoughts about Toby, I pushed the thoughts away, determined to keep hoping until there was some proof that no hope remained.

Focusing on the screen through eyes that threatened to cloud with tears, I concentrated on the film and soon found myself caught up in the plight of Polly Parrish, a young woman mistaken for the mother of an orphaned child with various uproarious results.

The film had been playing for a short while when I noticed a shadowy movement at the edge of my row, and then someone sat down in the seat directly beside me.

I turned, smiling to greet Felix. He was here earlier than I'd expected.

My smile faltered when I realized it was not Felix. It was, instead, Major Ramsey, the intelligence officer with whom my family and I had aligned to make use of our safe-cracking skills for king and country.

The last time I'd seen the major had been the morning after the second night of the Blitz, a night in which we'd robbed a bank and caught a ring of spies. Though I'd thought of him frequently over the intervening days, a cinema was one of the last places I would have expected to encounter him.

"What are you doing here?" I asked, rudely foregoing a greeting.

"Good afternoon, Miss McDonnell," he replied, his eyes on the screen. "You don't suppose I enjoy Ginger Rogers films?"

"No." I expected the major had neither the time nor the temperament to enjoy pictures, but if he did, he'd have gone to see one weightier than this. A war film, perhaps. Something with gravitas.

We sat in silence for a few moments as the film played. I waited for him to speak, the possible reasons for his unexpected appearance darting through my brain, but he didn't seem inclined to do so.

"You didn't come here to see this picture," I pressed at last.

"No. I need to speak to you. I went to the house, and Mrs. Dean told me where you'd gone."

Of course she had. Nacy had a bit of a crush on the major, and she was forever trying to push the two of us together. As fond as she was of Felix, in her eyes, he couldn't compete with an army major who was nephew to an earl.

"As my time is limited, I sought you out," he finished.

"Do we need to step outside?" I asked.

"No, this is as good a place as any. In fact, casual situations, such as this one, are an ideal way to pass along information. I don't want to draw more attention to you than necessary."

The implication was a bit alarming, but I was thrilled rather than frightened. It was clear that he meant to involve me in his work again, and I couldn't have been happier. I felt as though I'd been twiddling my thumbs since the last assignment, and, now more than ever, I had the urge to be useful.

His next words confirmed my hopeful assumption. "I have another job for you."

"What is it?" I asked, trying to keep my excitement tamped down. It was best, I knew, to maintain proper professional poise in such situations, even glad as I was to have a job to do.

"All in good time, Miss McDonnell. We're going to draw attention to ourselves if we keep talking without pause."

I did notice the glance the woman at the end of the row had

shot at us, annoyed at our whispering until she caught sight of the major. Now she seemed to be watching us with interest. Granted, the major did make a good impression, what with his impressive height and build and the irritating perfection of the features on his stern, handsome face.

"It's going to look rather odd for us to sit here stiffly watching the picture," I pointed out.

I thought he would agree that we should step into the lobby to talk. Instead, he surprised me by sliding his arm along the back of my seat and leaning toward me. "Is this better?" he asked in a low voice.

I looked up at him. He was very close now that his arm was practically around me. There was a challenge in his violet-blue eyes, and I had never been one to back down.

Rather than stiffening at the contact, as I was sure he would expect me to do, I settled against him, my eyes still on his. I could feel the warmth of him, the slow, steady rise and fall of his breathing against my arm, and the wool of his uniform sleeve brushing against my hair.

"That's much better," I replied, my brows shooting him a challenge of their own. Then I turned to look back at the screen just as Ginger Rogers and David Niven shared a romantic New Year's Eve kiss. I could feel a flush creep up my neck.

I wondered fleetingly what he was thinking about.

Perhaps it was a natural skill or perhaps it came with the housebreaking trade, but I had good instincts and the ability to sense the moods of people around me. I could normally sum up a person within minutes of meeting them.

The problem with Major Ramsey was that he defied all of this. I could rarely tell what he was thinking or feeling. There was never any indication of when he would be the stern military man or when he would soften into something a bit more human.

His expression had been as cool and imperious as ever when he'd taken a seat beside me. Now here he sat with his arm around me, as easy as you please.

He was disconcerting; even more irritating was that I knew he *meant* to be.

After a moment, he tilted his head slightly in my direction, as though he wanted to comment on the film—or perhaps whisper sweet nothings into my ear.

"Let me tell you why I've come before you respond. As I said, people will notice too much conversation. Tomorrow you'll be taking a trip."

I turned to look at him, not realizing just how close his face was. Our noses nearly brushed, and I turned quickly back to the screen.

"After the film, I need you to go home and pack a bag with enough clothing and necessities for perhaps a fortnight."

"Where am I going?" I asked.

"Sunderland. I have a packet here with your train tickets and the documentation you'll need. Can you fit it in your handbag?"

"Yes."

"Good. I'm going to hand it to you. Don't be obvious about it."

I nodded.

He reached into his jacket pocket with one hand, his other arm still perched on the back of my seat. I kept my gaze on the screen but was very aware of him as he shifted against me and then eased the packet into my lap. My fingers closed over it, and I adjusted my jumper to conceal it as best as I could. I would put it in my handbag after a few moments.

"The address of the lodging house in which you're to stay is there," he went on. "Make friends with the locals if you can, but be careful, and reveal as little as possible. I will join you in

Sunderland, but it may not be for a day or two. When I do, it will be under an alias. You're to pretend that you're just making my acquaintance."

My heart pounded with excitement. This sounded like proper spy work we would be doing, not just a locksmithing job. The secrecy, the packet of documents, his mention that he would be assuming a false identity. It all indicated something big.

He glanced at his wristwatch and then leaned his head toward me again. "As charming as this film—and the present company—is, I'm afraid I have a train to catch."

"But . . ." I began. I still had a great many questions.

"What you need to know at present is in the packet. I will make contact with further information. You're to share details with no one. Not your uncle. Not Felix Lacey. Understood?"

"But . . ."

"I don't have time to argue, Miss McDonnell. Do you understand?"

"Yes," I hissed.

"Tell your uncle I'll get you home in one piece. That's all he needs to know at present."

"Major . . ."

But he had already risen and strode from the theater.

I sat back in my chair with an annoyed huff. The major enjoyed this cloak-and-dagger stuff a bit too much. And I knew how much my uncle, Nacy, and Felix would worry about me. The major had put me in rather a tight spot.

The shadow fell across the row once again, and I thought he had returned. I was just preparing to give him a piece of my mind when Felix dropped into the seat beside me.

"Sorry I'm late, love," he said, sliding an arm along the back of my seat where the major's arm had been moments ago and leaning in to brush my cheek with a kiss.

I hazarded a glance at the girl at the end of the row, wondering what she would think of my multiple seatmates.

To my chagrin, she raised her eyebrows ever so slightly and then, with a wide grin, gave me an approving nod.

CHAPTER TWO

"You're leaving London?" Felix asked as we walked home. "Is he going with you?"

Major Ramsey had not forbidden me to tell Felix that I was leaving town, only that I couldn't share details, so I had confided in him that I was to do another job for the major.

"I . . . I was told I'm not at liberty to say any more. I'm sorry, Felix." It felt wrong, unsettling, to keep secrets from him. He was one of my closest friends and confidants. He knew more about me than anyone, aside from my family, and I didn't like secrecy between us.

We continued in silence for a few moments after that, my arm through his. I felt contented, walking along with him through the cooling evening air, but I also hoped to offer a bit of support. Felix had lost part of his left leg in a bombing and had been invalided out of the war. As with anything he set his mind to, he had adapted quickly to his artificial limb, and there was now only the barest perceptible limp as he walked. All the same, I knew that it was not entirely comfortable for him, and I did my best to make things easy where I could, without his noticing.

"It's certainly not my place to tell you what to do, Ellie," he said. "But I don't mind telling you that I don't particularly like it."

"You're going to Scotland tomorrow," I reminded him. "It's not as though we'd be together these next few days anyway."

"That's not the point, and you know it," he said. His tone was good-natured enough, but I could feel the tension in him.

"Felix," I said, giving his arm a little tug. "Don't be cross."

He stopped walking and turned to look at me. His expression was guarded, his eyes unreadable. "I'm not cross, Ellie. You know I always support your decisions."

"I know, Felix, and you're a dear to do so."

Felix was a boyhood chum of my cousins, and we had grown up together. It was only upon Felix's discharge from the navy after his injury and his subsequent return to London that our relationship had deepened—albeit, into one that was still without definite parameters.

We had been spending more time together in the past few weeks and had engaged in rather a lot of kissing. But we'd not really discussed if this was meant to be exclusive or if it was only a bit of fun. A part of me hated to ruin things by trying to put a definition on them. Everything was so uncertain in wartime. We liked each other very much. Wasn't that enough for now?

"I just . . . don't trust Ramsey," he said.

I looked up at him, surprised. "What on earth do you mean? If there's anyone in this country we can trust, it's probably him."

"Still purposefully misunderstanding me," he said with a smile. "All right. I'll put it plainly: I'm jealous."

"Felix!" I laughed. "Don't be ridiculous."

It had been clear from the outset that Felix and the major didn't particularly care for each other. While they had managed to formulate a mutually respectful working relationship, the undertone of dislike remained.

"It's not ridiculous. He fancies you."

"He does not." I felt a strange mix of emotions at the thought, not the least of which was guilt for having been so aware of the major's nearness in the darkened theater.

"I won't argue the point with you," Felix said. "After all, your life's your own. Just promise me you'll be careful."

"And you promise me the same." I still wasn't sure what Felix had been up to on his trips to Scotland, and I rather expected it was something outside the bounds of the law. He had hinted as much to me, though he would give me no details.

"I promise, sweet."

"Good. I'd like you back safe and sound by the time I return." We were alone on a side street, so I slipped my arms inside his jacket and around his waist, looking up at him.

As I thought it might, this seemed to ease the frown that had been lurking on his handsome brow for most of this conversation. His arms came around me. "You know I can't resist you when you look at me like that."

"I was counting on it," I said.

He leaned down to kiss me, and, for a few moments, I forgot to wonder about what tomorrow might bring.

Sunset was fast approaching when I finally returned to my flat. My stomach growled, but Nacy's stew would have to wait. If the Germans came again tonight—which was likely, given they had come every night for weeks—I wouldn't have much time to pack for my trip. A sense of purpose overcame the dreamy languor I had momentarily felt in Felix's arms, and I put the kettle on and then went to my room. Taking my suitcase from the closet, I set it on the bed and began to pack.

It didn't take me long to throw a fortnight's worth of clothes into the suitcase. I'd never been much interested in fashion and frills in the best of times, and these were not the best of times.

My serviceable wardrobe was followed by my hairbrush, a few cosmetics, a bar of soap, and a toothbrush.

That task quickly accomplished, I went to make my tea and settled on my sofa with the steaming cup and the packet the major had given me. I took everything out and spread it on the table before me.

There was a train ticket to Sunderland, leaving early the following morning, just as the major had said. No return ticket, I noticed. Then it seemed my job had no definite parameters as of yet.

There was also a small card with the name of a lodging house and an address printed on it in a neat hand. Constance's, no doubt. The major's secretary was highly capable and efficient.

This was further proven by the papers in the packet. An identity card and a ration book, both with the name Elizabeth Donaldson on them. It was an alias I had used before when working with the major. The papers looked very official.

The photograph was one of me that had been taken back when we'd first linked up with the major and signed the Official Secrets Act. I'd assumed it was the military intelligence equivalent of a rogue's gallery, but it seemed they'd had other uses in mind.

I studied my photo. My expression was serious, as it seldom was in real life, and it made me look older. My black hair contrasted sharply with my pale skin in the black-and-white photograph, and my eyes looked darker without their green tint. I wore no makeup, and the natural wave of my hair had ensured that stray curls had escaped around my face. All told, there was nothing especially remarkable about it. I appeared much like any other decent-looking Englishwoman you might pass on the streets. That was what had made me so adept at blending in, why I excelled at safecracking. It would also be what, I hoped, would make me good at whatever adventure lay in store.

The last item in the packet was the most interesting to me. It was a book: *The Birds of Northern England*. I frowned, flipping through the pages. I looked for words that might be underlined or words in the margins but saw nothing. The book appeared new, the spine uncreased. So what significance did it hold? Was it a codebook of some sort? Perhaps the key to a code I would have to solve?

It was just like the major to present me with something like this without explanation.

I slipped the documents back into the envelope they had come in and put it inside my handbag. I was as prepared for this impromptu trip as I was going to be.

I picked up my cup of tea and prepared to look a bit more into the bird book.

And then the air-raid sirens sounded.

I arrived at Victoria Station early the next morning. I'd left the house as soon as the all clear had sounded, hoping the roads would be passable enough and that the station hadn't been bombed overnight. Thankfully, it still stood when I reached it, and people were moving past the imposing brick façade and into the cavernous station beneath, carrying on as though we weren't facing death and destruction on a massive scale each and every night.

It made me proud of my country, proud of the people who refused to cower or give in. In a way, I almost felt a bit guilty about escaping to Sunderland. Granted, it was not immune from bombing, but thus far it hadn't been a constant bombardment.

I had only a small valise with me and opted to take it on the train. I boarded and put the bag onto the luggage rack and settled into my seat. The book of birds was in my handbag beside me, and I intended to use the train ride to peruse it. I was, surprisingly enough, not very tired.

I'd managed to drop off to sleep for a while on my makeshift bed in our cellar. We were fortunate enough to have this built-in shelter in the house, which Uncle Mick had reinforced with heavy beams. Thus far, it had protected us, and we had not yet taken to the Tube stations as many Londoners had.

Nacy had done her best to make the cellar comfortable for us, bringing blankets and pillows down from upstairs when it had become clear the air raids would be continual. Even with the distant booming and the rattling of the earth around us, I had drifted off the night before with a heavy quilt draped over me. A few weeks ago, I would never have imagined that I could sleep through such a thing, but the way the human body adapts in order to endure has always impressed me.

Uncle Mick and Nacy hadn't been thrilled with my announcement that I would be traveling alone. They'd always been overprotective, and my being a grown woman had done very little to change that.

"I don't like it, Ellie," Uncle Mick had said. "Are you sure I shouldn't come along?"

I smiled. "I'm to go alone. Major Ramsey's orders. And you know he expects his orders obeyed."

Uncle Mick frowned. "Well, I suppose we can trust him to look after you."

"You'll phone when you can, won't you?" Nacy asked. "So we'll know you're all right?"

I had made assurances that I would do the best I could to stay in touch, and I had made them promise me in return that they would take care and be safe. I had hugged them both extra tight before I left.

The train was about to pull away from the station and I had just opened my bird book when a voice asked, "Is this seat taken?"

I looked up to see a gentleman in an RAF uniform standing in the aisle. He was handsome in a rugged sort of way, with dark hair and sparkling dark eyes surrounded by slight creases. He was tall and tan, and his smile flashed white teeth. A very charming picture.

"No," I said. "It's not taken."

"Might I join you?"

"Certainly." The train was crowded, and I didn't object to a little company. A pleasant conversation with a handsome gentleman was likely to be more entertaining than a book on birds, after all.

He took a seat beside me and removed his service cap, brushing a hand through short-cropped dark hair that looked as though it would have the tendency to curl if given the chance.

"How far are you going?" he asked.

I considered and decided there was no reason to lie. After all, if he was traveling farther than me, he would see where I departed the train.

"Sunderland," I said.

"Really? So am I. I've been stationed at the air base for the past few months."

"Has the Luftwaffe done much damage?" I asked. There had been bombings in Sunderland, I knew, though the last had been a month before. It was natural, given that this was a port city, with mines and shipyards. Perhaps, however, now that they were focused on London, other areas of the country would be spared.

"Not as much as they'd like and not as little as we'd prefer," he answered. "But what takes you to Sunderland? Are you meeting your husband there?" He asked this with a flashing smile that told me he was aware it was not exactly a subtle question.

"No," I answered, reverting to the story that had been typed up in my packet of information. "I had a distant relation who died and left a house there. I'm going to tend to things."

"I'm sorry to hear that."

"Thank you."

"Captain Rafe Beaumont, at your service." He extended a hand, and I took it, my fingers enclosed briefly by his warm, rough ones.

"Elizabeth Donaldson," I said. "Pleased to meet you, Captain Beaumont."

"Call me Rafe, please."

"Then you must call me Liz." I wasn't sure why I was giving him an imaginary nickname, but it felt more natural to me than Elizabeth. After all, I was never called Electra, only Ellie. Saving, of course, the infrequent times Major Ramsey had seen fit to use my given name.

The train gained momentum, and we sat in silence for a few moments, looking out the window at the smoke rising up over the city after another night of destruction.

"We'll beat the blighters yet," he said.

I nodded and said a silent prayer that Uncle Mick and Nacy would be safe while I was away.

And then, in what seemed like no time, we were outside the city, and there were expanses of green flashing past the windows, sheep grazing in the distance. It was like an entirely different world from the one we had just left.

Captain Beaumont and I rode for a while in companionable silence, broken by occasional observations about the passing landscape, both of us clearly relieved to be out of the chaos of London but not quite wanting to admit it.

After a while, I took the bird book from my bag and began to skim through the pages. I still couldn't imagine what it was supposed to mean and why there had been no mention of it in my information packet. Then again, the packet had been rather sparse on details. I sometimes suspected Major Ramsey kept details from me for the express purpose of irritating me.

"Are you fond of birds?" Captain Beaumont asked, looking down at the book.

I hesitated for just a moment. I wasn't certain what this bird book was meant to convey in relationship to my assignment, but I couldn't very well pretend to be an expert in a subject I knew very little about. "Just beginning to be," I said. "I thought Sunderland might be a good place for bird-watching."

He seemed to accept this without any particular interest. "I've brought a book of my own," he said, pulling a small volume from the pocket of his uniform jacket.

I looked over and saw the title. "*The Allure of Greek Myth*!" I exclaimed, rather too excitedly.

"You know it?" he asked, surprised.

"It's one of my favorites."

He grinned. "I read classical literature at Cambridge."

I felt my first glimmer of real interest in the man. Greek mythology was one of the subjects closest to my heart. I had read the myths and legends from the time I was old enough to hold a book, and I'd always felt a connection to those characters who had lived out epics millennia ago. I was named Electra, after all.

We talked at length about Greek mythology, and the journey seemed to fly by. Before I knew it, we were pulling into Sunderland station. I hadn't spared more than a few glances at the bird book, but there would be time enough for that later.

He took my bag for me and carried it from the train.

Once we were on the platform, I turned to face him, wondering where we would go from here. While I had enjoyed his company on the train, I was not looking for male companionship. There was, after all, the matter of Felix. We weren't officially a couple, it was true, but I was growing ever more attached to the warm steadiness of his company. I felt no need to complicate matters with another suitor.

Perhaps the captain, too, had a sweetheart, or perhaps he read my reluctance in my posture. Whatever the case, he held out a hand to shake mine. "Perhaps we'll run into each other while we're here. Sunderland isn't so very large, after all."

"Yes, perhaps we shall," I agreed with a smile. "It was very nice to meet you, Rafe."

"And you, too, Liz."

He tipped his cap at me and then turned and walked away. I watched him for a moment, appreciating the set of his broad shoulders. Then I turned my mind to more important things.

I had reached the destination of my next assignment. I was anxious to see what sort of adventure was in store.

I exited the train station and stood outside for a moment, considering what I knew of Sunderland, which was not much. I had never even been to Tyne and Wear. I did know the city was located on the River Wear and had a port on the North Sea. It was a shipbuilding center, and there was also a mine. It had crossed my mind that the major had brought me here for some nefarious purpose. Was I to sneak into the shipyard for some reason? It had all been so very vague, and I found myself freshly annoyed that I didn't know what I was supposed to do or when he might contact me.

It was all very well to have a place to stay arranged, but I didn't relish the idea of twiddling my thumbs in the comfort and safety of a seaside town while my family was being bombed back in London.

Pushing down this natural inclination of mine to be easily riled by the major, I took a few calming breaths and then looked around to get my bearings. There had been a map to my lodgings in the packets that the major had given me, and I had memorized it in order to keep from drawing unnecessary attention to myself.

It was no more than a mile to the rooming house, and so I thought I would walk. It would give me a chance to get the lay of the land, so to speak.

As I neared the street where I would be staying, I encountered a busy road. I stood with a small crowd of pedestrians waiting to cross. There were several large, covered lorries, no doubt carrying supplies to or from those shipyards or the RAF station that was located somewhere nearby. I would need to look at a detailed map of Sunderland at some point. Perhaps it would give me some clue as to what the major might want me to do.

I was distracted by these thoughts when I felt someone bump into me from behind. It threw me off-balance, and I stumbled forward and into the path of an oncoming lorry.

CHAPTER THREE

I might have been able to catch myself before I was completely smashed to bits, but I was spared the necessity of testing my reflexes by a strong grip on my arm that pulled me backward onto the pavement.

"Careful there," said a good-natured voice.

"Thank you," I said, turning to the gentleman who had quite possibly saved my life. He was a tall, fair man with a thin mustache. His pale blue eyes searched my face, as though ascertaining that I had not purposefully thrown myself in front of an oncoming vehicle.

"Are you all right?" he asked. He was still holding on to my arm, but his grip had loosened now that I was no longer in danger of falling.

"Yes, fine. Someone bumped into me," I said, feeling a bit silly. "Thank you so much for your assistance."

"My pleasure." He released my arm and tipped his hat to me before walking away down the street. My gaze followed him for a moment, grateful that he had been there when he had. I then glanced around at the other people on the curb. Though there had been a few cries of alarm as I'd stumbled forward, there no longer seemed to be any interest in me now that I'd been spared a gruesome death.

I frowned as I considered what had happened. I was not a clumsy person; I had been knocked very hard. It had, in fact, almost felt like a push.

I hoped that I was merely imagining that there had been something more sinister than an ill-timed bump on a busy street. Whatever the case, I was thankful the man had been there to grab me, and I resolved to be much more careful.

The road was clear now and the lorries had passed, so I made my way gingerly across the street and recommenced my journey.

I'd always had a fairly good sense of direction—an asset in a profession that works primarily in the dark—and so I made my way without difficulty to the address given in the packet. I found myself glancing over my shoulder every so often to be certain that there was no one lurking behind me. The incident on the street corner had perhaps shaken me more than I cared to admit.

I noticed no one looming on the walk, however, and I soon began to feel reassured that the incident had been nothing more than an unfortunate accident.

The rooming house was an older building on a bustling street. There were several cars in the streets and people walking purposefully along in both directions. I had seen a few shops and restaurants along the way. It was certainly not a quiet residential neighborhood tucked away into a side street.

There was a sign on the door that read ROOMS TO LET, so it seemed I was in the right place. There was nothing particularly noteworthy about the building, which was, I assumed, why it had been chosen. It was painted a pale blue with dark gray shutters, solid and respectable looking. I walked up to the front porch and knocked on the door.

Almost immediately, I heard footsteps from somewhere inside the house. They grew heavier as they drew closer, and the door was soon thrown open to reveal a tall, buxom woman with dark hair drawn back tightly from a cheery red face. "Yes?" she asked in a tone that kept the single word from sounding curt.

"Mrs. James?" I asked.

"Yes."

"I'm Elizabeth Donaldson. I rang you about a room?"

"Oh, yes. Yes. Come in, Miss Donaldson. I've been expecting you."

It had, I assumed, been Constance who had phoned Mrs. James. But I supposed one strange woman's voice sounded very much like another. I did wonder what else Constance had told her and hoped it was nothing Mrs. James would expect me to remember.

"The parlor's there and the dining room there," she said, pointing at doors on opposite sides of the foyer. "Your room will be right this way."

She led me up a staircase and down a narrow hall to a small room at the back of the house. The walls were painted a pale yellow, and there was a cheerful quilt on the bed. The room smelled of fresh air and furniture polish. There was one window that overlooked a tidy garden behind the building. I could see a girl sitting on a bench reading below.

"As I said on the phone, it's not a large room, but it's the only one I have available at present. Will this do?" she asked. "If so, I'll take the sign down from the window."

"Oh, yes. This is very nice, thank you."

"I ask for each week's rent in advance, but since you may be taking up residence at your aunt's home, God rest her, we can wait and see about next week."

"Thank you," I said. The background information that had been written for my character stipulated that I would be going through my aunt's seaside cottage to prepare it for sale. Whether or not this cottage actually existed, I didn't know.

"Well, dear, I'll leave you to get settled. Just let me know if there's anything you need. I serve breakfast at seven in the morning and dinner at seven in the evening. Midday meals are up to you."

"That's wonderful. Thank you."

She left me alone then, and I hefted my valise onto the bed and opened it. Pulling out my clothes, I placed them in the wardrobe. It didn't take long to have my things in order.

I set the bird book on the bed and once again flipped through the pages, trying to see if it would reveal anything to me in these new surroundings. The birds stared secretively back at me from the pages, obstinately mute.

With a sigh, I tossed the book aside and decided to venture outdoors and look around. I wondered if whatever I was supposed to do was in some way connected with this house. There was, I had no doubt, some reason the major had chosen this particular location for me to stay. The job he had for me might even be in this neighborhood. If that was the case, I'd better get to know my surroundings.

I went back down the stairs and out the front door. I saw no one on my way out, and there was an air of quietness about the place. Mrs. James had said she had only one available room, but there seemed to be no one else about at present. Perhaps they were all at their jobs. This seemed to be a working-class neighborhood.

There was, of course, the girl who had been reading behind the house. She would, I thought, be a good place to start. If I could make conversation with her, perhaps I would be able to learn something.

There was no wall around the little garden behind the house. There were, however, paths among the foliage made of loose stones and bits of seashells. It was tidy and pretty, though nothing spectacular. Then again, it was the perfect sort of garden for a rooming house. Enough space for lodgers to walk about and get some fresh air without requiring too much maintenance.

As none of the foliage was much higher than my waist, it wasn't difficult to find the bench where the girl was reading, a book in one hand and a cigarette in the other. I walked toward her as casually as possible. I would have thought my footsteps on the gravel of the path would be enough to draw her attention, but she seemed to be engrossed in her reading.

"Hello," I said as I approached.

She looked up from the book she was reading. "Hello."

She was a lovely girl with flawless light brown skin and liquid brown eyes. Her hair was as black as mine and apparently long, for she wore it pinned up in a thick bun at the back of her head. If I'd had to guess, I'd say she was of Middle Eastern heritage—though, of course, one didn't like to generalize.

"I've just taken a room here," I said, by way of introduction. "Are you a lodger, too?"

"No," she said. "I live with my sister in that house there." She nodded her head toward the small white house on the opposite side of the garden.

"Oh, is this garden yours?" I was prepared to beg her pardon for trespassing, though I didn't intend to retreat until I learned a bit more.

"No, it belongs to Mrs. James," she said. "But she doesn't mind if I sit here and read. We're rather chummy."

"She seems a very nice woman."

"Oh, she's a lamb. But beware: there's nothing that happens within a ten-street radius that she doesn't know about."

I smiled. "I'll keep that in mind." This was good to know. I would have to be careful not to let my story slip. On the other hand, it might be beneficial to me if I could befriend the landlady and glean information from her.

"This is a lovely spot for reading," I said, by way of continuing the conversation.

She nodded, setting her book aside. I glanced down to see if it was, perhaps, a copy of *The Birds of Northern England* to match my own. Maybe it was some sort of signal between members of whatever scheme I was involved in.

No such luck. It was a tattered copy of *Jane Eyre*.

I really was cross with Major Ramsey for throwing me into this situation without giving me any sort of clue as to what I ought to be doing. He knew perfectly well how annoying I would find it. Furthermore, he had to know that I would try to work out the mission on my own.

"I come out here to smoke," she said, dropping her cigarette and grinding it out in the dirt with the tip of her shoe. "My sister can't abide smoking in the house."

I nodded. "My aunt never liked it either. She passed away. I've come to Sunderland to clean out her house."

"I'm sorry to hear that," she said. "My sister and I were raised by our aunt."

"I didn't know mine well," I told her. "But her house came to me. I wasn't sure if it was habitable, so I decided a rooming house was the best course of action. I'll be here for a fortnight or so, I suppose."

"I see," she said without much curiosity. That was one thing about the war that worked in my favor. People asked few questions. After all, everyone's life was uprooted now. There was very little interest to be found in the movements of others.

I had offered up more information than was probably necessary because I had learned it was a good way to gain a person's trust. If you were willing to tell them about yourself, you were more likely to be seen as trustworthy. Of course, I wasn't planning to steal from this woman. I only wanted to seem friendly. As

Major Ramsey had pointed out, having local allies was always beneficial.

"Is there anything fun to do in the area?" I asked.

Her eyes brightened. "Plenty. A lot of RAF men go through here. RAF Usworth is nearby, and there are always pilots at the clubs in the evening looking for a bit of company. We can go out dancing one night, if you like! You're not married, are you? It doesn't really matter, of course, but you might have a bit more fun if you're single."

I laughed. "No, I'm not married. I would like to go out dancing. My name's Liz, by the way. Liz Donaldson."

"Samira Maddox. I'm called Sami."

"I'm pleased to meet you." I was about to continue the conversation when there was, from the front of the house, a shout, followed by the screech of automobile tires and then a woman's scream.

Sami reacted before I did, abandoning her book on the bench and hurrying toward the front of the house. I followed close behind.

By the time we reached the street at the front of the building, a crowd had begun to gather. They seemed to be standing in the center of the street. Had it been an automobile accident? A thought occurred to me: What were the odds that two accidents might happen in my vicinity today?

We moved a bit closer, and it was then I noticed a man lying on the ground. I thought, at first, that he might have been injured and unconscious. Though there were already a few people gathered around him, I moved forward to see if I could be of some assistance. When I saw his face, however, I realized it was much too late for that.

His face was contorted, frozen in an expression of pain. White foam bubbled at his lips, and his pale blue eyes were wide open, staring sightless at the gray sky above. He was clearly beyond help.

It was so jarring a scene that it took me a moment to realize that I recognized him.

It was the man who had stopped me from falling into the street not two hours ago.

CHAPTER FOUR

I felt a jolt of horror and surprise. The man had saved me from being hit by a lorry, and now here he was, lying dead in the street. A strange sense of unreality threatened to creep over me, and my heart began to pound. It was not the first time I'd borne witness to violent death, but that didn't make it any easier. I concentrated on my breathing and forced myself to focus.

My heart rate steadied, and my thoughts became clearer. There was something wrong about all of this. The man had not followed me. I was certain of that. So what was he doing on this street? And how was it possible he had saved me from an accident only to die tragically a short time later? I had never been much of a believer in coincidences, at least not of this magnitude.

I looked again at the man. I wanted to go to him and close his eyes. This seemed the least I could offer him after the service he had done for me. I moved at once to his side and reached down to take his arm, to check for a pulse, even though it was dreadfully clear he was well beyond saving. The white foam on his lips quivered in the breeze, but he wasn't breathing, and his body was still. I felt a wave of sickness but tamped it down as I reached for his wrist.

The skin was still warm beneath my fingers, but, as I had

known since I first caught sight of his face, there was no life left in him. I pulled my hand away. It was then I noticed that his fist was closed around something. A piece of paper, it seemed.

I don't know what possessed me exactly. If it was some instinct or if I was simply still reeling from what had happened and did it without thinking. Whatever the case, I pulled the piece of paper from between his fingers and slipped it into my pocket. Everyone was still looking at the man's face, and I was adept at light pickpocketing, so it was no great feat.

I rose to my feet then and backed away from the body. There was nothing else I could do here. I looked around for Sami and saw her talking to a young woman, likely the one whose scream had brought us running. The girl was white as a ghost, and tears streamed down her face unchecked as she hugged herself. She was so deathly pale I was afraid she might faint, so I went to join them.

"He's beyond help?" Sami asked, her voice strangely flat.

"I'm afraid so."

The young woman whimpered.

"Are you all right?" I asked her. "Do you need to sit down?"

She didn't answer at first. Her eyes were still trained on the man on the ground. It was more difficult to see him now, with the people that had crowded around him.

"I . . . I can't believe it," she whispered.

My eyes went to Sami, and she shot me a worried expression.

"I think perhaps you'd better sit down," I said to the girl.

She made no protest, and Sami and I led her a short distance away to where a car was parked alongside the curb. She leaned heavily against the bonnet.

"Poor Hal," she said in a ragged voice.

"You know him?" I asked her.

She dragged her eyes to me and gave me a short nod. "His name is Hal Jenkins. He is . . . was . . . a friend of ours."

"We all had drinks together a couple of times a week," Sami

said, her expression set into the firm lines of composure. She was, I realized, very upset herself but determined not to let emotion take the reins.

"Did you see what happened?" I asked the girl.

I knew it might not be a good idea to press her when she was clearly in shock, but I also knew the police would be along at any moment, and this was my chance to ask questions of a witness. I would need to report this to the major. Things like this didn't happen without a reason.

"I . . . I was going to the shops, and I saw him across the street. I waved, but he . . . he didn't seem to see me. He was staggering, and then . . . he collapsed." She burst into sobs then, and I put an arm around her shoulders, angling her away from the sight of the dead man.

"My name's Liz," I said gently. "What's yours?"

"Nessa," she said with a sniff. "Nessa Simpson."

Her face was still a ghastly shade of white, but at least she wasn't hysterical. I didn't blame her for being upset. Death was not an uncommon thing these days, not in wartime, but there was something clearly shocking about a man dropping dead in the middle of a thoroughfare.

No doubt the consensus would be that he had suffered a seizure or something of the sort, though he had seemed strong and healthy enough at a glance. But it seemed clear to me that it was something less natural. Something more sinister.

Two police officers arrived then. One of them knelt beside the body, and the other began to push back the crowd.

"They're going to want to question the witnesses," Sami said. "You'd better talk to them, Nessa."

Nessa sniffed again but nodded. "All right."

Sami linked her arm through Nessa's, leading her to where a policeman stood at the curb, talking to an excited group of onlookers.

I wondered briefly if I should approach the group and listen to what they had to say. But, given Nessa's description of the incident, it didn't seem there could be much more to learn about Hal Jenkins's last moments.

I remembered the slip of paper in my pocket. Did I dare draw it out?

Glancing around, I saw, as I had expected, that no one was paying me the least bit of attention. And so I slipped it out of my pocket and opened it.

It was a small scrap, apparently torn from a piece of good-quality stationery. The writing on the paper was in bold, dark strokes in black ink: *WE KNOW YOU HAVE IT.*

I considered this. Despite the somewhat dramatic nature of the missive, it was not very telling, as far as things went. Perhaps it was simply something to do with his work or a note from a friend. He might merely have had the piece of paper in his hand when he was overtaken by whatever malady had killed him.

I couldn't help but think, however, that the way he had clutched it, even as he died a gruesome death, meant that it was something important.

What had Hal Jenkins been in possession of that was so important? I wished I'd had the foresight to search his pockets, but it was much too late for that now.

As Sami detached herself from the group, I slipped the piece of paper back into my own pocket.

"That officer will take care of Nessa," she said when she returned to my side. "I've already told them that we arrived after the fact, so we needn't stay."

I nodded, glancing once more at the still form of Hal Jenkins on the ground. Someone—the policeman, I assumed—had covered him with a blanket, and two more officers had arrived and were directing cars away from the scene and telling newly arrived gawkers to move along.

There was, as Sami had said, nothing we could do. All the same, I felt a bit guilty leaving him lying in the road. He had saved my life today; it felt wrong that there was nothing I could do to help him. Unless there was some way I could discover how and why he had died . . .

"Are you all right?" Sami asked. "You're rather pale."

I blinked and returned my focus to her. "Yes, I'm all right. It's just . . . a shock."

She looked back in the direction of the accident. "Yes. One always thinks death will get easier, and it never does. Especially not when it happens to people you know. Poor Hal."

"Did you know him well?"

She shook her head. "He was part of the regular crowd at The Silver Sextant—that's the pub down the street. Everyone from the street frequents it, so we've all got chummy. I wasn't very close to him, but it's still ghastly to see him that way."

"Yes. Horrible."

She gave a deep sigh. "Come, let's see if Mrs. James will give us some tea."

The tea Mrs. James made for us was very strong and very sweet, just as I liked it. She tutted and fussed, just as Nacy would have done under the circumstances, and I was comforted. I had never known my mother, but with Nacy looking over me, I'd never wanted for motherly love and affection.

Sami, for all the coolheadedness she had displayed at the scene of the accident, seemed rattled now that we were at the table, the cup and saucer shaking ever so slightly in her hands. I was, unfortunately, familiar with the aftereffects of coming across a dead body unexpectedly, and I sympathized with her.

"It's just so shocking," she said. "I thought at first he might have been hit by an automobile, but it doesn't appear that he was."

"No. Nessa Simpson saw him crossing the street," I said. "She said he was staggering and then fell down."

"Perhaps it was his heart," Sami said. "There's a great strain on men these days."

"There was nothing wrong with Hal Jenkins's heart, in my opinion," Mrs. James said. "Not a sturdy young man like that."

I looked up, surprised. "You knew him, too?"

She nodded. "I know everyone in this neighborhood. I've lived here for over forty years."

"Then he lived nearby," I said. I was trying not to appear too inquisitive. I didn't think that Mrs. James would notice, as she was likely to enjoy a bit of gossip.

Sami, however, was a different story. She was sharp, observant. I had noticed how quickly she had taken the situation in hand, how she had stayed alert and kept her poise. She would notice if I appeared too keen to get information or didn't keep my story straight. I was going to have to tread carefully when I was with her.

"Yes," Mrs. James said, warming to the subject. "He lived in Mrs. Yardley's rooming house, just at the end of the street. The big gray house." She shook her head. "Mrs. Yardley will have his room vacant by the end of the week, mark my words. Even though no one wants an attic room, she'll find a willing lodger to keep from losing any money."

"You don't think she'll be upset about Mr. Jenkins's death?" I asked.

"Well, as to that, I don't think she knew him all that well. Mrs. Yardley isn't the type to befriend her boarders. Besides, he hasn't been here long—on this street, I mean. He was a Sunderland boy, but he'd only been with Mrs. Yardley a few weeks. Couldn't join up on account of hearing loss in one ear, he said. He was working at the shipyard, though, doing his bit. Must have been a change for him, poor dear. He worked with books before the war, I think."

I tucked this piece of information about his war job away. Had the mysterious possession referred to in the note been something he might have procured at the shipyard? Something he, perhaps, had not been meant to have?

After we had finished our tea, I excused myself and went up to my room to rest and to plan. Already this trip was proving to be much more than I had bargained for, and I had a busy night ahead.

Clearly, I was going to have to do a bit of breaking and entering.

CHAPTER FIVE

I waited impatiently for darkness to fall. If Mrs. James was right, there would be limited time to search Hal Jenkins's rooms before his things were cleared away to make room for a new tenant. That meant I would need to go tonight, before his landlady had a chance to interfere.

The more I thought about it, the more certain I was that the paper clutched in his hand with the mysterious reference to an unnamed possession had something to do with his death. And, if that was the case, the window of opportunity to discover what that possession had been was very small.

I wished the major had given me some way to get in touch with him. Though I usually resented his supercilious manner, the death of Hal Jenkins was an urgent matter, and I would have liked to consult with him. After all, what were the odds an un-natural death had taken place right on the street where he had planted me?

I briefly considered ringing Constance, the major's secretary, to see if there was any way she could get in touch with him. I doubted, however, that he had left any contact information. He was a cagey fellow and would no doubt check in with Constance on occasion rather than telling her how she could reach him.

Well, perhaps I would ring her tomorrow and leave a message if I discovered anything tonight.

Barring that, the major had said that he would meet me here in Sunderland in due course, so I supposed that there was no choice but to wait. I would just have to hope that nothing else drastic happened in the meantime—and that I was in no danger myself.

To be fair, I didn't think the major would knowingly have left me in danger. He was not the sort of man to take undue risks, especially with other people's lives. All the same, he probably hadn't been anticipating that Hal Jenkins would drop dead in my general vicinity, and I would be glad when I could relate the details to him.

Until then, I would just have to proceed on my own. If he grew angry about it, which he no doubt would, he would have no one to blame but himself.

I dressed in black trousers and a black shirt for the job. I was glad I had thought to bring trousers, because I was going to have to climb a tree.

I'd taken a walk after dinner to case the house. Never go in blind. That was a rule of Uncle Mick's. The house was at the end of the street, as Mrs. James had said. It was a Victorian-era house, two stories plus the attic. Since it was a rooming house, I thought it would be risky to attempt to enter the house and take the stairs to the attic. Therefore, it seemed best that I take advantage of the large oak tree growing near the house. There were sturdy-enough-looking branches that went all the way up to the attic windows, and that would be my point of ingress.

This certainly wasn't my first time breaking into a house, but it was my first solo job. Every other time, I'd had Uncle Mick or my cousins at my side. It was a bit daunting being alone. Without backup, I would be at the mercy of my own abilities and whatever fate might have in store.

I'd taken note of the steps that creaked in Mrs. James's house (the third and fifth steps from the top) and I avoided them as I made my way down the darkened staircase.

I had considered climbing out of my window and dropping to the ground below, but there were hedges below my window that would be sure to make the landing unpleasant and leave scratches. This had seemed a drastic measure to take when I could easily walk down the stairs and out the front door. After all, this wasn't finishing school; I could leave in the middle of the night if I chose to.

The streets were dark and quiet, the blackout curtains doing their job to keep any light inside the houses at bay. It had the added advantage of there being no potential witnesses glancing out a window to see me making my way down the street.

I reached the house and, with another quick glance around, slipped into the shadows of the tree I had selected. I slipped off my shoes, leaving them at the base of the tree. It was easier to climb without them, and it would be quieter once I was walking around the attic room, too.

The tree itself was no trouble. I'd grown up with boys, tagging along with the neighborhood gangs of roughhousing hooligans until Nacy decided I needed to start acting like a lady. I'd climbed more trees than I could count, and this one posed no difficulty. I was up it in no time.

I found firm footholds and took just a moment to survey the neighborhood through the branches, appreciating the moonlight and the gentle breeze.

Then I turned to more important work. The window was a Victorian-era sash window, and it was fastened from the inside. I had assumed it would be fastened. If Hal Jenkins had had something worth hiding—something worth killing for—it made sense that he would have been cautious.

Unfortunately, this meant the easiest way in was to break one of the panes of glass. This went against all my training, as Uncle Mick had always stressed the importance of leaving no evidence of our entry behind. That was not to say, however, that I was unprepared for this eventuality. After all, I was Uncle Mick's girl, wasn't I?

This was standard burglary stuff, not much skill required. I pulled the glass cutter from my tool kit and began to scrape a small square in the center pane on the top sash, right above the fastener. I waited for gusts of wind to rattle the tree branches and conceal as much of the sound as possible. When I'd made deep enough grooves, I used the little ball on the other end of the cutter to gently tap against the glass along the inside of the grooves.

This was to be the noisiest part of the operation, but it couldn't really be helped. The only possible precaution was patience, a few light taps at a time to draw as little attention as possible. Finally, I gave one last, firm tap, and the square of glass clattered inward onto the floor, slowed a bit in its descent by the blackout curtain inside the window.

I held my breath, waiting to see if the sound had drawn any attention, but there was no movement on the street and none inside the house as far as I could tell.

Reaching carefully through the small square I had made in the glass, I released the latch. Withdrawing my arm, I put my hands against the panes of glass on the undamaged lower sash and pushed to raise the window.

It didn't budge.

I pushed harder and felt only the slightest give. It was no longer locked; this was a problem with the window itself. Likely the casement had swollen in the seaside air. It was the kind of thing that happened often enough with old windows.

Removing a thick file from the tool kit, I slipped the edge beneath the sill and gave a sharp downward push on my end. This aspect required more brawn than brains, but the angle mattered, too, and I knew what was required to break the seal. There was the little snapping sound as the wood gave way, and the window opened a few inches.

Slipping my fingers in the crack, I began to jiggle the frame, working the window upward. It was slow work, as I'd already made more noise than I'd like, and so it was a few minutes before I'd widened the opening far enough to fit through.

Balancing on the tree branch, I leaned forward and slipped my torso through the opening and then, my hands on the floor, slid the rest of my body through, landing almost soundlessly on the wooden floor inside.

I rose to my feet and stood still for several minutes, just listening. The house was quiet, and there was little sound except the occasional gust of wind through the tree outside.

When I was at last sure that my entrance hadn't been noticed, I pulled a torch from my pocket and switched it on. It was another benefit of the blackout curtains: that no one would notice my light shining around the room from outside.

Moving the light around, I took stock of Hal Jenkins's last residence.

The room was neat and sparse, which was disappointing somehow. It would be easier to search, but the orderliness also made me suspect that Hal Jenkins would not have been careless with his secrets. If there was something he was hiding, he would no doubt have done a good job of it.

Lucky, then, that I had experience rooting out valuables.

I searched the bed first since it was near the window, pushing down on the mattress to feel for anything hidden inside. I was met with only the squeak of the springs. There was nothing beneath the mattress or under the bed either.

Next, I went to the little writing desk in the corner. The top was empty except for a desk blotter. I flashed the light to see if I could make out the impression of any writing on its surface like they did in the detective stories, but the entire thing was a scramble of words, probably written across decades or more, and there was nothing easily discernible in the dim glow of the torchlight.

I pulled open the drawer. There were a few pens and pencils, a razor-sharp paper knife, a small bottle of glue, two postage stamps, and a few sheets of plain, inexpensive stationery, as well as envelopes. I flipped through the sheets of paper quickly to see if anything might be written on them. They were disappointingly blank.

On impulse, I placed a piece of paper atop the blotter and rubbed the pencil over it. One summer when we were children, the boys and I had picked up the somewhat macabre hobby of making rubbings of old tombstones in London. It became a competition to see who could find the earliest dates and the strangest inscriptions.

I didn't know if there was anything useful that might be gleaned from the blotter, but it was worth a try. The rubbing complete, I folded the sheet of paper and tucked it into my pocket to be contemplated when I had more time and light.

After confirming the absence of any hidden compartments or secret drawers in the desk, I moved to the little bookshelf next to it. There were several leather-bound books.

My light skimmed across the spines, and the title of one of them caught my attention: *The Art of Bird-Watching*. It was obviously not the same bird book I had in my possession, but it was similar enough to give me pause. As soon as I saw the major, I would have to ask him about that book and what it meant.

I slipped each of the books from the shelf and flipped through the pages, but there was nothing secreted in any of them. A cursory examination proved they were also empty of notes, markings, or even bookmarks.

The wardrobe was my next target. It felt a bit disrespectful, somehow, to rifle through the man's clothes. Being a thief doesn't allow for a lot of sentimentality about other people's possessions, however, and I was able to push those thoughts away without too much difficulty.

There weren't many clothes. Everything was laundered and in its rightful place.

I searched the pockets of his jackets and came across a few pence, a stub of a pencil, and two matchbooks. The matchbooks were both from nightclubs, and I slipped them into my pocket in case the locations might prove worth investigating later.

I did a quick sweep of the rest of the room: the floor beneath the rug (no loose floorboards), the bedside table (empty except for a lamp and an ashtray), and a wooden chair (cushionless).

One might have been tempted to draw assumptions about Hal Jenkins as a person from the state of his room. On the surface, it appeared that he was neat and frugal, a man of few passions or hobbies who lived an almost depressingly tidy life. There was another interpretation, however. One I found more likely: it was suspicious. The room was too tidy, too sparse. It seemed to me to be indicative of a man on the move, a man who did not intend to be held down. Perhaps a man who was ever ready to make an escape. There was nothing in this room that he could not have abandoned at a moment's notice.

The same could be true of my room at Mrs. James's house now, and perhaps that was why this interpretation seemed so fitting. After all, I was here on secret and temporary business; it seemed Hal Jenkins had been, too.

I remembered the firm grip on my arm, pulling me back from the oncoming lorry. He had been quick to help a stranger. That was a point in his favor, wasn't it? All the same, my brief survey of his nearly bare room had only increased my suspicions about the man.

It seemed this dicey foray into his room had been an unnecessary risk. There was a door at the other end of the room, probably leading to the toilet, and I decided to have a look.

It was no great surprise that the room was clean and almost bare, save for a towel on the rack and a bar of soap in a dish at the sink.

I opened the medicine cabinet behind the mirror and looked inside. There was nothing to see but some shaving soap, a razor, and a comb. Not even any hair tonic or aftershave, nothing that would leave even a lingering scent as an indicator of his presence. Hal Jenkins had not been looking to make any sort of mark on the world around him.

I closed the cabinet and was about to leave the room when I stopped dead, my skin prickling. Something was wrong. My finely tuned inner alarm was banging as loud as an air-raid siren, though I couldn't quite be sure why. Had I heard something out in the bedroom?

Quickly, I switched off my torch and moved silently to the bathroom door, listening. Though my eyes were still adjusting to the total darkness, I looked in the direction of the door that led out of the room, presumably to the stairs or a landing of some sort.

Was someone out there? Had they heard me moving about in Hal Jenkins's room and come to investigate? I waited with bated breath for the sound of a voice or keys in the lock. There was nothing but silence.

My eyes grew focused in the darkness, and I suddenly noticed a large shadow in the corner of the room, darker than everything else around it. There hadn't been any furniture there, had there? No, I hadn't overlooked anything, I was sure. Then I saw it move, and a cold chill swept through my veins.

Someone was in the room with me.

CHAPTER SIX

The shadow moved with alarming speed in my direction. I didn't know who they were or what they wanted, but it didn't take a genius to realize it was best not to wait around to find out.

I sprinted toward the window, hoping I could sail through the opening without getting stuck, but the shadow was fast. The intruder grabbed me from behind, even as I lunged at the sill.

I kicked out at him—it was clearly a man, and a big one at that—with absolutely no effect. He propelled me back into the room and we landed on the bed, the creak of the springs loud in the silence. I struggled violently, but it was no use. He was immovable, his weight pinning me down with rock-hard force.

A scream rose up in my throat, despite the fact that this was contrary to a lifetime of training to be silent. Screaming would bring the police, but that was a better alternative than death. Even as the thought crossed my mind, however, a hand clamped over my mouth.

I struggled harder, the first hint of genuine panic beginning to well up in me, and I tried to think of what I could do to free myself.

Then the beam of a torch shone into my eyes, and I was effectively blinded.

There was nothing wrong with my hearing, however. I heard a curse, irony and anger melded together in a familiar voice, as the weight holding me down eased.

"I ought to have known it was you, Miss McDonnell."

Major Ramsey let go of me, and I pushed him back as hard as I could, the residue of adrenaline lending added strength to my angry shove. Admittedly, it did very little to move him, though he did give me space to wiggle out from under him and off the bed.

I shot to my feet, though my legs felt numb, and whirled to face him. "What do you think you are doing?" I demanded in a harsh whisper. Truth be told, I was almost surprised I could speak with my heart still in my throat.

"I think it's I who should be asking you that question," he said, his tone and his expression maddeningly bland.

My heart continued to pound at an alarming rate, and I felt suddenly a bit light-headed.

To my annoyance, the major seemed to notice that I was not quite steady on my feet, and he took my shoulders and sat me back down on the edge of the bed.

"Put your head between your knees," he instructed.

"I'm not going to faint," I said, the irritation helping to clear my head. "I've never fainted. You just . . . scared the life out of me."

"I thought you were an intruder." He paused. "I was not altogether wrong, of course, but I didn't know it was you."

"But what are you doing here?" I demanded.

"The same thing as you, I imagine."

He moved away from me then and to the door of the bedroom. Had he come in that way? If he had done, he'd been incredibly quiet about it. Still, it seemed the most likely option. I didn't imagine Major Ramsey was a skilled tree climber at his size, but he'd surprised me before.

He put his ear to the door and then, after a long moment, pulled it open and looked out into the darkness beyond. Apparently satisfied, he closed it again and came back to where I still sat on the edge of the bed.

"The room below this one is, luckily, unoccupied this evening, or we might have drawn attention to ourselves with that scuffle," he said.

My head had cleared now, and my hands had almost ceased their shaking. My anger was still fully intact, however. How dare he manhandle me in that fashion, tossing me about like a rag doll?

"You might have killed me," I said accusingly.

"If I had intended to kill you, you'd be dead." While I'd become accustomed to such charming pronouncements from Major Ramsey, these words rather gave me a chill, and for a moment I was speechless.

"Did you find anything?"

I looked up at him and blinked, surprised by the question. I had thought he would berate me for breaking in here, but I supposed there would be time enough for that later.

"Nothing of note," I said. "In fact, the entire place is suspiciously spartan."

He nodded, but he gave the room a quick yet thorough going-over just the same. I watched from where I sat on the edge of the bed, noting with satisfaction that he checked all the same places I had and found nothing new.

I had a great many questions about the major's relationship to Hal Jenkins, what my assignment here in Sunderland was, and if the two were connected. I knew, however, that now was not exactly the best time to ask them. And even if I did, the major probably wasn't in the mood to be forthcoming.

I was still more shaken by our tussle than I cared to admit. Not by what had happened, but by what might have. The truth of the matter was that, if the major had been Hal Jenkins's killer, I might not have survived our encounter.

I had known there was some risk involved in this escapade of mine, but I had let my guard down once I was in the room, a stupid mistake. I didn't like to admit that my actions might have been foolhardy, but mistakes were never a total loss if you learned from them, as Uncle Mick liked to say.

Well, lesson learned. Next time I would bring a weapon of some sort.

The major returned to my side. "How did you get in?"

I nodded toward the window. "I climbed the tree."

His brows rose ever so slightly. He went to the window and, flicking off his torch, pushed aside the blackout curtain. He took in the hole in the glass and the gap I had crawled through. Then he pushed down the sash and secured the latch. The cut in the glass would be noticed, of course, but everything else was as I had found it.

"Let's go," he said.

I followed him across the room. He opened the door, looked out, and then motioned with two fingers for me to precede him, then, once I was in the corridor, he held up a hand for me to stop. Like he was directing traffic in Piccadilly Circus, I thought irritably.

He closed the door to Hal Jenkins's room and moved ahead of me across a short landing to the top of the stairs. Again, we paused to listen and then began to descend. It was a good thing I was barefoot, though the major seemed to be quiet enough in whatever shoes he was wearing.

We went down one set of stairs and then another. The major had clearly come in this way, for he knew the layout of the house. There was no hesitation in his manner, though there was caution. Finally, we reached the front door. It pulled open on mercifully silent hinges, and we were outside.

Once on the street, I turned back toward the side of the house and the big oak tree.

The major caught my arm. "What are you doing?" He could manage to sound demanding even when his voice was barely a whisper, I noted.

"My shoes are under the tree."

He looked down at my bare feet—I'd foregone stockings, as they weren't apt to hold up to tree bark when climbing—and released my arm. I hurried into the shadows and slipped my shoes on. The major had continued down the street, and I walked quickly to catch up with him. Neither of us spoke until we were a good distance from the house.

Unsurprisingly, it was me who broke the silence. "I have a lot of questions."

He didn't break his stride, didn't even look at me. "I'm sure you do."

"Can we go somewhere to talk?"

There was the slightest pause. "I don't think that's a good idea. Go back to your rooming house, and don't leave again until morning."

I let out an irritated sigh. "Major, I . . ."

He stopped then and turned to me. I don't think he'd quite realized how close behind him I was following, because when he turned, our bodies nearly touched. He drew back slightly.

"I appreciate that things have become . . . complicated, but I don't have time for this tonight. Will you please do as I ask?"

It was the *please* that threw me off guard. I wasn't certain I'd ever heard him say it before, and even if his tone wasn't exactly pleading, there was no sharpness to it.

"Fine," I said, before I could think better of it. He had his reasons for all this shadowy business, no doubt. I'd just have to be patient.

"Good. I'll contact you soon."

I nodded, slightly mollified by this assurance. I was being

dismissed, but at least I knew he was nearby and that he knew Hal Jenkins was dead. Importantly, my instinct had been correct; the dead man was related to my mission.

"All right," I said, tamping down the hundred questions I wanted to hurl at him. I would take my leave in quiet dignity. "Good night, Major."

I turned and began to walk away from him, toward Mrs. James's establishment.

"Miss McDonnell."

I looked over my shoulder.

"Stay out of trouble," he said, instantly erasing whatever goodwill I'd had toward him.

Major Ramsey did not appear the next morning. I hadn't really expected he would arrive at the crack of dawn, but I found myself eating my porridge quickly and hurrying out to the garden in case he decided to make an appearance.

Instead, it was Sami who called to me as I wandered the little shell-strewn paths.

"Liz!"

I looked up to see her waving to me from the back door of her house. "Come and meet my sister."

I waved back. "Coming!"

Sami was standing with another woman just outside the back door of their house as I approached.

"This is my sister, Laila. Laila, this is Liz Donaldson."

Laila Maddox looked very much like her sister, though her coloring was slightly different. She had the same dark eyes, but her hair was brown rather than black, and her skin was slightly lighter than Sami's. They were a striking pair, and I could imagine they would turn plenty of heads when they went out together.

"It's a pleasure to meet you," Laila said. Her voice was soft, and lower than Sami's. The immediate impression I had of her was one of elegant reserve. She wasn't going to be as keen on a bit of gossip over a cuppa as her sister was.

"Samira tells me you've just come to Sunderland."

"Yes. Temporarily. I've come to take care of some business related to my aunt. She recently passed away."

"My condolences," Laila said.

"Thank you."

"And speaking of condolences," Sami said, "we're all going to the pub tonight for a farewell of sorts to Hal. Will you come? It won't be too maudlin. Hal wouldn't like that. We're just going to have a drink in his honor. And you can meet some of the others on the street."

"I'd like that," I said.

I looked at Laila, who hadn't spoken since her sister had mentioned Hal. "I'm sorry about the loss of your friend."

"He wasn't my friend." She said this in a tone that was difficult to read. There was no particular emotion in it, just a smooth statement of fact.

"Laila doesn't come to the pub with all of us much," Sami said, seeming to feel an explanation was necessary. "But she'd met Hal a few times."

"It was terrible what happened to him," Laila said in the same cool voice.

"What did happen to him?" I asked. "Has there been any more word on how he died?"

Sami shook her head. "No, I don't think so. I spoke to Nessa Simpson last night. She said the police asked some questions, but no one seemed to know much. It seems as though Hal just took sick suddenly and collapsed."

"Are you late for your shift, Sami?" Laila asked.

Sami looked at her watch. "Blast! I've got to dash. My boss

at the chemist hates it when I'm late. I'll see you tonight, then? I'll come to collect you at eight and we'll walk over together."

"That sounds perfect."

"You'll be home right after work?" Laila asked. "No special errands for the chemist today?"

Sami rolled her eyes. "Yes, Mother."

Then she was gone, leaving only the trailing scent of jasmine behind her.

I smiled at Laila for want of some other appropriate response to the exchange between the sisters. "It was nice to meet you."

"And you, Miss Donaldson."

"Call me Liz. Please."

She smiled her agreement, and then, with nothing much else to be said, we parted ways. Laila certainly didn't have her sister's easy way with strangers.

Returning to the house, I made my way back to my room. I had a sneaking suspicion Major Ramsey was not in a hurry to come over and share whatever information he had with me. Granted, he probably was displeased he had caught me sneaking around Hal Jenkins's room in the dead of night. I was rather surprised he hadn't dragged me off somewhere for a stern lecture last night. I had no doubt it was coming.

Thinking of last night's escapade reminded me: I wanted to look over the rubbing I had made of the desk blotter in the bright light of day. I didn't expect to find anything of use, but Uncle Mick had taught me to leave no stone unturned.

I fished the paper from the pocket of last night's trousers and went to the desk near the window and sat down. Unfolding it, I set it on the desk and smoothed out the creases as best as I could.

Daylight didn't make much difference in the readability of the paper. The rubbing had been successful. A little too successful.

It had picked up all the scribbles and scrawls left by hundreds of letters, a tangle of loops and swirls.

There were very few legible words, though I made out a few innocuous ones with no clue as to when or why they'd been written: yesterday, dearest, coffee, sea.

I suddenly wished Felix was here. He was good with this sort of thing, of taking in the nuances of handwriting, because, among his other talents, he was an accomplished forger. It was an illicit skill that he'd put to use in one of my past dealings with the major. Though, looking at this tangled mess of words, I knew he probably wouldn't be able to decipher it any better than I could.

And then I saw one word that stood out from all the others. Mostly because it was written in capital letters and underscored by deep grooves, as though the writer had pressed his pen down hard as he underlined it: <u>KILL</u>.

CHAPTER SEVEN

Well, that was curious.

I leaned closer, squinting at the word. It clearly said *KILL*, but whatever else the sentence might have said seemed lost in the swirl of words around it. I thought perhaps I could make out part of another word in line with the rest of the sentence. It said *VON*. That might be part of a name—a German name, at that.

Another idea occurred to me. I would mail the rubbing to Felix to see if he could make anything of it. It was a long shot, but it was worth a try. I didn't know how long he would be in Scotland, but hopefully he would find the letter awaiting him upon his return.

I folded up the paper again and then wrote Felix a brief letter, asking if he would look it over. I was about to sign off when I paused and decided to add a bit of what I was truly feeling to the lighthearted note.

I hope you're safe and behaving yourself. Please be careful, Felix. There isn't much news I can share with you, but I'm ever reminded how dangerous things

*are at present. I miss you and look forward to being
reunited soon. I expect you to take me dancing.*

xx,
Ellie

*P.S. Address the envelope to Liz Donaldson when you
write me back.*

I sealed the envelope and then realized that I didn't have any
stamps. I went downstairs to ask Mrs. James.

"No, dear, I'm afraid I haven't any. But the post office isn't
far. I have a bicycle in the shed, if you'd like to take it."

I liked that idea very much. I'd been meaning to get the lay of
the land in the area, to see what sort of things Hal Jenkins may
have got up to in the neighborhood. I also wanted to have a look
at the places he could potentially have gone between where I had
encountered him and where he had died. The bicycle would make
it easier to cover more ground.

My only reservation was that I was expecting Major Ramsey.
This reservation lasted less than half a moment. If he did show up
while I was gone, it would serve him right. Let him wait around
for me for once.

I gathered my handbag and jacket and, on a whim, brought
along the birding book. Then I took the bicycle and set off down
the street. I passed The Silver Sextant—the pub where we would
be meeting tonight—a bakery, a florist, and the chemist where,
presumably, Sami was employed.

Eventually, I wanted to see more of the city. Sunderland was,
of course, much too big a place for me to tour on the bicycle, but
I could take a cab. I wanted to see the places that had the most
potential to be involved in my mission: the RAF base and, if possible, the locations of the shipyards and coal mine.

The RAF base was, from what I'd gleaned so far, the closest of these locations. I'd heard the planes flying overhead often since moving into Mrs. James's.

These were all, naturally, places that would be heavily guarded, so it wasn't as though I could waltz up to any of them asking questions, but I could still gather intelligence.

A life of crime had taught me that reconnaissance was key in any job. It wasn't enough to know the house you were going to break into; you needed to know the neighborhood.

Mission objectives aside, I found that I enjoyed riding the bike along the streets, the physical exertion and the wind in my hair doing wonders to clear my head, if not to bring answers.

I rode as far as the River Wear, glancing east to where it ran into the sea. I couldn't see the sea from here, but I could smell the salt on the breeze. As much as I loved London, there was a part of me that was drawn to coastal living. Perhaps it was my heritage. Uncle Mick and my late father came from Galway.

Turning from the river, I pedaled the bicycle in the direction of the curb where I had nearly met a grim fate beneath the wheels of a lorry. It was a busy area, as it had been that day. I then turned back toward the street where I was staying, taking note of the buildings between.

There were houses and many of the same sorts of shops I had seen at the end of my street. Nothing seemed out of the ordinary.

I posted the letter to Felix and then stopped at a café for lunch, ordering tea and a cheese sandwich. As I ate, I brought out the birding book, once again flipping through the pages. I liked birds as well as anyone, and I'd always found it easy to lose myself in books of diverse topics, but this one was fairly dull.

If I was meant to know something about birds for this mission, however, I could do the job. Thankfully, I had a quick mind and an excellent memory. It had been an asset to me in our professional pursuits as well as the illegal ones. But never had it been more useful than when I'd decided to spy for king and country.

And never let it be said that I wasn't game to take on a challenge. Granted, this one wasn't particularly exciting, but that was immaterial. And at least the watercolor illustrations were pretty.

I took a bite of my sandwich and studied the painting of a capercaillie.

A moment later, movement not far from my table caught my eye, and I looked up. I was surprised to see Captain Rafe Beaumont, my train ride companion, standing just inside the doorway, waiting to be seated. He hadn't seen me yet, but I decided his company would be infinitely preferable to my current reading.

"Hello, Rafe," I called, closing the book.

He turned, smiling when he saw me. "Liz. This is a pleasant surprise. I didn't expect to run into you so soon. May I join you?" he asked, indicating the seat across from me.

"I'd love it," I said sincerely.

He settled into the seat, placing his service cap on the empty chair beside him. "You've found my favorite café."

The waitress came quickly, smiling prettily at the handsome RAF captain as he ordered coffee. When she'd gone, he turned his attention back to me. "How is everything going with your aunt's house?"

"I haven't started yet," I said, injecting a rueful note into my voice. "I was settling into my rooming house and then I . . . got a bit distracted."

I half considered telling him that a man had been killed the day I arrived, but I decided against it for the time being.

"What part of the city does she live in?"

I gave vague whereabouts of my imaginary and dearly departed aunt's house. A location had not been specified in the packet of information the major had given me. In any event, growing up among thieves had given me a naturally guarded disposition, and such information wasn't something I would have been likely to share. Even if the dead aunt and the house had been real.

"And how is everything in the RAF?" I asked.

He smiled easily. "Much the same as usual." It was an equally vague answer, but that sort of thing was expected, necessary even. Even the slightest slip of information could be disastrous in times like these, and Rafe Beaumont was too clever to share anything in casual conversation.

His coffee came, and he sipped it.

"Would you like to have dinner with me tonight? I know an excellent club, The Gale. Good food and music. Dancing."

"I . . . that sounds very nice, but I have an engagement this evening."

"Oh. Well, perhaps another time, then." He took my declining of his offer in stride and didn't press for a future date. I was glad. He was charming and handsome—and my relationship with Felix wasn't exactly exclusive—but all the same, I hadn't come to Sunderland looking for dates. Even an added friendship would distract from my mission, whatever it was, and perhaps make it more difficult to move unobserved throughout Sunderland. Already I was bumping into acquaintances.

Then again, I reflected, Nacy hadn't raised me to be rude, and Uncle Mick hadn't raised me to throw away possible sources of information. Besides, it wouldn't be a bad thing to know someone in Sunderland. The major had told me to make friends with the locals, after all.

"I'll probably be busy with my aunt's house the next day or two," I said, thinking I would no doubt link up with Major Ramsey at some point. "But if you'd like to take me driving one day later this week, I'd love to see more of Sunderland."

He smiled. "Shall we say Friday, then?"

"That would be nice."

I gave him the telephone number to Mrs. James's house and then, my tea finished, bid him good afternoon.

Sami picked me up at eight o'clock sharp. She looked stunning in a dress of deep garnet red, and I felt a bit underdressed in my tweed skirt and white blouse.

"Shall we wait for your sister?" I asked when we were outside. The sky was a dark, dusky blue, the sun long gone down behind the horizon, and the nightingales were chirping in the hedges.

"She's already there, I imagine. Laila treats punctuality almost like a religion."

We walked down toward the pub together, chatting about the events of our day.

"I have a bicycle, too," Sami said. "We should cycle down to the beach one day. Well, most of the beaches are closed, but we can get near. We can have a picnic."

"That would be nice." Two days in Sunderland and already my social calendar was fuller than it usually was in London.

We went into The Silver Sextant. We were engulfed immediately by the atmosphere of the place. Dark, smoky air, the smell of ale and food, raucous laughter. It was not, perhaps, the atmosphere that might appeal to a gently bred girl, but, despite my time at finishing school, I was not gently bred, and I felt immediately at home. It reminded me of nights spent at home, with the boisterous voices of my cousins and the scent of Uncle Mick's pipe.

Sami took my arm, ushering me through the crowd toward a table in the corner. There were four people sitting there.

Laila was the first person I noticed. Like Sami, she was so striking that the eye was instantly drawn to her. But it wasn't only that. There was something that set her apart from everyone around her, an aloofness that created the illusion of physical distance, as though she were a china doll protected beneath a bell jar.

She seemed a bit put off by the atmosphere of the place, and none of her companions seemed to be engaging with her.

"Hello, loves," Sami said as we approached the table. "This is my new friend, Liz."

They greeted me, and Sami made introductions. "You know Laila, of course. And Nessa," she said, pointing to the blond girl beside her sister, the one I'd met on the afternoon of Hal Jenkins's death.

"Nice to see you, Liz," Nessa said. I hadn't taken much note of her appearance in the excitement of our first meeting. She had a broad, pale face with a smattering of freckles across her nose and pale blue eyes.

"And this is Carlotta Hogan." Carlotta was a small brunette girl who reminded me of the watercolor of the garden warbler in *The Birds of Northern England*: dainty with sandy-brown hair and dark eyes.

Inwardly, I cursed the birding book and the unwanted avian knowledge it was foisting upon me.

"And this is Alfred Little. He lives at Mrs. James's, too." I looked at the young man, sure I hadn't seen him before. He was an extremely pale, thin boy with white-blond hair and gray eyes who looked as though he was barely old enough to be allowed in the pub. He offered me a shy smile and his eyes flickered away from mine almost instantly.

"I'm pleased you let me join you tonight," I said. "I didn't know Hal, but it was a tragic thing that happened to him, and I'm glad to take part in honoring his memory."

Sami and I took our seats, and I found myself seated between Laila and Nessa.

I had been trying to get a read on Laila, and, as the others talked, I realized one thing about her. She wasn't simply reserved. She was watchful. I ought to have recognized it sooner, for it was a quality I also possessed. In my line of work, watchfulness was a necessity, and I had cultivated the habit even when I wasn't working. I was constantly aware of my surroundings, taking note of the people around me and what they were doing.

Laila had the same air of studied attentiveness. She was keeping tabs on everything that went on around her. Why was that? Was it simply a natural inclination, or something more?

But perhaps I was making something out of nothing. That was the trouble with war. It made you look for trouble where there might be none. But it wasn't paranoia when the danger really existed, was it? After all, a man was dead.

I turned my attention to Nessa and started up a conversation.

She was friendly and forthright, talking in an easy manner about the neighborhood and her war job.

"I work at the shipyard," she said. "I'm a welder."

"Impressive," I said, and I meant it. We'd worked a few times with Sparky Spellman, a fellow who used a blowtorch instead of combination work to open safes. I had always been fascinated at the way the ferocity of fire could be bent to one's will, that most destructive of nature's elements made an accomplice in productivity.

"It's better than the job I had before the war," she said. "I was a shopgirl; I had no patience for it."

"I almost hate for the war to be over," Carlotta said from across the table. "It'll be back to business as usual for us women with nary a word of thanks."

"Carlotta!" Laila said.

Carlotta shrugged, defiant. "Well, it's true. I don't want to be a teacher, and I don't intend to be. When the men come back from war, they can't have my job."

"Don't tell me you ladies are taking up with suffragettes again."

I looked up to see that another member of the group had arrived. He was a strapping young man, tall and broad-shouldered with coppery hair and a ruddy, expressive face.

"And here's Ronnie Potter to round out our little wake," Sami said cheerfully. "Ronnie, meet Liz Donaldson. She's staying with Mrs. James."

He stretched out a hand to shake mine. "Pleased to meet you, Liz. I'm called Ronald," he told me with a smile. "No one but Sami has called me Ronnie since I left the nursery."

Sami handed him a mug of ale and he picked it up, clearing his throat to begin a speech. I wondered if he was the de facto leader of this little group. I would have thought it might be Sami, but they had all waited for Ronald to arrive and were waiting now for him to speak, their attention focused on him.

"Hal wasn't the rowdiest of blokes, but he was a good friend and the life of the party, in his way. He was always there with a smile and a cheerful word or a joke. I'll always remember the first time I met him . . ."

He launched into the story, and I looked around the group, taking in their expressions, their reaction to Ronald's words. I didn't know the nuances of their individual relationships with Hal Jenkins, how close each of them had been to him. From what I had learned of Hal Jenkins—and indeed from the tenor of Ronald's speech—Hal didn't seem the type to get too close to people.

Laila was still and stiff beside me, and I hadn't quite worked out yet whether she was sad or annoyed. Nessa looked sympathetic yet stoic. Carlotta's face was grave. Alfred looked uncomfortable. More than once, I saw his finger slip into his collar as if to loosen it.

They all seemed genuine enough reactions, varied responses to sadness based on the little flickers of personality I had seen so far. Of course, I knew that a spy or a murderer would be careful to hide his true feelings.

I realized that I had begun to think of Hal Jenkins's death in such terms—that he was a spy and that he had been murdered. Perhaps this realization ought to have surprised me, but it didn't. After all, Major Ramsey was involved in this somehow. That much was clear from last night's encounter. And Major Ramsey did not tend to involve himself in matters of little consequence.

Speaking of the major, I was cross he had yet to make contact. It was irresponsible of him to leave me waiting for him.

Not to put too fine a point on it, but there was also the possibility that I might be in danger at this very moment. I'd never been overly concerned with my own safety—thieves didn't have the luxury of a strong self-preservation instinct—but I couldn't help being a bit put out with the major that he knew there had been a suspicious death, and he had still left me to my own devices.

My attention was called back to the present as the group chuckled collectively at Ronald's retelling of one of Hal's jokes.

"I suppose I'll be telling that one for the rest of my life. In Hal's honor. Here's to you, Hal." He lifted his glass.

"To Hal," Sami said, raising her glass. She had done it so quickly that a little spilled over the side.

"To Hal," we all repeated.

The toast completed, the group relaxed and began talking and joking with one another. Though I was clearly the outsider, they made an effort to include me in their conversations. I thought it couldn't hurt to buy the next round to further my good standing—and perhaps loosen their tongues a bit.

I looked to flag down a barmaid, but the place had grown extremely busy in the time since we'd come in, and the only one I could see was laden with a tray full of sloshing ales.

"I'll go and get some more drinks," I said, rising from my seat and waving down the men as they began to rise.

"Sami and I don't drink alcohol," Laila said. I caught a flash of annoyance on Sami's features, but she didn't contradict her sister.

"I'm not much of a drinker myself," I said. "Perhaps some ginger ale?"

Laila nodded.

I walked to the bar. There were several people crowded around it, and I was waiting for the barman's attention when I felt someone move up very close behind me.

"Hello," a man's voice said directly into my ear.

I didn't turn around, though I was fairly certain the greeting had been directed at me.

It wasn't the first time I'd been approached by a man in a pub. Uncle Mick and the boys had always formed a sort of protective barrier when they were with me, but I'd learned to take care of myself.

"I'd like to talk to you," he said, his voice close to my ear.

"Sorry," I said, without turning around. "I'm here with someone."

"You don't suppose you could make an exception?"

"No, I . . ." I looked up at him for the first time and blinked. I didn't recognize the major at first. For one thing, he was not in his usual army uniform. Instead, he was wearing RAF blue, which, I had to admit, suited him immensely.

But there was something markedly different about him. His carriage, normally rigid with duty and disapproval, had the swagger of a pilot, and even his voice had sounded different. The warm, charming tone had been so unlike the usual clipped pitch of his voice that I hadn't even registered Major Ramsey as the possible owner of it.

I remembered he had told me that I was to act as if we were strangers, so I smiled up at him. "I might," I said, answering his question.

The barmaid appeared then, and I turned back to put in my order for the drinks. When I turned back, the major had moved even closer.

"You said you're here with someone?" he asked.

I nodded toward the table in the corner, where the group laughed loudly at something Ronald was saying. They were engaged in his story and were paying no attention to me. "I'm having dinner with my friends," I said. "Would you like to join us?"

"I'd rather just talk to you." He said this in a tone that, to anyone in the crowd around us who might be listening, would sound flirtatious. Knowing the major as I did, this change in manner was taking a bit of getting used to.

"Maybe you should ask me to dance," I said, lifting my brows ever so slightly. A woman at the piano in the corner had started up a tune, and several couples had moved to a makeshift dance floor in one corner of the room.

"Perhaps I shall."

"I'll look forward to it." I flashed him a smile and then moved past him without a backward glance.

CHAPTER EIGHT

I considered this newest development as I made my way back to the table. What was he doing here in an RAF uniform? I knew him better than to believe his appearance at this pub was a coincidence. He had followed me here. I was a bit annoyed it had taken him all day to do it, but now was better than never.

Laila and Sami were standing a little way off from the table talking in hushed, urgent tones when I approached. I caught a glimpse of Sami's face and saw she looked exasperated. Catching sight of me, Laila cut off the conversation and stepped back from her sister.

"I've got to be going," Laila said. "I have a headache. It's rather loud in here." Trombone and clarinet players had appeared as if out of nowhere to join in the lively jazz tune. They were rather good, I thought.

"Yes, I suppose it is a bit loud," I answered. "Though, I confess, I sometimes think it's nice to have a bit of noise and atmosphere. It's so quiet, living alone."

"We wouldn't know about that," Sami said, a slight edge to her tone.

"No," Laila agreed, shooting a meaningful glance at her sister. "We've always had each other."

It was clear that they'd been arguing about something. Sami was still angry, and Laila was attempting to mollify her. Or was she reminding her that they were allies, not enemies?

"I'm going home to take some aspirin," Laila said. "I hope you have a nice time. Good evening, Miss Donaldson."

"Good evening," I said, watching her leave.

"Everything all right?" I asked Sami.

She waved a hand dismissively. "It's always something with Laila. She thinks she needs to run my life as well as her own."

I wondered which of them was the older sibling and had to guess it must be Laila. I was beginning to get a read on their dynamic. Sami was clearly the more outgoing and social of the two. Laila held more traditional values and disapproved of her sister's more modern behaviors. It was an old tale.

I'd experienced a bit of that myself, with my cousins. Colm and Toby, despite the shenanigans they engaged in, were forever trying to keep me out of trouble and felt they had the right to lecture me about things because I was younger than them. It could be very trying to be the youngest in the family, and it seemed natural enough that Sami would push against the boundaries her sister was trying to set.

"I'm sure she means well," I said.

Sami pulled a face and then went back to her place at the table. She and Carlotta began talking in low voices, and I supposed Sami was complaining about her sister. Carlotta appeared sympathetic.

Our drinks arrived, and we sipped them and continued to talk.

Part of me remained attuned for the major's approach, but it seemed he was going to take his time about it. Well, I could make use of the time anyway.

"What do you do?" I asked Ronald. He'd had his drink, the

one I'd bought, and had managed to flag down a barmaid for a third. He wasn't drunk, but his eyes had the slightly shiny quality of a man who was on his way.

"I work at the docks," he said. "I've been thinking about signing up, but they keep telling us we're doing important work there."

"Of course you are," I said encouragingly. "I suppose there must be a lot of ships coming in and out of the port now, more than usual."

He nodded. "The quays are teeming most days. And Alfred there works in the mines. Accounts for his complexion."

Alfred smiled weakly at the joke, and I supposed it must be one he had heard often.

"Will you dance with me now?" I looked up to see the major standing at the side of the table. Sami looked up at him, and I could see the interest in her gaze. The major seemed to attract female attention wherever we went. I had noticed it often, but he seemed to be unaware—or at least deeply unconcerned about it. Usually, that was. Tonight, he was leaning into it. He was aware that he was attractive, and he was using it as part of his costume as much as he was those RAF blues.

I glanced at my companions. Carlotta had joined Sami in admiring the major, her dark eyes sparkling. Nessa was much less obvious, but I could see that she, too, appreciated his charms.

I smiled up at him as I would have if he'd truly been a dashing RAF man and not my grim handler playing a part. "I'd love to."

He pulled back my chair for me and then took my elbow as he led me out to the dance floor. He pulled me into his arms, and we began to dance.

Naturally enough, I'd never had cause to dance with Major Ramsey, but I wasn't at all surprised to find that he was an excellent dancer. He was, underneath his hard military shell, rather posh. The nephew of an earl would surely have attended his share of society soirees. What was more, he had a natural athleticism to him that made him physically adept at most things.

"You dance beautifully," I said, before I thought better of it.

"Thank you. So do you. Some aspects of finishing school seem to have been a success for you."

For an instant I was surprised at this remark, but then I remembered the major's dossier on me, the one that had put my life into a neat little list of facts and dates. He knew, of course, that Uncle Mick had sent me to finishing school. But there had been a bit of a dig in there as well.

"Some aspects were successful?" I repeated. "Meaning, I suppose, that some things didn't take?"

He leaned a bit closer. "They did not succeed in subduing that little tilt of your chin when you get angry. Or the flash of defiance in your eyes."

I wanted to be cross with him, but I couldn't stop the smile that came to me. He'd summed me up very accurately. "It was not, after all, meant to alter my personality," I said.

"No," he answered. "We wouldn't want that."

For a moment, neither of us spoke as we settled into the rhythm of the dance. I had a good deal I wanted to say to him, but we were surrounded by people. This was not the ideal meeting place, but it occurred to me that he'd probably done it this way to establish our acquaintance.

He'd approached me in a pub, a thing RAF men did every day in the city. We'd have to pretend to be interested in each other romantically in order to account for our time together. We'd done it before, as it was, quite naturally, the best cover story for a man and a woman working together.

His voice pulled me out of my thoughts.

"Making friends, I see."

"I'm good at making friends," I said. "It comes easier to some than to others."

We danced in silence for a moment after that. Then he leaned closer. "What made you search Hal Jenkins's room?"

"I was there when he died. There was something strange about it. And that's not all," I said. "He saved me from being run over by a lorry an hour or two before he died."

If he was surprised by this, he gave no sign of it. "Where did this happen?"

"A few blocks from my lodging house," I said. "I'm not entirely sure someone didn't push me intentionally."

"What did he say to you? Did you talk about anything?"

"No. I only thanked him for saving my life. But later, when I saw his body, I noticed that he had something clutched in his hand. It was a piece of paper, and it said 'We know you have it.'"

"You ought to have told me this last night." His expression was perfectly pleasant, though there were daggers in the words.

"You didn't give me time!"

"I suppose I was a bit distracted encountering you in the middle of an unauthorized burglary."

I gave a little laugh, and it was genuine. "Looking at your face, one would never know you're reading me a lecture. You're a very good actor, Major."

"Captain," he corrected.

I looked up at him. "I suppose you had better introduce yourself."

"Captain John Grey, RAF." John Grey, a suitably unimaginative name for the major. No doubt he'd always longed to be a simple *John* but had been forced to contend with the more glamorous *Gabriel*.

"A pleasure to make your acquaintance, Captain. I'm Liz Donaldson."

"The pleasure is all mine, Elizabeth," he said, ignoring the shortened form of the name I'd chosen for myself. "Do you still have the note?"

"Yes. I'll bring it the next time I see you. Now it's time for you to answer some questions," I said. "Did you know Hal Jenkins? Was he working for you or against you?"

"Now isn't the time to discuss this."

"I think he was murdered," I pressed. "His expression was . . . unnatural, and he had a sort of white foam coming from his lips." I managed to suppress the shudder I felt at my memory of the expression on the dead man's face.

"Yes, I saw him. I was there."

I looked up at him, surprised. "I didn't see you."

"You weren't meant to."

I stepped on his foot, and he pretended not to notice.

We danced in silence for a few moments.

"I want to talk to you," I said at last, when it became apparent he didn't mean to share any more information with me. "I *need* to talk to you. After all, I was very nearly pushed in front of a lorry, and a man has been killed. I think I deserve some explanations."

"That's why I'm striking up your acquaintance. So we can be seen together." He paused, seemingly considering something, and then he spoke. "I'll come and collect you in the morning."

I studied him. It was suspicious that he had given in to my demands. "Just like that?"

"You're going to make a nuisance of yourself until I agree. So consider it a date."

"A date?"

"Yes. Isn't it perfectly obvious I'm courting you?"

I laughed outright at this, and I thought there was even a hint of amusement in his eyes, which, against the color of his uniform, looked distinctly blue tonight.

Despite my general irritation with his refusal to share information, I found that I enjoyed the dance. I didn't get out dancing much these days. Felix had taken me a time or two, but, though I would never have dared to say it to him, I worried that it was too much on his leg. He was naturally graceful and moved easily, even with the artificial limb, but I sometimes worried that it pained him more than he would admit.

The dance concluded, and Major Ramsey escorted me back to the table.

The girls looked at me expectantly, and I made introductions all around. Neither Alfred nor Ronald seemed much enthused about the major's appearance. Then again, Alfred was shy, and Ronald had consumed another glass or two during the dance and was slightly slumped in his seat.

"Have a drink with us, Captain," Sami said.

"I'm afraid I have somewhere to be, though I find myself tempted by such delightful company," he said, with this newly assumed charm. "Perhaps another night?"

"Yes," Sami agreed, a slight smile on her full lips. "We'd like that."

She was flirting with him right in front of me, but I supposed I technically had no claim on his attentions in her mind. We'd only just met. In any event, she was going to be disappointed.

Or perhaps not, I thought suddenly. I knew nothing about his personal life. There could be any number of women, and perhaps he would enjoy getting to know Sami better while getting information from her.

Working so closely with the major and for such high stakes gave the illusion of intimacy. But we weren't friends. We were colleagues, working toward a common goal. That was the whole of it.

He was an extremely attractive man, and though he had made it clear to me on more than one occasion that he didn't have time for relationships, perhaps he preferred more casual encounters. What did I know?

I realized that this line of thinking was not at all productive, and so I pulled my attention back to the conversation just as Major Ramsey turned to me and took my hand in his. "I look forward to tomorrow, Miss Donaldson."

"Me, too," I replied, and batted my lashes a bit for good measure.

With a smile and nod at the table, he took his leave.

When he had faded back into the crowd, Sami gave a quiet whistle. "You've snagged a dreamboat, Liz. I don't remember the last time I've seen such a good-looking man."

"He's very fine looking," Carlotta agreed.

"Did you give him your telephone number?" Sami asked.

"We're going out driving tomorrow morning," I said.

"Even better," Sami said. "You're a quick worker. I'm a bit jealous!"

Sami winked at me, and we went back to our drinks. I felt my fondness for the group growing. They were all warm and funny. Even Alfred, who said little, began to warm to me and told me a bit about his work in the mines.

Surely none of this group would have had reason to kill Hal, would they?

All the same, I couldn't help but notice they were all doing war work with potentially sensitive information. Ronald at the port, Alfred in the mines. Nessa worked at the shipyard, and I learned that Carlotta had a job at the chemist where Sami worked.

Was it possible that Hal Jenkins had found out something that one of them didn't want the others to know? Had Hal been working with one of them in some sort of nefarious scheme?

I had so many questions, and I didn't feel the night had gotten me any closer to solving the mystery of Hal Jenkins's death. I hoped that the major would finally be able to answer some of them tomorrow.

CHAPTER NINE

Although I had felt troubled about everything that was happening, I found that I slept well. Perhaps it was because the safety of my bed was much more assured than it had been in London these past few weeks.

Not that Sunderland had escaped either. This was a port city and thus a good target for Nazi bombs. Thus far, however, my nights had been quiet, and I had been lulled to sleep by only the occasional call of some nocturnal bird outside the window (a nightjar, perhaps?) and the sea breeze in the trees.

My guilt at the luxury of it reminded me that I needed to call home. I asked Mrs. James if I might use the telephone before breakfast to make a quick call to London. I thought doing it early would lessen the chance of my call being overheard.

"Hello," Nacy answered after a few rings, and I felt a swelling of love at the sound of her voice—and also relief. If she was answering, that meant they were all right and that the house was still there.

"Hello, Nacy," I said. "It's Ellie."

"Oh, Ellie, I'm glad you've called."

"Is everything all right?"

"Yes, dear. All's well here. I've just been worried about you."

"I'm sorry I haven't called sooner, but things have been so busy here. You're both safe?"

"Yes. The bombing has been going on as usual, but we're all right."

I felt another stab of guilt that they continued to face the danger of nightly air raids while I enjoyed what was essentially a trip to the seaside. I knew, of course, that I was doing my part to fight the war here, but it didn't make it any easier to think about the bombs dropping around my family.

"Have you heard from Felix?" I asked. I had told him he could ring Nacy if he had any messages he wished to relay to me, and that I'd get them eventually.

"No, we've not heard anything from him."

I hadn't really expected that he would ring me from Scotland, not unless there was something wrong. I wondered what he was getting up to. More than once, he'd evaded the topic, even going so far as to tell me that he didn't want to talk about it.

It was strange and a bit unsettling.

Besides, I wanted him to look at the rubbing I'd taken from the desk blotter in Hal Jenkins's room.

"I can't talk long, Nacy. I just wanted to check in with you, to make sure you are all right."

"Yes, dear. We're fine. Are you taking care of yourself? Have you had enough to eat?"

I smiled. "Yes, on both counts."

"Oh, Mick wants to speak to you. Be careful, dear."

"I promise."

There was a moment of silence on the line, and then I heard my Uncle Mick's voice. "Hello, Ellie girl. How are you?"

"I'm fine, Uncle Mick. It's good to hear your voice."

"Yours, too. I wanted to tell you there's a letter that came for you in the post yesterday." There was something a bit off in his voice, I realized suddenly.

"Oh?" I asked.

"It's from Clarice Maynard."

I stilled. Clarice Maynard had been my mother's best friend before my mother's death of the influenza when I was very young. I had only just learned of Clarice's existence and was eager to talk to her about my family's secret past, the story I had never confided to anyone except Felix.

The grim facts were that my mother had been sentenced to death for the murder of my father before I was born. The sentence had been commuted when her pregnancy was discovered, but she had died when I was still much too young to remember her.

Uncle Mick and Nacy had raised me—along with Colm and Toby—in a loving household, and I'd never wanted for love or affection. But I had lived beneath the shadow of the family tragedy nonetheless.

My mother had gone to her grave protesting her innocence, and, no matter how much evidence I had read against her, I could not bring myself to believe that she had killed my father.

Recently, I had spoken to two people who had led me to feel these weren't empty hopes on my part. One was a fellow prisoner, who said my mother had confided to her that, though she suspected the identity of the real killer, the truth would do more harm than good.

The other was my mother's barrister. He, too, had told me that he believed in her innocence but that my mother was hiding something. He had said that her friend, Clarice Maynard, would be my best shot at learning something new about her.

After a good deal of searching, I had found her address and written to see if I might come and visit her at her home in Lincolnshire to talk about my mother.

I didn't know what I expected to do about my mother's case now. There was no bringing her back, no saving my father from the fate that had befallen him. Nevertheless, I felt that I had to know. If I could prove her innocence, it would at least remove the stain from her name, take some of the weight off our family.

Uncle Mick and my father had been very close, and, though he had never spoken a word against my mother, I knew that he must believe that she had done it.

Now the letter had arrived when I was absent, and it was clear from his voice that he recognized the name.

I didn't want to lie to Uncle Mick. I'd never lied to him about anything. And so I told him half the truth. "I ran into someone a while back who knew my mother, and they mentioned Mrs. Maynard. I thought . . . well, I thought it wouldn't hurt to get in touch with her."

There was a pause at the other end of the line. Uncle Mick was seldom speechless, so I grew uneasy in the silence. At last, he said, "You know I'll tell you anything you want to know about your mother, love." I tried to gauge if it was hurt or disappointment in his voice. Maybe it was a bit of both.

"I know," I said. "You've always been wonderful, Uncle Mick. I just . . . I know talking about . . . everything must be difficult for you. But we don't have to discuss it now. We'll discuss it when I get home."

"Do you want me to forward the letter?"

I considered. I was curious what Clarice Maynard had to say, and now that I knew the letter was there, I thought it might prove a distraction if I dismissed it.

"Yes, you might as well." I told him to send it to the post office where I had mailed Felix's letter. I didn't want anything coming to Mrs. James's house with my real name on it. This also helped me to avoid directly disobeying the major's order not to share anything about the mission. After all, the general location of Sunderland could give little away.

"All right," Uncle Mick said. "I'll send it along."

"Thank you." There was another pause, and I found I couldn't ring off without asking. "Uncle Mick?"

"Yes?"

"You're not . . . angry with me?"

"Of course not, love," he said, his voice as warm and gentle as when he'd comforted me as a child. "It's just . . . there are certain things . . . well, we'll discuss it when you get home, like you said. And if there's anything in that letter you want to talk about before then, you've only to phone me."

"All right. Thank you."

That would have to suffice for now, but I didn't want to end the conversation on that note. I didn't want him to think I felt he hadn't done enough for me, that I didn't appreciate his role in my life. He had done as much as any parent ever could, even more. All the same, this was something I had to pursue. I needed to know the truth, whatever it might be.

I didn't have time to put all these feelings into words, so I simply related the feeling that was strongest.

"Perhaps I don't say it often enough," I told him, my throat tight with emotion. "But you know I love you, Uncle Mick."

I heard the smile in his voice. "I love you, too, Ellie girl."

I ate a breakfast of warm, thick porridge with Mrs. James's other lodgers, none of whom seemed overly interested in conversation. Alfred Little was not there. I had yet to see him since I'd begun lodging here, but I knew miners kept long hours.

I had just set down my spoon when Mrs. James came bustling into the dining room, her cheeks flushed and eyes twinkling.

"Liz, dear, your gentleman friend is in the parlor," she said. "Calling rather early, isn't he? He must be smitten."

"Thank you, Mrs. James." I was glad to hear the major had arrived early. I was ready to see why I had been called to Sunderland

and what it had to do with Hal Jenkins's death. In fact, the major had a good deal to explain.

I walked into the parlor and found him standing near the window, looking out at the back garden where I had first met Sami.

He turned at the sound of my footsteps and smiled at me, catching me off guard. I had forgotten he was meant to be a charming RAF officer and not his usual commanding self. His smiles always threw me, the infrequent flash of those straight, white teeth a reminder that he was capable of human warmth after all.

"Good morning, Elizabeth," he said.

"Hello, John," I replied. I knew in a rooming house this size and with a landlady who loved a good gossip as much as Mrs. James, there was every chance this conversation would be overheard. And so I gave him the closest thing I could to a reprimand. "You're here earlier than I expected."

"I couldn't wait any longer to see you," he replied smoothly. "Are you ready?"

I didn't know where we were going, but there wasn't much use in protesting now. "As ready as I'll ever be," I said. "Just let me run upstairs and get my jacket and handbag."

"Don't forget the book," he said.

For an instant, I was confused. And then I realized what he meant. *The Birds of Northern England.*

"All right." I found myself excited at the prospect of finding out what the bird guide was truly for.

I went up to gather my things and hurried back down the stairs. The major was waiting for me in the foyer, and Mrs. James had found him. They were chatting amiably.

Major Ramsey was smiling again, charming Mrs. James, and she was enjoying every moment of his attention. I felt a stab of annoyance that the major never wasted any of that charm on me. Not that I particularly wanted to be charmed; I would much rather know where I stood with a person than deal with false pleasantries. All the same, it was a sharp reminder that he didn't seem to view me as worth the effort of being anything more than civil.

I plastered a pleasant expression on my face as I approached them. "All set."

"Have a good time, dear," Mrs. James said.

"Thank you."

"She may not be home for dinner," the major said to Mrs. James as he took my arm. "But I'll have her home at a decent hour."

She beamed at him, and we took our leave.

He had a car parked at the curb, and we said nothing as we walked toward it, his hand on the small of my back.

He opened the door for me, and I slid inside. He went around to get in, and a moment later, we were driving away from the house.

"You owe me several explanations, Major Ramsey," I said.

"I'm sure you think so, but let's not deal with them all at once, shall we?"

He was himself again, the charm having been tucked away until it was needed again. It really was impressive the way he could pretend to be so warm and personable when his natural state was cool and distant.

"If the army hadn't been to your taste, you could have had a career onstage," I said. "The way you can turn your pleasantness on and off like a switch is really marvelous."

"Surely you don't mean to suggest that I am habitually unpleasant?"

"I'm not suggesting it. I'm saying it."

He smiled, one of the rare genuine smiles I had seen from him. "I don't have to pretend with you, Miss McDonnell, just as you clearly don't have to pretend with me."

We were silent for a few moments as he drove down the street, past the pub, and toward the river. He then turned in a northeastern direction, toward the sea.

"What's this bird book all about?" I asked him.

"It's a part of your cover story."

"Is that all?" I asked, annoyed that I'd imbued the book with more significance than necessary.

"A cover story is an important part of any mission, Miss McDonnell. Let us not discount it."

"That's easy for you to say. You haven't spent hours memorizing inane bird facts."

"Then let's put that hard-earned knowledge to good use, shall we?"

He reached his arm behind me into the backseat and then set something heavy in my lap. A pair of binoculars.

I looked over at him.

"We're going to watch some birds."

CHAPTER TEN

We continued toward the seaside but away from the city proper, and the view grew more scenic, the green vista stretching out into the distance, dotted with trees and the occasional rocky outcrop.

The major wasn't going to give me any information until he was ready, and neither of us seemed inclined to small talk, so I put my window down and enjoyed the gusts of salty air that were interspersed with the cool afternoon breeze. I had never been to the northeast coast. In truth, I hadn't often ventured far from London. Our lives and our work were there, and we'd never been a family of holiday-goers.

"Hal Jenkins was poisoned." The major broke the silence in a startling fashion. "Potassium cyanide."

I drew in a sharp breath. I remembered the contortion of his face and the foam on his lips. "That's awful. Poor man."

"It's quick," the major said. "Spies operating in enemy territory often keep capsules on them in case of capture."

I looked up at him. "Do you think he was a spy?"

"That remains to be seen, but it's not something lay people often have on hand."

"No," I agreed reflectively. There had been a deadly toxin

involved in our last mission. It seemed the Germans had a large supply of deadly potions on hand.

I thought back to what little I knew about Hal Jenkins. He hadn't seemed nefarious to me, and I had a good instinct. Having been raised around criminals, I was very good at reading people. My own brief interaction with him had shown him to be a man of, if not conscience, at least consideration. He had quite possibly saved my life, after all. Even my late-night perusal of his residence, the word *kill* etched into the blotter aside, had given me no actual proof of wrongdoing.

It occurred to me that I should probably tell the major what I had discovered on the desk blotter, but then I remembered that I had sent the rubbing off to Felix. It had seemed like a good idea at the time, but now I was fairly certain Major Ramsey would be cross with me if I admitted it.

Perhaps I would just hold aside that bit of information for now. After all, it hadn't actually been anything concrete. That single word was not even necessarily written during Hal Jenkins's stay at that lodging house. Perhaps the word *kill* had been a bit of hyperbole in a love letter or something of the sort, entirely innocent and unrelated to Hal Jenkins or his death.

All the same, he had been killed, hadn't he? How else would he have been poisoned? It wasn't likely he had saved me and sent me on my merry way only to swallow a cyanide capsule a short time later. That didn't make sense.

"But surely he didn't take the capsule himself? Why would he do that on a crowded street? Unless he was in danger of being caught by someone?"

"No, I don't think so," the major said. "I think it far more likely that it was administered without his being aware of it. It would have to have been a very short time before he died, however."

Some parts of this scenario were still unclear to me. Indeed, a lot of things were still unclear, but I decided to start at the beginning while the major was in the right frame of mind for answering questions.

"So why did you bring me to Sunderland?" I asked. "What's my purpose in all of this? Was it something to do with Hal Jenkins from the beginning?"

"In a manner of speaking. I have an informant who heard rumors about some activities Hal Jenkins might have been involved in. It appears the informant was onto something."

"What sort of activities?"

"We'll discuss that in more detail later."

I ought not to have been surprised that the major was playing his cards close to his chest. As usual, I'd been left in the dark as much as possible. I could never be sure if this was simply because of the clandestine nature of our work or because he didn't quite trust me. I was a thief, after all.

Or had been, at any rate.

These days I was no longer sure exactly where I fell on the spectrum of law-abiding citizens. We hadn't pulled a job of our own since getting involved with Major Ramsey, and I found that these dalliances with espionage were providing me with more than enough danger and excitement to quell my less legal impulses.

All the same, the secrecy rankled. I sighed. "Why all the mystery, Major? You can trust me a little by now, can't you?" I kept my tone light, but the question was in earnest. I'd done enough to earn at least a bit of trust by now.

He glanced over at me. "It isn't that I don't trust you, Miss McDonnell. It's simply that there are a great many factors at play here. There are a few things about which I have no definite answers, and what I do know will be best explained when we get to where I'm taking you."

I accepted this and pressed onward. "Is that why you chose Mrs. James's lodging house for me? Because Hal Jenkins lived on the same street?"

"It was preferable to keep you near him. There were no vacancies at Mrs. Yardley's rooming house. Alas, not everything can be arranged according to ideal specifications."

"Then you meant to have me monitor his activities?"

"I was doing that myself. He's been on my radar for some time. I did, however, hope you would get to know some of his associates. The only people that he seems to have spent any amount of time with recently are your little group of new friends. He met with them regularly at the pub. You saw for yourself that it's crowded and noisy. It would be an ideal place to exchange information or even small packages without drawing much notice. As I suspected, you've made better inroads with his group of friends than I might."

I shot him a smile. "Don't undersell yourself, Major. I'm sure you could get a lot more information out of Sami Maddox than I could."

He said nothing. For some reason, I couldn't resist pressing the issue just a bit, however. "In fact, you ought to have courted Sami rather than pretending to court me. You would have had better access to the source of information."

"I don't care for those sorts of tactics," he said.

I couldn't resist teasing him a little. "Do you never mix business with pleasure, Major?"

His eyes met mine and held for just a moment, and I felt the heat creeping up my neck.

"I find it generally ill-advised to do so," he said at last. "And I think it especially distasteful to use romance as a means to an end. I don't make promises I don't intend to keep."

Sometimes I forgot that there was that aristocratic heritage underneath the military bearing. He would, no doubt, have been raised on the ideas of honor and chivalry.

"It's wartime," I said. "Most romances don't require promises these days."

Even though I believed what I said, a little part of me admired his unwillingness to play with a woman's heart just because it might prove useful to him. Enough men did just that without noble motivations, so the fact that he avoided it even when it might have made his job easier was commendable.

He ignored my observations on the nature of wartime romance, and we drove along for the next few moments in silence. Just to show him that I could, I refrained from asking any more questions. For the time being, that was.

Finally, the major pulled the car over, far enough into the tall grass that lined the road that it wasn't in danger of being hit by anyone who might drive this way. He did nothing to conceal it, so it appeared that this was not going to be a clandestine mission, at least not at present.

He got out of the car and would have come around to open my door, but I didn't wait for him. I got out myself and surveyed the landscape.

It was a pretty spot, though there was nothing much to see. It looked much the same as the road we had just driven along. In the distance I could hear the sea, though I couldn't see it here, for we were in a slight dip in the land and there was a wooded area between us and the shore.

It was a lovely day, and for the briefest of moments, I allowed myself to appreciate it. The sky was bright blue overhead with only a few wispy clouds floating dreamily along above us.

I was caught by the silence of it all. There was no noise but the rustle of the wind through the tall grass and the leaves of the trees, and the distant sound of the sea.

"It's always so strange for me to be away from the city," I said as Major Ramsey came around to where I stood. "I'm not used to the quiet."

"Especially not now," he agreed. "I've grown so accustomed to bombs, I can scarcely sleep without them." It was almost a joke! Well, he was in a fine mood today.

"I've told you before, Major. I'm firmly under the impression you don't sleep," I said.

"I manage it occasionally." He nodded toward the binoculars, left behind on my seat. "Don't forget those."

And so we were back to business.

I retrieved the binoculars and slung them by the strap around my neck. "Now what?"

"Now we look for birds."

He turned and began walking away, so he didn't see me roll my eyes and tramp irritably after him. I glared hard enough at his back, however, that he could probably feel it.

We walked along through the field for several minutes in semi-companionable silence. The major paid me no attention whatsoever, but he did look interestedly at any birds that darted past us, and there were quite a few.

I pointed out a wood pigeon and starling, just to prove that I had been doing my lessons like a good student.

Every so often, I lifted the binoculars to my eyes for effect. Well, I hoped the major would think I was doing it for effect. I was really doing it to find out if I could catch sight of why he had brought me out here.

At last, I lowered the binoculars and stopped walking. "Are you going to tell me what this is all about or not?"

He stopped, too, and turned back to me. "Reconnaissance."

I glanced around at the stretch of fields around us. "There's nothing to see here."

He didn't answer but resumed walking. I considered refusing

to move until he gave me more information, but after a moment, I followed. There was a barely discernible path through the tall grass, as though someone had tread here recently. Had that been the major?

We reached a copse of trees, and the major stopped, turning to me once again. "It's possible that we may be observed. We should try to appear to be on friendly terms."

I couldn't help but laugh. "I don't think I'm the one who gives people the impression that I'm unfriendly, Major."

His eyebrows lifted ever so slightly, and he held out his hand. I looked at it for just a moment and then placed mine into it. He gave me a short nod and then led me from the copse of trees. We walked along at a leisurely pace, up a short incline. The grass was even taller here, and the occasional bramble snagged at my skirt.

"It's not much farther," he said.

"It's all right. I like a good trek." That was true enough. I'd always loved walking. Even in London, I could spend happy hours wandering the city and taking in the sights. There was something relaxing about using one's own two legs to get around while the mind roamed free.

Of course, this wasn't entirely relaxing, not with Major Ramsey clasping my hand like we were lovers out on an afternoon stroll. Not that it was exactly uncomfortable either. Major Ramsey's utter lack of self-consciousness kept me from feeling awkward. Besides, I knew where I stood with Major Ramsey; there was no danger of misinterpreting his motivations.

We crested the small rise, and now I saw the place we were likely headed toward. The barbed-wire perimeter fence was a dead giveaway.

I took a quick look at the layout of the place before pointing my binoculars toward the sea, as though I wasn't the least bit interested in the buildings. The sea was visible from here, the sunlight glinting on the water.

"What is that place?" I asked the major.

"It's ostensibly a small publishing company, Pavonine Press," he said. "At least, it was before the war. Operations have slowed due to paper rationing and other war-related factors and the fact the market for their specialty isn't incredibly in demand."

"What's their specialty?"

"Ornithology."

I looked at him, finally understanding more of what was going on. Or, at least, in theory. I was still a bit fuzzy on the particulars.

"So bird-watching isn't just our excuse for being out here," I said. "But don't tell me Hal Jenkins was killed because of something to do with birds?"

"It's unlikely the subject matter got him killed. It's more likely related to what's going on in that compound."

I glanced toward the fence again. "Rather high security for a printer, isn't it?"

"So it would seem. The owner of this particular press is a man named Sheridan Hall. He lives in a manor called Vangidae a few miles down the coast. He is, by all accounts, wealthy, eccentric, and thoroughly obsessed with birds. He's been a bit vocal about his annoyance that his press has been forced to close, and about the disruption to birding patterns caused by increased RAF activity in the area."

"Fairly typical behavior for a rich man, in other words," I said dryly.

"Those things aside, as far as I have been able to discern, he is living a quiet life, quite unremarkable in the sense that there has been no shadow of any sort of suspicion attached to his name. The same cannot be said of this facility. My informant also says there have been rumors about odd behavior at the press."

"Like what?" I asked.

"Comings and goings at odd hours. More activity than there should be at a defunct printer. And there has been additional security added to patrol the perimeter, men discharged from army service for the most part. Men invalided out that are still able to hold a gun."

I thought of Felix. I was glad he hadn't taken on security work upon his return from the war. The thought of his putting himself in additional danger caused a tightness in my chest, and I tried not to think about what he might be up to in Scotland.

But now was not the time to focus on that.

I considered everything the major had told me, and it all began to fall into place. It was certainly curious that there should be so much activity at a temporarily deserted printing press. Also, why were there so many guards? It was natural enough that the owner might want to protect the investment of his machinery and supplies. But why would he go to the trouble of hiring such a large contingent of guards if he wasn't hiding something?

"What does all of this have to do with poor Hal? Was he involved with the printing press in some way? I thought he worked at the shipyard."

"He worked at the printer before the war but moved to the shipyard when the printer closed."

I remembered the *VON* I had seen on the blotter. Had that been part of *Pavonine*? Had Hal meant that someone within the operation would be willing to kill? The pieces did seem to fit.

"But he's still linked to what's going on inside," I said.

"Yes. He has been seen making trips to this facility by my informant, sometimes carrying a large bag or suitcase in and out."

"A black market in bird books?" I asked dubiously, though, in truth, my mind was beginning to turn in another direction.

"I have to imagine it isn't books they're printing, Miss Mc-Donnell."

"Counterfeiters," I guessed.

He looked at me approvingly, as he sometimes did when I

connected the dots quickly. I never knew whether to be pleased or insulted. "Excellent conjecture," he said.

It hadn't been that far of a leap. After all, it was a printer. They'd need special equipment to make money, ink and paper of a different sort than for printing books, but the disused printing equipment would still come in handy.

Everything I knew about counterfeiting was from Notes McNulty, a man Uncle Mick had sometimes played cards with who ran with a counterfeiting ring; they'd double-check all his money before they'd let him play.

"But isn't this a job for the police?" I asked. "What's your stake in all of this?"

"Intelligence I've received indicates these counterfeiters may be involved in espionage," the major said. "We need to be sure of what is happening in there before we decide how to act."

We stood for a few moments, taking turns looking at the facility and the surrounding area through the binoculars.

"Well?" he said at last.

I looked at him. "Well, what?"

"Are you going to help me break into that facility?"

I smiled brightly. "Major Ramsey, I thought you'd never ask."

I had been hoping this was the sort of thing the major had in mind, and I was glad that I'd been his first choice to carry it out. I felt the familiar humming in my blood that came at the start of a job, at the knowledge that there was a challenge—and perhaps even danger—ahead.

The next course of action would obviously be to case the joint, so to speak, to get the lay of the land and figure out the best place to get in.

"I suppose a nice romantic walk around the perimeter is in order," I said, flashing him a smile.

Without hesitation or comment, the major moved to my side and took my hand in his again. "Let's go," he said. He was getting better about not grasping me by the elbow and leading me about like a prisoner; our working relationship had definitely improved.

Hand in hand, we began ambling in the direction of the facility.

"It's lovely here," I said, turning to look up at him. It would look strange if we were walking around without saying much to each other. "Such wide-open spaces."

"Yes. Sunderland has some very fine shoreline."

"I don't get out of London much. I would have loved to travel the world. I ought to have started before the world descended into chaos."

"The war won't last forever."

"I hope you're right. Sometimes it seems as though there is no end in sight."

"A thing I learned in the deserts of North Africa: when the horizon seems too distant, it's best to focus on just putting one foot in front of the other."

I glanced over at him. It was a comforting reminder, and I was cheered by it. It was the sort of thing Uncle Mick would have said, that there was no use in borrowing trouble from the future. Occasionally, it occurred to me that Uncle Mick and the major were not as different as they seemed.

"Do you miss the desert?" I asked the major. I wasn't sure where the question had come from. We didn't generally engage in personal topics. I was curious, though. I knew he had not been happy to have been called back to the relative safety of London from his post in North Africa. I wondered if he was still longing to go back.

"Sometimes. It's beautiful in a brutal way. Especially at sunset. There's always a moment when the sun gives a final flare and the sand glows like the embers of a dying fire." The corner of his mouth tipped up. "I'm sorry. I don't often wax poetic."

I was oddly touched by this vivid description. "I've always suspected you might have a bit of poetry in you, Major."

He gave me a faint smile. "I contain multitudes, Miss Mc-Donnell."

We started along the perimeter nearest the sea, occasionally raising the binoculars to our eyes and pretending to look around for birds. The inside of the compound seemed deserted today. Of course, just because I didn't see anyone didn't mean there was no one there.

Upon closer inspection, the perimeter fence was not as daunting as one would suppose. It was perhaps ten feet tall and topped with barbed wire, but it wasn't extremely heavy duty as such things went. I'd definitely broken into more difficult places.

A good pair of wire cutters would do the trick. All the same, if we wanted to get in without being detected, we would have to find a way to cut through in a place that would cause the least amount of notice or damage.

The back of the facility, on the south side of the compound, seemed the best spot. The feasibility of this depended on how often the guard patrols made the rounds, of course, and we also needed to make sure that whatever we did in the dark would not be easily discoverable in the daylight.

As far as I could tell, there were three buildings within the fenced area. The largest building was, I surmised, where the main printing operations took place. It was roughly the size and shape of a warehouse, boxy and tall, with only a few windows dotting the sides. There was a smaller building nearby that looked a bit more like a comfortable cottage. This I guessed to be the location of the offices and, perhaps, the temporary guardhouse. The third building, a good distance back from the others, seemed to be a storehouse of some sort, for there was a large rolling door and a loading dock.

All told, it looked to be a small but well-equipped little operation. I wondered how much money could be in a publisher devoted primarily to books about birding. Had Sheridan Hall funded the majority of the operations as a hobby, or had it actually been a profitable enterprise?

We walked past the compound a good distance, still pretending to be enjoying our birding adventure, and then we walked back on the other side, so we'd made a full circle by the time we were done. I still had yet to see a soul.

"Are the guards on duty during the day?" I asked.

"There is usually at least one, but generally they remain inside the guardhouse unless a car arrives. I haven't seen them patrolling the compound much in the daylight, mainly just at night."

So the major had already been doing his reconnaissance without me. Perhaps that was what he had been up to the last few nights when he couldn't be bothered to let me know what was happening.

"All right, so when do we do the job?" I asked.

The major looked at me. "How soon do you think we can do it?"

I shrugged. "I'm at your disposal, Major." In truth, I was game to get started. Uncle Mick had drilled into me the importance of patience and planning, but I thought I had seen all I needed to of the layout of the place.

"The sooner the better would be optimal. With Hal Jenkins dead, there is no telling how the organization might be affected. They might even decide to close up shop now that his death has the potential to attract attention to them."

"How about tonight?" I asked.

He considered. "It's a quarter moon tonight and the weather should be clear, so I think tonight would be as good as any if you think you can be ready. What will you need?"

"I brought along the tools I might need to get into the building," I said. "I knew you wouldn't have called me this way if it didn't involve a certain set of skills. But you might bring a pair of wire cutters for the fence."

"Very good. Let's go somewhere we can map out the plan."

CHAPTER ELEVEN

Once again, I crept from Mrs. James's house in the dead of night. I was really quite surprised I hadn't been caught by one of the other lodgers yet. Or, even more disastrous, Mrs. James. She would surely be curious as to where I was going at this time of night, and the only plausible but innocuous excuse was that I was sneaking out to see a man.

That would preserve the secret nature of my mission, but it might also cost me my lodging. I knew many a landlady who'd thrown a girl out for less.

No sense in worrying about that at the moment, though. I hadn't been caught.

I slipped out into the street and walked down to where the major was waiting for me, concealed beneath the branches of a willow.

"Ready?" he asked in a low voice.

I nodded. "Ready." The plan was simple enough. Almost too simple. All the same, I was looking forward to our evening's adventures. After our reconnaissance was complete, the major had taken me to a small tearoom where we had cemented the stages of our plan for the remainder of the afternoon. Now I was eager for action. He led me on a circuitous route until we reached his car. The headlights were hooded, and we cast very little light as we made our way down the darkened streets. I half expected that we would be stopped and asked what our business was traveling by car at this time of night, but we encountered no one.

I glanced over at the major, but I couldn't see him well, as dark as it was. We were both dressed in black. It was the best sort of attire for our purposes, but it was also a bit conspicuous if we were seen wandering around together. Then again, there were a lot of funerals now. Perhaps anyone who happened to observe us would merely think we had been to one.

I'd pinned up my hair and tied a kerchief around it, as I did to keep the curls at bay when I was doing a locksmithing job.

Once we had nearly reached our destination, he pulled the car off the road and into a little copse of trees. The night was dark, and I didn't think that there would be any chance of it being spotted.

He got out, and I did the same.

"We're going north," he said. "Stay close, and don't talk unless it's an emergency."

I nodded.

We started walking. The major set a steady pace. I liked that he didn't treat me with any special courtesy when it came to the jobs we did. He knew that I could keep pace with him, and he expected me to do so. I had grown up being treated that way by my cousins, though, as I'd become a woman, I'd realized this was an anomaly. Most men underestimated women. I liked that the major didn't act as though I was capable of less because of my gender.

The night was cloudy, and it made for good cover as he crossed toward the more open ground.

At last, he stopped, holding up a hand. I stood still where I was until he motioned me forward and leaned close to speak in a low voice.

"We're nearly there. Remember: there are guards that roam the perimeter. Their patrols are well spaced, but we still need to be watchful and as quiet as possible."

I nodded.

"Prepare your tools now. We may not have much time."

I reached into my pocket for my little lockpicking set. It was a near-replica of the one Uncle Mick carried, wallet-sized, with little leather hoops that held picks and other tools of different sizes. I didn't know exactly what sort of locks we would be facing once we were inside the gates, of course, but I was ready for nearly any eventuality.

Except for one, I realized. "What will we do if we're caught?" I asked in a low voice.

"Let's not get caught," he answered.

"Brilliant. Why didn't I think of that?"

We reached the perimeter fence at the back of the compound, and the major pulled a pair of wire cutters from his pocket. Near the bottom of the fence, he began cutting the chain links. It was not exactly silent work, but it wasn't loud enough to draw much attention. At least, I hoped it wasn't.

He snapped the links as quickly and efficiently as though he'd been born to a life of crime.

When he'd finished, he pulled back the flap of the fence and motioned for me to go first. I crawled through on my stomach and then moved away and sat with my back to the fence to keep watch while Major Ramsey entered.

When he had done so, he pushed the piece of the fence back into place so it wouldn't be noticeable at a cursory glance, and then he motioned for me to follow him.

Major Ramsey, I had often noted, moved with a grace and agility not common in a man of his size. He slipped soundlessly from shadow to shadow, only the occasional glint of light bouncing off his fair hair. If he had been the proverbial "dark" to go with tall and handsome, he would have been undetectable.

We reached the back door of the storeroom building without seeing or hearing anything, and we stood for a moment, catching our breath and looking out over the quiet darkness of the broad expanse of lawn we had just traversed. I had expected there would at least be spotlights we would need to dodge, but everything remained dark and still.

"There's no one here," I whispered after several moments of stillness and silence.

"They're here."

I would take his word for it. He knew more about this place than I did, after all. I'd been kept in the dark about most of it, except for the brief visit today.

"All right," he said after a long moment. "Follow me."

Without waiting for my reply, he disappeared into the shadows.

I followed along behind. We skirted the building and then crossed another patch of open ground before reaching the back door of the large warehouse-type building. I went at once to examine the lock. It was a padlock. I could have picked this in my sleep. It was not exactly the heavyweight sort of security I had been expecting. Then again, if the efficiency of the guards was any indication, I shouldn't have been surprised.

"This won't take long," I said.

He nodded. "Work as quietly as you can. I'm going to keep an eye on the perimeter."

I turned my focus on my padlock. It was large and impressive to look at but not at all difficult to unlock. I slid my tools from my pocket and set to work.

It took only a few moments. With the right tools and technique, there were few padlocks that could withstand an experienced locksmith for more than a minute or two. I opened the lock and then tucked my tools away. I looked back over my shoulder for the major. I wasn't sure where he had gone off to, but I knew better than to go into the building without him.

"That was quick work," he said, appearing at my side a moment later.

I slipped the shackle of the lock off the hasp and staple and slipped the lock in my pocket. Then Major Ramsey grasped the door's handle. He looked at me for confirmation, and I gave him a short nod. I was ready.

Pulling the door open slowly, he gave a cautious glance inside before motioning for me to precede him. I entered the building. It was already very dark inside, and once the major slipped in behind me and pulled the door closed, it was pitch black. We stood for a moment in silence, listening. There was no sound but the wind and the sea. The major flicked on a small torch.

I took a look around the place. It seemed larger on the inside than it appeared on the outside, and the light did not penetrate far beyond a small circle.

"What are we looking for?" I asked.

"Evidence of counterfeiting," he said in a low voice. "Just let me know if you see anything suspicious."

I glanced around and saw that there was a stack of finished books sitting on a large table. I didn't know much about bookmaking, though I'd read a few things about it. My best guess was that we were at the binding station. There was an industrial-sewing-machine-type thing nearby and, behind it, shelves of leather and a great many spools of thread in different colors.

I went and looked at the books. They all had bird-related titles, but I didn't have time to investigate any more before the major moved farther into the room, taking the light with him.

By the light of the major's torch, we began making our way around the warehouse. I supposed what we were looking for would be located near the actual press. After all, that's where the money would be made.

We skirted a shelf laden with large sheets of copper used to make molds and the dangerous-looking saw used to cut the copper plates apart. The place didn't have the dejected air of abandonment, and there was the lingering scent of ink and hot metal in the air. If I had to bet on it, I'd say the machines had been in use, and recently.

I saw the giant typesetting machine, and I pulled out my own torch, switching it on. Curiosity pulled me over to look at the tiny letters that would be slotted into molds and covered with metal to make the first draft of a book's page, so to speak.

A stack of larger plates at the station caught my attention, and I went to look at them to see if they might be what we were looking for. Was there, perhaps, a picture of His Majesty's face on them that might be used on counterfeit money?

I picked up the plate and almost laughed when I was presented with a picture of a bird. I couldn't escape the things. I sifted through the pile, but they were all various birds, used to illustrate the books that had been printed here.

The major appeared at my side, and I held up one of the plates. "Ruddy shelduck," I explained. "I could tell you all about them."

"Some other time."

We turned toward the press itself, still looking for any signs that money was being made here. It would have been nice to see the stuff stacked up like some miser's hoard, but so far there was no sign of it.

"What do they use this money for?" I asked. "Spies, I mean."

"Living in our country, mainly. Spies need money to live like everyone else," the major said. "Although, on a larger scale, it is possible to pump enough counterfeit money into the economy to cause inflation at a catastrophic level."

I would have to take his word for it. National economics was one thing I'd never had much interest in.

"I don't think that's what they're doing here, though," he said, looking around. "It's not a big enough operation. They'd need to be working around the clock."

"I wonder why they aren't working tonight," I mused.

"They may have been instructed to lie low for a few days after the unfortunate death of Mr. Jenkins," he said. "But, even then, I'd think there would be more evidence."

He wandered away, having a closer look at the press. He put his fingers to it, and they came away clean. No wet ink. He began to go around the front end of the machine and then went around the other way.

There was a table there against one wall, and I went up to it, shining my light across its surface. Quickly at first, and then slower.

"Major," I said. I didn't turn to look for him. I couldn't take my eyes away from the items spread out before me.

I felt him come up beside me, and we looked down at the table together. It appeared someone had used this table for practice, because the printing was slightly crooked on the paper, the ink a bit smeared. All the same, it was clear enough what they were: National Registration Identity Cards.

"They're not just counterfeiting money," I said.

"No. They're printing false documents for German spies."

I had a sinking feeling in the pit of my stomach. This was not good, not at all. Granted, a ring of counterfeiters attempting to destabilize the economy was also bad, but this was frightening in a different, more immediate way. These items were enabling the enemy to walk among us.

Once the cards were printed, it would be a matter of filling in the information with different inks in different handwritings and snapping pictures of the spies to place inside.

"What now?" I whispered to the major.

"Hold this."

He handed me his torch and pulled a small camera from his pocket. While I trained both lights on the table and the offending documents, he snapped a series of photographs of everything as it lay.

As he did so, I looked around for completed cards. I didn't see any. Had they yet to print them? Or had they been given to spies already?

I studied the printed covers of the National Registration Identity Cards, looking for some telltale mark I would be able to remember. It was a trick I'd picked up from Felix. When items were printed on the same machine or from the same plate, there were small irregularities that would identify them if one looked closely.

And sure enough, there, just under the right-hand lion on the crest, was a tiny smudge. It was barely noticeable, some minuscule flaw in the plate they had used, but it was enough that I would notice it if I saw it again.

"Did you see this irregularity?" I asked, pointing it out to the major.

He studied the place where I pointed out the flaw. "Very good, Miss McDonnell. That will likely prove of use to us."

He finished with his photographs and began to straighten the piles again. I helped him, and soon everything was back as it had been.

It was just then that we heard the sound of voices outside the front door to the warehouse, not far from where we stood.

"Did you hear something?" the first voice asked. He was speaking in a low voice, nearly a whisper, but he was close enough to be audible, which wasn't exactly comforting.

"Thought I did," a second, gruffer voice replied. "Sounded like voices."

Well, this was less than ideal.

I looked at the major for instructions.

He jerked his head toward the back of the warehouse, the direction from which we had come.

I turned and began to move rapidly but soundlessly through the warehouse. I got a good mental picture of the path to the door in case it became necessary to switch my torch off.

It was a lucky thing, for a moment later, I heard the sound of the lock being undone at the front door of the warehouse. The major and I switched our torches off at the same time, and he took my arm, leading me unerringly through the maze of equipment and machinery.

We slipped quickly through the back door, and I had the presence of mind to slip the padlock from my pocket and replaced it, clicking the shackle back into place. *Leave things as you found them.* Uncle Mick had drilled that into me from the beginning, and good training held up in a tight spot.

"I'll go around!" the gruff voice called from somewhere on the west side of the building.

Major Ramsey's lips pressed against my ear, and he whispered one word: "Run."

CHAPTER TWELVE

I dashed in the direction of the fence, and I could feel the major was hard on my heels. We were both running as silently as possible, but I was afraid we were still going to attract notice. Somehow, however, I did not hear any movement behind us, and there were no shouts of alarm that would indicate the man had seen us.

Unfortunately, we'd done such a good job of camouflaging the cut in the fence that, at first, I was unable to determine where it was. Especially now that we were working in the dark after our eyes had grown accustomed to the torchlight.

The major, however, did not seem to have lost his sense of direction in the fray, and he led me to the spot, pulling back the flap and motioning for me to go through.

I slid through the opening as fast as I could. The major came through behind me and pulled the flap back into place. We had agreed to tie the fence back together with tiny pieces of wire to obscure our entrance, but I didn't know if we had the time.

I looked back toward the warehouse and saw a man there shining a torch over the back door. He didn't seem particularly interested in the padlock. Indeed, there was no reason why he should be. I had left everything just as I had found it.

I looked at the major, but he wasn't looking at me. And then I saw what he *was* looking at: my kerchief had fallen from my hair on the scramble and was lying on the other side of the fence. It was black, so it blended with the ground in the darkness. But if either of the men came around with torches, they'd spot it. And possibly the cut in the fence.

That was, of course, unless I could get it back.

I glanced at the major, and this time he was looking at me. He gave a slight shake of his head. My eyes darted back toward the warehouse. The man was no longer by the back door, and I thought for a moment that they may have decided it was a false alarm.

And then I realized they had met up and were walking along the fence, shining their torches searchingly into the darkness outside it.

I darted at the opening before I could think better of it. With one quick movement, I slid through and back into the compound and snatched at the kerchief. It wasn't far enough that I had to go all the way back in, but, once I had it in my hand, it was harder than I'd expected getting through the fence backward.

As I scurried in reverse, my shirt caught on the fence, and I had a terrifying moment in which I thought I might be stuck. I jerked myself free, out of the way, and back into the cover of the taller grass outside of the fence.

The major pulled the flap of fence back into place. I reached into my pocket for the precut piece of wire and tied it quickly along the links near the bottom. That would have to do. The men were getting closer, and we were out of time.

"Go," the major hissed. I turned and began making my way at a crouched run through the tall grass. The sound of voices was still audible behind us, but I hadn't heard any shouted alarms as of yet.

I couldn't hear the major behind me. He was moving so quietly that I had to glance over my shoulder to be sure he was there. I looked back just as he tackled me.

I hadn't even seen him coming. There was just a flash of darkness a split second before he reached me and the impact of his body hitting mine, knocking me to the ground.

"Someone's coming." The words were too low to even be called a whisper. He breathed them into my ear even as he pressed a finger to my lips.

It was not as though I was going to make a sound. My breath had left my body as I'd hit the earth, and his not inconsiderable weight pressing me into the ground wasn't making it easy to suck it back in.

I nodded to show him I understood.

He took his hand away from my mouth, but he didn't shift positions.

It was only then that I heard the sound of footsteps very nearby. I realized then why the major didn't dare move. We were perhaps three meters away from whoever it was. He had come from around the other side of the compound. Outside the walls. They were more competent than we had believed.

I stilled, doing my best not to make a sound, not even to breathe. Which wasn't difficult considering the major was a dead weight. In his defense, he likely couldn't shift if he didn't want to make any noise, but I still hadn't got a good breath since I'd hit the earth, and I felt a bit light-headed.

And so I lay very still, the cold ground against my back and the warmth of the major pressing into me from above.

There was the sound of a voice from inside the compound and an answering call from whoever was near us.

"No, nothing!" he called, and I could tell that the footsteps were moving away. He was going to meet his companions, thankfully. We hadn't been caught.

We were still for a moment longer, and then the major rolled his weight off me. He stayed on his side beside me, motioning for me not to move.

I frowned at him, though he probably couldn't see me in the darkness. Sometimes he gave me the most ridiculous instructions, as though I had no common sense.

I'm not certain how much time passed. To be honest, I had begun to daydream a bit. I could hear the sound of the sea from where we lay, and there was a cool, salty breeze that was blowing the grass. The clouds had parted, and the sky was a mass of stars overhead. For a few moments, I couldn't help but enjoy the peacefulness of it all, the tranquility. Perhaps we city girls are easily led astray by the beauties of nature.

At last, Major Ramsey sat up a bit from the grass and looked around us. After a long moment, he rose to his feet. I saw with surprise that he was holding his service revolver. It must have been in his hand when he tackled me. He moved quickly, I'd give him that.

He tucked the revolver back into the shoulder holster he was apparently wearing beneath his jacket.

"I think we're in the clear, but we'd better hurry," he said.

He held out a hand to help me up. I stood and began brushing the dirt and grass from my clothes. "We've got to stop making a habit of this, Major," I said. It was the second time he'd tackled me this week, and it had been only a little less alarming the second time.

"You're not hurt?" he asked.

"No," I assured him quickly.

"Good. Let's go."

We hurried back the way we had come, only faster. I didn't think we were being followed, and I knew the major would likely be able to spot a tail if we had one, but we kept up a steady pace nonetheless.

By the time we reached the car, I was a bit winded. Major Ramsey pulled open my door, and I sank with a relieved sigh into the seat.

The major got in his side and pulled away as quickly as he could without making a racket. We drove, lights off, down one winding road and then another. I had to hope there was no one else stupid enough to be out on the dark roads at this time of night, or there would be the potential for a catastrophic collision.

I saw the major's eyes flicker frequently to the mirror, and I couldn't resist looking over my shoulder from time to time. But there were no lights behind us. No warning signals that I could see from the compound.

"I think we did it," I said.

"I apologize for my roughness," he said, his eyes still on the road. "I didn't have time to give you a proper warning."

"No apologies necessary, Major," I assured him. "It was a lucky thing you spotted that man when you did. Besides, Colm and Toby were never gentle with me because I was a girl. I've been tackled often enough."

He looked amused. "I sometimes forget your rather rough-and-tumble upbringing."

I laughed and reached up to straighten my errant curls, which were bobbing around my face as the car jostled over ruts in the road. With the kerchief discarded, I could only imagine how very rough-and-tumble I looked at the moment.

"You're bleeding," he said suddenly.

I looked down at the hand I had just lifted to see that my wrist and the back of my hand were streaked with blood that had run down from my upper arm. Apparently, I'd scraped my arm when I'd snagged my sleeve on the fence scrambling through. Only now that the adrenaline of the moment had passed did I feel the sting.

I pressed my fingers to a tear in the fabric. "I think it's just a scratch from the fence," I said.

But the major had already pulled the car over to the side of the road. "Let me see."

"Really, Major, it isn't . . ."

"Let me see."

I sighed and extended my arm. He quickly rolled up the sleeve. It was an ugly little scratch, just above my elbow, and it had bled quite a lot, as evidenced by the blood staining my arm. Even now, it was still welling with a fresh line of crimson.

Major Ramsey pulled a handkerchief from his pocket and took my arm in his free hand, dabbing at the blood.

"It's not too deep," he said. "It won't need stitching."

"No," I said. "I'm fine."

He wrapped the handkerchief around my arm and pulled it tight. I winced slightly, but I knew the pressure would stop the bleeding.

"That should be all right for now," he said, his thumb rubbing the skin above the bandage as if to soothe the pain. I felt an unexpected tingle on my skin where he touched me.

"Yes," I said, suddenly a bit breathless. "I'll clean it up once I get to Mrs. James's. Thank you."

His hands were still on my arm, and when I looked up, our eyes met in the dim interior of the car.

And there it was. That uncomfortable little jolt in my chest that I sometimes felt when we were in close proximity. I could no longer deny to myself that it was attraction on my part, and sometimes, in moments like these, it was getting harder for me to believe that he wasn't feeling something, too.

But just because I could no longer deny my attraction to him did not mean I wasn't going to ignore it.

I shifted slightly back in my seat. "Thank you," I said again.

He released my arm, his eyes lingering on mine for just a moment longer before turning to put the car back into gear. "You're welcome."

He pulled us out into the road, and we drove along for a few moments in silence.

"So what's the plan now?" I asked when the quiet began to wear on me.

Major Ramsey said nothing for a moment, and he didn't take his eyes from the road when he finally spoke. "I am going to have to reevaluate based on the new information. You need to lie low and keep from drawing attention to yourself until I figure out what our next move will be."

I had known he would say something like that. I also knew what it meant: he would disappear for several days while I sat there waiting to hear from him.

"Before you argue with me," he said, "I still need you for the purpose for which I placed you in Mrs. James's establishment. You can get to know what you can about Hal Jenkins's associates. I still believe one or more of them was in league with him and, in all probability, had something to do with his death."

This wasn't exactly a cheery thought. I liked Sami and the others, and I didn't like to believe that they might be involved in treachery or murder.

All the same, I knew very well that, in such matters, everyone had to be looked at closely, as if under a microscope. I had seen before the lengths to which some people would go, for inscrutable reasons. I had seen people whom I never would have suspected of betraying their country do so for profit or revenge.

"Ask what questions you can, but don't make yourself obvious," the major said. "And it would be best for you to remain on your guard, Miss McDonnell."

He was making it sound dangerous to mollify me, and I was annoyed to realize it was working.

I didn't want to stay tucked away, somewhere safe, when there were so many other important things I could be doing. But it was true that I would be able to further use my acquaintance with Hal Jenkins's group of friends to see what I could learn from them. I would not be idle.

I also didn't tell him, of course, that I had sent the letter to Felix. I highly doubted it would provide any useful information, but it was worth a try.

"All right," I said. "But you promise not to desert me now that I've done the locks bit?"

The corner of his mouth tipped up ever so slightly. "You may have noticed, Miss McDonnell, that you have proved useful beyond the 'locks bit' several times."

He really was laying it on thick, and it hadn't escaped my notice that he had made no promises. All the same, it was probably as much of a guarantee as I would get out of him.

"Why couldn't they have printed those things in Germany?" I asked suddenly, my mind going back to what we had uncovered. "Wouldn't that be the usual procedure? Send the spies in with the relevant papers?"

"I assume they believe that those printed here will be more accurate and up-to-date than those printed in Germany. And they have the equipment here, so they might as well make use of it."

It was as good an explanation as any. At least for the time being. But one thing still didn't quite fit. "Why did they kill Hal? If he was often seen going in and out of the building, presumably to collect and then deliver the false documents to spies, why did they want to get rid of him?"

"There are several possibilities that occur to me, but the most likely seems that he double-crossed the wrong person."

I shivered, unable to erase the picture in my mind of Hal Jenkins lying dead in the street.

"What about the note?" I asked, remembering the piece of paper he had clutched in his lifeless hand. "'We know you have it.' What did he have? Was he killed because he was in possession of it? Or because he took it? And why would they kill him before they got it back, whatever it was?"

"All excellent questions, Miss McDonnell," he said unhelp-fully. I suspected he had ideas about this, too, but felt no inclination to share his theories with me.

"I wonder what Sheridan Hall knows about all of this," I mused. "If he was closely involved in the workings of his press, it seems strange he wouldn't know what is going on there now. You said he lives close to the press?"

"About a mile to the south."

I looked at him. "Do you suppose we should pay him a visit?"

"We'll consider it," he said, surprising me. "But you're not to do anything on your own. Do you understand?"

I nodded.

"I need verbal confirmation, if you please."

I narrowed my eyes. "I understand."

"Good."

He parked the car a short way down the street from my lodging house. We sat in silence for a moment, as he seemed to be considering something.

At last, he said, "I'm staying in a cottage not far from Hall's manor house, Vangidae. He goes out walking every morning and afternoon, but I haven't yet approached him."

I waited.

"I'll pick you up tomorrow at thirteen hundred hours," he said. "We'll see if we can't make his acquaintance."

I smiled broadly. "Excellent."

"Until tomorrow, then."

I opened the car door and got out, but his voice followed me. "Miss McDonnell."

I ducked my head back into the car.

"You did well tonight," he said.

I smiled. "Thank you."

"Good night."

"Good night, Major."

I closed the door with the barest click so as not to draw prying eyes to windows.

I got to Mrs. James's house quickly and, taking my shoes off at the front door, slipped inside. I was about to sneak back up the stairs when I heard a noise. I wasn't quite sure whether it had come from inside the house or behind it. I stilled, listening. Perhaps Mrs. James was up early to get things ready for breakfast. It would be dawn soon, I realized.

There was no sound for several moments, so I took the steps slowly, avoiding the squeaking ones, and made it to my bedroom door. I slipped inside and sighed with relief.

It had been an eventful night, and I still wasn't sure what to make of everything that had happened. Hal Jenkins had clearly been involved in something more devious than we had assumed.

It was then I heard another noise. This one had definitely come from outside the house. I moved to the window, pushing aside the edge of the blackout curtain and looking into the garden behind the house.

The light had just begun to turn the smoky dove gray of predawn, and I could clearly see two figures standing on the back porch of Sami and Laila's house.

Were the sisters out so early? But no. One of the figures was a man. The other was Sami.

They were clearly having some sort of heated discussion. The man seemed to be holding a metal case of some kind, and, as if to emphasize a point, he slammed it against the porch railing, creating the muted clanging sound I had heard.

This clearly angered Sami, and I heard her raised voice, though I couldn't make out what she was saying. She glanced around, as though afraid they would be seen. They certainly weren't being very clandestine about whatever was going on.

She said something else to the man, and then she went into the house and closed the door firmly behind her.

The man stood there for a moment, as though debating whether he should bang on the door or accept defeat. Eventually he chose the latter, stalking away with a clearly angry stride.

I closed the curtain and turned toward my bed, wondering what all of that was about. What was Sami Maddox involved in?

CHAPTER THIRTEEN

I slept later than I intended the next morning and missed break-fast, so I decided to take a walk to the tea shop.

It occurred to me that Sami might be free to grab a bite be-fore she went to work. I wasn't sure of her schedule, exactly, but it was worth a try. I wanted to start talking to the potential suspects as soon as possible, and, after what I had witnessed between Sami and the mystery man, I also wanted to see what I could find out from her.

I felt a bit guilty thinking of Sami as a suspect, but the fact was I couldn't rule her out, not yet. The confrontation with the man at her door had been strange, and with strange behavior came suspicion. If she was, as I hoped, innocent, then the sooner I could prove it, and get us all out of danger, the better.

The major was to pick me up at one o'clock, and I hoped I might learn something before then.

My plan was to talk to each person in the group about Hal Jenkins to see if they'd let anything slip. I also planned to get a look at their identity cards to see if any of them had the telltale smudge marking it as a forgery, making them a German spy. That seemed far-fetched—even if one of them was linked to Hal Jenkins, it didn't mean they were a spy—but I intended to explore every avenue.

The scratch on my arm still looked inflamed this morning, but it was no longer bleeding. I'd cleaned it thoroughly before bed, and I rebandaged it now. I wished I'd thought to bring a tin of Nacy's salve with me. It worked wonders. In lieu of that, I'd just have to pick up some antiseptic ointment later on.

I didn't want to ask Mrs. James, because I was fairly sure she would ask a great many questions. In my effort to keep from drawing notice from her, or anyone else, I dressed in a long-sleeved blouse and blue skirt.

There was no one about when I went downstairs, and I crossed the garden toward Sami's house without seeing a soul.

I went to the door and knocked.

It was Laila, however, who opened the door. She was wearing a gold-colored dress and a thick gold necklace. She looked terribly chic, and I fought the urge to pat at my wayward curls.

"Hello," I said, giving her an overbright smile. It didn't seem that I had been making much headway as far as winning Laila's trust was concerned, but I didn't intend to give up. There were few people we McDonnells couldn't make friends with, once we set our mind to it.

"I suppose you're looking for Sami," she said. "She's not here."

"Oh, well, I missed breakfast and was just calling to see if she wanted to go to the tea shop with me. I'll drop in and see her again this evening."

She hesitated a moment and then said, "Would you like to come in? I've just put the kettle on, and I've some toast and jam."

I was surprised by this invitation but tried not to show it. "I'd like that very much, if it wouldn't be too much trouble."

"No trouble at all."

Laila was another of the suspects, after all. I had expected it to be difficult to have a private word with her, so this was a bit of a lucky break.

She led me into the house. It was small, but tidy and cheerfully decorated in bright colors and patterns.

"Take a seat, and I'll bring the tea and toast out here."

I didn't mind eating in the kitchen, but I didn't think that Laila was much on informality. Besides, it would give me the chance to look at her identity card if she'd left her handbag about.

She went to get tea and toast, and I scanned the room. There was a dark pink sofa and chairs that sat before the fireplace. The rug beneath my feet was clearly expensive and shot through with a host of vibrant-colored threads. Rugs weren't really my specialty, as they weren't exactly easy objects to steal, but I knew a quality rug when I saw one.

There was a piece of art above the fireplace; it looked to be ebony inset with a pattern of glossy iridescent tiles. On another wall, there was a large painting, this one also colorful and depicting several women in a garden, a profusion of flowers and vine-laden trees around them. Under other circumstances, I would have gone over and examined it in more detail, but I had a handbag to rifle through.

It was sitting atop an ornately carved wooden table near the door, the same green handbag she'd been carrying when we had all gone to the pub. With a glance in the direction of the kitchen, I went over to it and unfastened the clasp.

Everything was neatly arranged inside. There was a small purse, a tube of lipstick, a pencil, and the little green card holder that held her identity card. I pulled it from the purse.

I could hear the rattling of cups as she set them on a tray in the kitchen, and I knew my time was limited.

The identity card stuck in the holder, as they were wont to do, and it took me a moment to prize it out. A quick glance at the crest of two lions on the cover showed that the smudge I was

looking for was absent. Laila Maddox did not have a false identity card, whatever else she might be hiding.

I quickly replaced the card and the handbag, and I was sitting
on the pink sofa when Laila came back into the sitting room with
tea-things on a tray.

"You have a lovely home," I said.

"Thank you." She set the tray on the low ebony table before
the sofa. "How do you take your tea?"

"Sugar and a bit of milk."

She gave me a generous scoop of their sugar ration, and I felt
myself warming to her a bit. Sweets had always been the way to
my heart, even more so with a war on.

She poured herself a cup of black tea and then took a seat
in the chair across from me. It occurred to me, of course, that
I should be careful what I ate and drank since Hal Jenkins had
been poisoned, but I didn't suppose Laila Maddox would kill
me in her own home. After all, what reason would she have to
eliminate me?

We both sipped our tea in silence for a moment.

I was still trying to find a way to get a read on Laila. Samira
and I had such an easy rapport, but her sister was much more
reserved. It was difficult for me to figure out what made Laila
Maddox tick. Sometimes she felt cool and aloof, and sometimes
there was a warmth in her eyes that it almost felt like she willfully
suppressed.

"I love the painting of the women in the garden," I said at
last, for something to say. I looked over my shoulder at the piece.
"Where did you get it?"

"It was painted by my mother," she said.

"She is a wonderful artist," I said, impressed.

"She painted a good deal before her marriage and was somewhat celebrated when she was young. She was Persian. She married my father and came to England before we were born, but

things were difficult for her here. She never really felt as though she belonged."

It was the most personal thing I'd yet to hear her say, and I knew I must tread carefully while she was opening up to me.

I nodded. "I imagine it must have been hard."

"She might have been happy if our father had loved her, but he grew, I think, tired of the novelty of a foreign wife."

There was a slight edge to her tone as she said this, but she went on in a steady voice, as though she were telling someone else's story.

"She grew ill, and he hadn't the inclination to take care of her. He was home very little. When she died, he left us in the care of my father's aunt. Samira and I were never really happy there. Or, perhaps, I was less happy than Samira. She is more . . . adaptable than me."

I considered this, and it put a new perspective on the women's relationship. Laila and Sami were so different that, at times, it was almost difficult to believe they were sisters. Oh, I knew well enough how divergent sibling personalities could be, but there were certain elements that those raised together often shared. Even though Colm and Toby were not my brothers, we had the same upbringing, the same memories, some of the same idiosyncrasies.

Sami and Laila seemed to lack this quality. There was a disconnect between them, as though they were not quite in sync. It was their divergent approach to their traditional upbringing, I thought. The split between the life with their mother and the life with their British aunt. Laila had been older when their mother died and had attempted to retain something of her mother's culture. Sami probably had few memories of her mother and found life with the aunt easier.

I found I could sympathize with both of the sisters. I knew

what it was like, grappling with a legacy. Not in the same way, perhaps. But both our mothers had left a mark on us.

"My mother died when I was very young, too," I said. Now was neither the time nor the place to trot that story out, of course, so I added, "The influenza." It wasn't a lie.

"I'm sorry."

"I don't remember her at all. I don't know whether that's better or worse."

We sipped our tea in silence for a few moments, both of us thinking about our dead mothers. And then I remembered that I had not come here to commiserate about the past.

I had to find a way to bring the topic around to Hal Jenkins. There had been something a bit strange about Laila's reactions when Hal was mentioned. Certainly, she hadn't seemed overly upset about his death. Of course, that didn't necessarily mean anything one way or the other. One thing I knew about Laila Maddox: she was adept at hiding her feelings.

"I came to Sunderland to go through my aunt's house," I said, "but I'm afraid I've been rather distracted. You see, I've met a man."

"Oh?" She didn't seem particularly interested in my romantic life, but I plunged ahead as though I was like most girls in love, oblivious to the disinterest of those around them. "He's an RAF pilot. We went out yesterday, and I feel as though I'm quite smitten already."

She offered me a small smile. "That's very nice for you."

"Do you have a beau?"

"No."

Well, it didn't seem we would be getting anywhere along those lines. I would have to be more direct.

"Oh, well, I'm sure the right man will come along eventually."

She sipped her tea and said nothing.

"I hadn't thought to find romance here," I said. "In fact, the way things started, I rather thought it was going to be an ill-fated trip."

Her brows raised slightly as if in inquiry. Laila Maddox was not a chatty woman. Well, that was all right. I could be chatty enough for the both of us.

"I had just reached Mrs. James's house and met your sister in the garden when we heard the commotion and ran out to see that Hal Jenkins had died."

There was a reaction, though it was difficult to gauge exactly what it was. Some emotion flicked briefly in her eyes, and then it was gone. She nodded. "Yes, that was terrible."

"I didn't know him, of course, but it was so dreadful. I didn't like to talk to Sami too much about it because, well . . . I had the impression that she and Hal were close?"

This did elicit a reaction. Laila's face grew hard. "There was nothing between Hal Jenkins and my sister. If anyone told you that, they were lying."

"Oh," I said, feigning surprise at this reaction. "I didn't mean to insinuate anything. I only thought . . ."

"You thought wrong." She smiled to soften the words, but I could tell that our conversation was coming to an end. A moment later, she confirmed this.

"I'm so glad you stopped by, Miss Donaldson," she said, setting her cup and saucer on the table. "But I'm afraid I have to go out soon. I'll tell Samira you came by."

"Is she at work? I might stop by and see her later."

There was a short pause.

"No," she said. "She had some errands to run today. She'll be back this afternoon. I'll tell her to call on you, shall I?"

"Yes, that would be nice."

I thanked her for the tea and took my leave.

That was one visit checked off my list. I hadn't gotten far with Laila Maddox, but at least I'd gotten a look at her identity card.

Now on to my next mark.

I decided to visit the chemist shop where Sami worked next. If Laila was telling the truth and Sami wasn't working, I thought now might be a good time to talk to Carlotta alone. Besides, I needed to get a new bandage for the scrape on my arm.

It wasn't a long walk to the chemist, and the day was clear and warm. It occurred to me how often I had taken days like these for granted before the war, bright days with the first hint of autumn on the breeze.

The chemist was small, but fairly well equipped given the shortages of certain supplies. There was the peculiarly distinct smell of liniment and herbs, soap and candy in the air. I glanced at the counter, but there was a gentleman in a white coat behind it. The chemist, I assumed.

Perhaps Carlotta wasn't here either? But then I spotted her in a corner of the shop. She was helping a customer, so I moved away and pretended to browse the shelves, feigning interest in various salves and balms.

At last, I rounded the corner and approached her. "Oh! Hello, Carlotta," I said.

She smiled when she saw me, and it was an easy smile. Either she had nothing to hide or, more likely, she didn't think she had anything to hide from me.

That was something I had to my advantage, after all. I didn't present much of a threat when one looked at me, and I had the knack for putting people at ease.

That was one advantage I had over the major in matters like these. He could, I had to admit, shift his personality rather well when the situation called for it. All the same, there was a commanding air to him that left people on edge. I, on the other hand, was a woman of the people.

"Hello, Liz. Can I help you with something?"

"Oh, I was stopping by to get some plasters," I said. "I scratched my arm, and I needed to replace the bandage."

"Oh, I'm sorry. We have some right this way," she said. She led me to a small shelf of the things needed to care for minor wounds.

I selected what I needed.

"This is rather embarrassing," I said. "But you don't suppose you could help with the bandage, do you? It's my right arm, and I'm rather clumsy with the left."

"Oh, of course! Come with me."

As I had been hoping, she led me to the back room. I glanced around. It was used mostly for storage, shelf upon shelf of bottles and boxes, potions and powders. There were several metal tins of first aid supplies that looked as though they had been packaged to ship, perhaps to the military or local hospitals.

There was also a coatrack in the corner with a hat and Carlotta's handbag hanging from it.

She led me to a wooden chair in the corner, and I pushed up my sleeve.

"Oh, that looks as though it must have hurt," she said, examining the wound.

"It did," I admitted.

"This might sting a bit," she said as she dabbed a bit of boric acid ointment onto a cloth and patted it on the scratch.

It did sting, but I was used to Nacy's thorough cleaning of cuts and scrapes, so I was prepared.

"How did it happen?" she asked.

"I snagged it on a sharp edge of a fence," I said, seeing no reason to lie about the source of my injury. "I'm afraid I've been a little jumpy lately."

She smiled. "Aren't we all?"

"I suppose so." I leaned slightly toward her, as though imparting a confidence. "I think the death of poor Hal Jenkins rattled me more than I like to admit. It was just so shocking."

She looked closely at me then, and I wondered if I had overstepped my boundaries. Would she wonder why I was here? But no. The moment passed quickly, and she seemed to let her guard down once again.

"It was horrible, what happened to Hal. It's still hard for me to believe he's gone."

"I wonder what the doctors will say," I said. "He was young, wasn't he?"

"Yes, I think so. I didn't really know him all that well." She glanced toward the door back into the shop then, ostensibly to see if any other customers needed her. But there was a bell over the door, and it hadn't rung since I'd come in.

Why was she interested in ending the conversation?

Of course, it was possible the chemist didn't like her chatting while she was working. This, however, seemed to be something else. She was nervous.

This assumption was confirmed by the fact that her hands were trembling as she wound the bandage around my arm.

There was a jingle then, and she jumped. "I'll be right back," she said.

She went back into the shop, and I shot up from my chair. Hurrying to the hat rack in the corner, I took down her handbag. It was much less tidy inside than Laila's had been, filled with candy wrappers, used train tickets, and loose aspirin tablets. It was easy enough to locate her identity card, however. It wasn't even in the card holder. I looked at the seal on the front. No smear. Carlotta's card hadn't been printed in the warehouse either.

I heard the murmur of voices, and the bell jangled again as the customer left. I shoved everything back into the handbag, hung it up, and returned to the chair. I was ineffectually trying to tie the dangling bit of gauze with my left hand when she came back in.

"Sorry about that," she said brightly. "Let me finish that up for you."

She tightened the bandage and tucked it into place.

"Thank you," I said.

"Glad I could help."

She led me back out into the shop, and I paid for my items.

Carlotta seemed lost in thought, as though she was contemplating something. As she handed me my items, she placed a hand over mine.

"Listen," she said quietly. "I don't think you should be asking these sorts of questions."

I raised my eyebrows, as if in surprise. Though, truthfully, this response had caught me off guard. "What do you mean?"

She looked around again and then leaned closer, though I was fairly certain we were the only ones in the shop besides the chemist on the other side of the room. "You shouldn't be asking questions about Hal's death," she whispered.

The bell above the door rang again, and she released my hand suddenly.

"Just mind your own business," she said, not unkindly. "It's safer that way."

CHAPTER FOURTEEN

I left the chemist with more questions than answers. I had been tempted to stick around and ask Carlotta what she had meant, but several customers had come in, and the opportunity had been lost. What was more, it was clear she was scared of something. Or, more likely, someone.

The fact that she had been willing to warn me, however, gave me hope. It signaled that she might be willing to talk more later if I could convince her that it was safe.

It was nearly noon, so it would be time to meet with Major Ramsey soon. I turned back toward the house, my thoughts swirling.

He was punctual as ever, parked at the curb in front of the house as I reached it.

When he saw me, he got out to come around and open my door.

"You don't have to do that," I said in a low voice, though there was no one about. "I can get in on my own."

He shook his head. "It would drop me in Mrs. James's esteem if I didn't display the manners of a proper gentleman."

"So you're forced to use the ruse of courting me once again,"

I said as we drove away. "One wonders that it doesn't try your nerves, Major Ramsey."

"It's a very convenient ruse when a man and a woman are working together," he said.

"Yes," I said. "I suppose that explains why you brought me instead of Uncle Mick."

"A man and a woman moving about together draw less attention than two men of disparate ages." He glanced at me. "Did you object to this trip?"

"No," I said truthfully. "But I do hate to have left Uncle Mick and Nacy in London. I worry about them."

He nodded. "That's understandable, but I'm sure they understand that you're doing important work."

"They do," I agreed. A question suddenly occurred to me. "But why did you instruct me to pretend that we were strangers? Couldn't we have come as a couple?"

"We're less conspicuous as a pair if we meet here in Sunderland and strike up a romance rather than having arrived together. Besides, that would have required us to put up the pretense of marriage, and I thought I'd spare you that necessity."

I didn't tell him that I had brought his ring along, the ring he had bought for a former fiancée and that I had used once when we were undercover. It had occurred to me that we might be able to make use of it again, and it was tucked into a secret compartment inside my suitcase.

We both knew what he was not saying, of course. That that ruse would have required sharing a room.

The major and I had posed as a married couple at a rooming house for a few hours once before, and though cards had proved distraction enough, I didn't suppose it would be comfortable to stay with him for any length of time.

"How's your arm?" he asked, interrupting my thoughts.

"My . . . oh, it's fine."

"Are you sure? You've cleaned it properly?"

I smiled. "Yes. If there's one thing Nacy taught me to do thoroughly, it was bandaging scrapes. It's fine."

"Glad to hear it."

"I went to the chemist to buy some bandages, and I talked to Carlotta Hogan," I said. "She told me to be careful about asking questions . . . because it's safer that way."

Major Ramsey glanced at me. "A friendly warning? Or a threat?"

"I don't think she was threatening me, but she's hiding something."

"Perhaps you can talk to her again," the major said. "But be careful."

"I always am, Major."

"You almost *never* are, Miss McDonnell," he replied. There was no censure in the words, and I smiled.

"'Risks net rewards,' as Uncle Mick always says."

The major parked us in a secluded field not far from the beach, and we walked along the dunes together like a young couple in love—or the nearest approximation we could manage, at any rate.

Most of the beaches were closed now, blocked off with rolls of barbed wire—whether to keep citizens in or the enemy out, I wasn't entirely sure. The grassy dune eventually rose to a more rocky bluff above the beach, and we occasionally stopped to look out to sea as though we enjoyed the view.

Finally, I was met with the sight of a large manor house looming in the distance.

"Don't look at it too closely," the major said, his hand on my lower back, his expression a mask of pleasantness. "Although you may be interested in those birds flying in that direction."

I lifted the binoculars I was carrying and pointed them in the direction of the house. "Birding was the best you could come up with?"

"It's a good excuse for binoculars."

"Yes, I suppose it is."

Vangidae was an imposing sandstone manor set on a slight rise overlooking the North Sea. I could see smoke rising from multiple chimneys.

"Are we going to break into there, too?" I asked.

"Not unless we have reason to," he replied, as though I went about breaking into houses without good reason.

"First you got me involved with a group of collectors of Chinese porcelain," I said, recalling our first mission. "And now an amateur ornithologist. You couldn't make use of your uncle's connections this time?" The Earl of Overbrook had been our entrée into a porcelain collectors' event that had been instrumental in our mission. I wouldn't be surprised if he was chummy with a few bird-watchers, too.

"My uncle is more interested in shooting birds than studying them, I'm afraid," Major Ramsey said. "We'll have to make our own introductions."

"What time does Sheridan Hall usually go on his walks?" I asked.

"Early in the morning and again after lunch. His second walk occurs at around fourteen hundred hours."

I looked at my watch. It was just after one o'clock. "Then we'll have about an hour to wait."

I sat down on a grassy spot atop the bluff, opened the birding book on my lap, and looked expectantly up at him.

He lowered himself to the grass beside me. Despite his very stiff bearing, he didn't look as out of place in situations like this as one might expect. I tried to imagine him, tan and weathered, in the deserts of North Africa, and I could picture it easily enough.

"Did you always want to be a soldier?" I wasn't sure where the question had come from. I hadn't expected to ask him, it had just come out.

"Yes. From the time I was very young, I knew it was the life I wanted."

I could understand that. After all, I'd known when I was very young that I wanted to follow in Uncle Mick's footsteps. I had never considered anything else, despite his urging to choose a field less steeped in risks.

I wondered if the major had followed his own father's path. "Was your father a career soldier?" I asked.

"No, though he fought in the last war. He was wounded at Amiens."

"I'm sorry. Was it serious?"

"His shoulder gives him trouble to this day, though he will admit it to no one. Even when it happened, he couldn't bear my mother and sisters fussing over him. I remember he called me to sit by his bedside and read to him as he recovered because the women would leave him alone if I was with him."

I smiled, both at the memory and at the fact he had shared it with me.

"I suppose it was alarming for a young boy to see his father like that."

"Yes. I worried that he would die, even after the doctors had said there was no danger of that."

This was a new side of Major Ramsey, a new key to unlocking that tightly padlocked personality of his. And it suddenly made sense to me how he ended up a career military man, how his life had been shaped by that early experience.

I had been born just as the Great War was ending. I had no memories of it. Though I'd never asked him his age, I judged Major Ramsey to be six or eight years older than me. He would have been old enough to have at least vague memories of the way the war had changed his family. It was the sort of thing that would have made an impact on a young boy.

"That must have been difficult."

"Not so very difficult," he said. "I got to keep my father. It was a lot more than millions of other children could say."

I nodded. I knew what it was like to be fatherless. Though it wasn't the war that had taken my father.

Silence fell for a moment, and I found myself surprised by the easy way we had been talking. There had been a lot of friction between the major and me since the beginning of our acquaintance, so it sometimes took me by surprise when we had a comfortable conversation.

"Is your family all right now?" I asked.

He nodded. "My parents and my sisters and their children are in Cumberland."

"How many nieces and nephews do you have?" I asked. I realized how very little I knew about him. Not that it was really necessary for us to know each other on a personal level; the work we did didn't require it. All the same, I was curious about him, about his life outside of the military. He was so seldom anything other than the stern, unyielding major, but I knew there was more to him than that.

"I have two nieces and four nephews," he said. "The eldest is ten, the youngest six months."

If he found my sudden questions invasive, he didn't show it. He didn't seem to mind discussing his family with me. This was nice, talking to him as a regular person.

"How fun they must be," I said. I thought of Colm and Toby. I hoped one day they would be home and married, and that there would be little ones running around.

The longing for it, for that sense of normalcy, put a lump in my throat. I missed the way things had been, missed it so desperately

I felt almost as though I couldn't breathe. But, of course, I could. We all went on breathing and longing and hoping.

I wrapped my arms around my knees, looking out at the sea as the wind set several curls that had made a break for it billowing around my face. I'd never been caught up in my appearance, but my unruly hair had always been the bane of my existence. I disliked things I couldn't have control over.

Glancing back at the major, I saw that he was looking at me. His eyes today were exactly the color of a twilight sky, a dusky blue-gray that hovered on the verge of violet.

I don't know why I chose that moment, but I suddenly wondered if Major Ramsey could do anything to find out about what had happened to Toby. Surely, with his connections, he could discover more than we had been able to.

"Major . . ."

Now was not the time for this conversation, perhaps, but we were being friendly today, and he suddenly seemed more approachable than he normally was. I felt that I could ask him. "Is there any way you could . . . do you suppose you could find out anything about what happened to Toby?"

There was a brief pause. I wondered if he was trying to find a way to tell me that he didn't have time to waste doing such things. But what he finally said was worse.

"I've already looked," he said. "I'm sorry, but I haven't been able to find any trace of him on the lists of German prisoners or through any of my other contacts."

I realized what that meant, and I felt myself go numb. "Then he's probably dead," I said.

"I've found no evidence of that either." He meant to comfort me, but it didn't do much good. I realized now that I had secretly been holding out hope that my association with Major Ramsey would someday prove useful in bringing my cousin home.

"I don't know how I'm going to tell Uncle Mick," I said.

"You've nothing new to tell," he said. "You knew his name wasn't on any of the lists of prisoners that have been released."

"Yes," I said. "But in your official capacity . . ." My words trailed off. It was a lot to digest. I hadn't expected to come face-to-face with this sort of realization today. With everything else that was on my mind, it felt like grief was jockeying for its place at the head of the line.

"It's possible that he escaped capture and is being hidden in France while he waits to make his way home," Major Ramsey said.

I considered this. It was something Toby would be likely to do. He and Colm had always had a daring streak. As boys, it had caused them to do foolhardy things, risking their necks and incurring Nacy's wrath.

Was it possible it could also be the trait that would push Toby to escape, to elude pursuers and make his way toward England? If he had escaped at Dunkirk, he wouldn't have been able to cross the Channel without a boat. So perhaps he had gone farther into France until the opportunity for getting back to our shores presented itself.

It wasn't much, but it was something. The major had given me hope.

I looked up at him. "Thank you," I said.

"I haven't done anything."

"You looked into his imprisonment, and you've given me something to hope for. That's quite a lot."

We looked at each other for a moment.

Then suddenly, he smiled down at me and, to my astonishment, pulled me against him, his mouth moving near my ear. "We're being watched," he murmured.

To my everlasting annoyance, my heart had begun an irregular rhythm that had nothing to do with possible danger.

I plastered a smile on my face instantly and leaned into him. "Let me go and speak to him first," I said.

"I don't think so."

"It'll be less conspicuous if it's just a woman talking to him about birds," I pointed out. "Just give me a few minutes."

He let out a short breath. "Five minutes. And don't do anything to alarm him."

I rose with a laugh, using his shoulder to pull myself up, and dusted the sand from my clothes. "I'm much less alarming than you are, Johnny."

He frowned at my use of a nickname for his alias, and I blew him a kiss as I walked away over the dune.

CHAPTER FIFTEEN

Mr. Hall had spotted us in deep conversation and had gone in the opposite direction—better to give us privacy, I assumed. Now I walked hurriedly in the direction he had retreated, trying not to appear as though I was following him.

I walked along the bluff, giving special attention to the birds that soared overhead. This really was a good spot for birding, if one was interested in such things. I saw a sanderling hopping along the shore below, if my memory of that wretched book served.

I went over a dip in the dune and saw him standing there. He saw me, too, so it was perfectly natural to wave hello and move in his direction.

"Good afternoon," I said.

"Good afternoon."

Mr. Hall was not what I had expected. I had assumed he would be a doddery elderly man, but this gentleman, while slightly stooped and of weathered complexion, had sharp eyes, and his manner and movements were animated. I realized that I would have to adjust my expectations of him. *Never assume, Ellie girl.* Uncle Mick had told me that often enough, and it would do me well to remember it.

"It's a lovely day," I said.

"Indeed." He was looking at me expectantly, wondering, I supposed, what I was doing on this deserted stretch of beach.

"My husband and I are renting a little cottage back that way," I said, pointing vaguely to the north. "He's on leave from the RAF, and we've come here for a bit of privacy."

"Well, I suppose a secluded spot like this is just right for privacy," he said, a twinkle in his blue eyes. "Young married couples like to be alone together, don't they?"

"Yes, I suppose so," I said, trying to muster up a blush.

"There's a lot of good deserted beach along here," he said. "And just half a mile or so to the south, there are some old smuggler's caves worth exploring. Do be careful, though. There are one or two deep pits inside it, I believe. Where is the young man now?" he asked, his eyes moving from me to scan the beach behind me.

"Oh, I've left him alone to think," I said. "He's a writer, you see."

"Ah!" His interest seemed piqued at this. "And what kind of books does he write?"

I tried to think of what Mr. Hall might be least interested in. The less interested he was, the less likely he would be to ask too many questions.

"He writes mystery novels," I said at last.

"Ah." I appeared to have chosen right. The flicker of interest evaporated from Mr. Hall's expressive face.

"I would never tell him," I said. "But they're not much my cup of tea."

"No?"

"No. I'm not much for reading. I like to be outside, in nature. I've been looking for birds today . . ." I held up the birding book and then wondered if I was laying it on a bit too thick.

His gaze was suddenly sharp, and I didn't know whether I

had roused his academic interest or his suspicion. I would have to tread carefully.

"Interested in birds, are you?"

"Well, I'm a novice, but I'm trying to learn. They're such marvelous creatures."

"That they are, my dear."

"I spotted a sanderling just now," I offered.

"There's a falcon nest on the cliffs a mile to the south. You know they've made it legal to kill falcons in this country," he said, eyeing me with a stern expression. "They're eating homing pigeons. I think it's a crime to kill the falcons, myself. It's all well and good that the pigeons are being used for sending messages and so forth, but what about when the war is over? Are they going to put this much effort into rebuilding the falcon population?"

"I agree with you entirely," I said. "I think it's criminal that such beasts are being destroyed. They're magnificent."

This was clearly the right thing to say, for his brows lifted ever so slightly from where they had been lowering, and he nodded his head emphatically. "Precisely. Precisely."

"Elizabeth!" I heard the major calling before we caught sight of him. I considered not answering and seeing if I could make any more headway, but Sheridan Hall was already looking in the direction of his voice.

"This way, darling!" I shouted.

He appeared then and caught sight of us. He gave a wave and a friendly smile. Really, it was remarkable the way he could change his entire personality at the drop of a hat.

"Don't tell him I've been speaking disparaging of the genre," I whispered to Mr. Hall.

He gave me a conspiratorial wink. "I wouldn't dream of it, my dear. Your secret is safe with me."

I smiled brightly at him and then turned to watch the major approach.

"Finished contemplating your chapter already, darling?" I asked as he reached us.

"Nearly," he replied without missing a beat. "But I grew lonesome without you and came in search of you."

He reached me and slid an arm neatly around my waist as he offered the other hand to Mr. Hall. "Captain John Grey," he said.

"I'm very pleased to meet you, Captain," Mr. Hall said. "And I don't blame you at all for coming to search for your charming wife. Were she my wife, I shouldn't like to let her out of my sight."

The major smiled. "She does tend to wander off."

"Well, I'm delighted that she wandered in my direction. Perhaps I shall see you both again before your leave is over."

"We would love that," I said.

He smiled at us. "Until next time, then."

Major Ramsey turned me in the opposite direction and began leading me away.

"You ought to have given me a bit longer. We were getting along famously."

"I have no doubt of that, but we don't want to rouse his suspicions."

"Nothing suspicious about a novelist and his wife renting a secluded cottage by the sea."

"You decided to tell him I was a writer, did you?"

"He was wondering why you let me go out walking alone, and it was the first thing that came to my head. You were pondering your next chapter."

"Not a bad idea," he said. "That fits in with his interests."

"Well, as to that," I said. "Not exactly."

He looked at me, and I could see the suspicion lurking in his eyes. "No?"

"No," I said. "You write mystery novels."

"It's you who should be writing novels, Miss McDonnell. That imagination of yours knows no bounds."

We arrived back at the lodging house just as dusk was falling.

He opened my door, and I remembered to put a cheerful expression on my face. I was just about to walk away when he caught my arm. "Wait a moment."

I looked up at him.

"Come here." He pulled me against him, and I was too surprised to argue. I knew at once, of course, that it must be a part of our ruse, but I wasn't sure who we were meant to be playing this scene for.

"Your friend is watching us," he said, answering my question, leaning close as though whispering into my ear.

I smiled up at him, as I might have if he had said something charming or romantic. He was very close, his eyes on mine, and I thought for a moment he might kiss me.

My heart sped up, traitorous thing that it was. There was no reason why I should be anticipating a kiss from Major Ramsey.

But he didn't kiss me. He stepped back suddenly and released me, reaching up to tuck a stray curl behind my ear. "I'll see you later."

I nodded up at him, remembering to keep the besotted expression on my face.

"Hello, Liz!" I turned and saw the familiar figure of Nessa Simpson approaching. She smiled broadly as she reached us.

Her eyes ran appreciatively over the major and she smiled at him, revealing a dimple in one cheek I had not noticed before. "Hello, Captain."

The major had switched immediately back into his more charming mode, and he smiled at Nessa in return. "Good evening, how are you?"

"Very well, thank you." She beamed under his attention like a flower in the sun. It really was ridiculous how women responded to him.

"Thank you so much for a lovely day, John," I said, smiling up at him. "I look forward to seeing you again soon."

To my surprise, he leaned forward and brushed a kiss across my cheek. I caught a whiff of his shaving soap, still warm and slightly spicy even after a day spent out in the sea breeze.

With another smile and a tip of his cap at Nessa, Captain John Grey went back around to the driver's side, got in, and drove away.

Nessa grinned at me in a conspiratorial way now that the major had gone. "He really is rather magnificent," she told me. "I know Sami is just green with envy that you spotted him first." There was nothing malicious in the comment, but all the same I wondered if she and Sami had competed over a man before.

Nessa was pretty, but she wasn't stunning like Sami was. I'd never been insecure in my looks, but I didn't flatter myself that, were the major really just an RAF pilot on the prowl, I would have attracted his notice more than Sami.

"Did you have a nice time?" Nessa asked as she walked me toward the front door.

"Lovely," I said. "We went for a drive out along the seashore."

She looked at me with a bit of a twinkle in her gaze. "Have you been lying in the grass?"

I looked at her, surprised. "Why do you ask?"

She gave me a sly smile. "You naughty thing. Don't worry. I'm not one to tell tales. But you might want to brush off your bottom before Mrs. James sees you."

I flushed at the implication. While I had, in point of fact, been lounging in the grass with the major, it was not what she thought.

"It wasn't . . ." I began, but she held up a hand.

"You needn't deny anything to me. I'd do the same, if I had a handsome fellow like that. After all, there's a war on. You've got to experience life while you can."

"But I . . ."

"You're smitten with him," she said. "Not that I blame you, of course. He's enough to make any woman lose her head."

"I suppose I'd better be careful," I said. "After all, I don't know him very well, and he probably won't be in Sunderland much longer."

She shrugged. "My own motto is to think as little about the future as possible. One can't afford to in wartime. There is only the present moment, and one must live life to the fullest."

"Do you have a beau?" I asked.

There was the briefest shadow that crossed her face, and then she smiled. "There are too many handsome pilots around here to settle on just one."

There was something behind the statement, but I could tell that it wasn't anything she wanted to discuss. Most likely, she had lost someone she cared about. I recognized that look well enough these days. The haunted look of sadness in the eyes of young women who had lost their true loves too early.

We focused so much on the day-to-day now, on survival and making it through, that thoughts of the future, when they appeared, felt like a frightening dark void. It was dreadful to think of what life would be like when the war was over. When we were expected to go back to our normal lives when so many of the people we loved were lost to us.

What would life be like after all of this if Toby was truly gone? I couldn't bear to think about it. And that was, I supposed, why living day-to-day was the best strategy right now.

"Anyway," Nessa said, "I'm glad you had a nice time."

"The seaside is lovely. It's not something I get to see every day in London."

"I would give my right arm to live in London," Nessa said

wistfully. "Well, perhaps not now, with the bombing. But I've always wanted to escape Sunderland, and it's never been much of an option for me. Perhaps when the war is over, I'll build up enough fortitude and funds to chase my fortunes elsewhere."

"I suppose a lot of us have dreams for what we hope to do after the war," I said. I was trying to get the conversation around to Hal Jenkins, and it seemed Nessa had given me a way to go about it. "Of course, the war is changing so many things, and so many people won't see the end of it. I feel so bad about Hal Jenkins. I didn't even know him, but it was such a shock to see him fall in the street like that."

Nessa nodded sadly. If she saw anything suspicious in my shifting the topic to something so solemn, she didn't show it. "Poor Hal. I never would have expected something like that to happen to him."

"Something like what?" I asked, pretending I had misunderstood her in hopes that she might say something telling.

"Well, that he would . . . die like that," she said, lowering her voice, as though we were at a funeral. "It was just so unexpected."

"Did he have any family that you know of?" I asked.

She shook her head. "He didn't talk much about his personal life. I'm not even sure if he had a girl. He flirted a bit with Sami, but most men do." Again, there was the lighthearted acknowledgment of Sami's appeal to men. Did I imagine the slight edge beneath the words? Even if that were the case, it might not mean anything. It was usual for women to be a bit jealous of the most popular woman in their set.

All the same, I decided I might as well pursue that angle and see what could be learned.

"Did Sami fancy him, do you think?" I asked. "She seemed upset that he died, yes, but I didn't know that there was anything in the way of romance between them."

Nessa waved a hand dismissively. "No, nothing like that. Sami wouldn't have looked twice at him under normal circumstances. I think she just flirted with him because she knew it made her sister mad."

Now that was interesting. "Did Laila disapprove of Sami spending time with Hal?" I asked.

"Well, you might say so," Nessa said. "Laila was sweet on Hal."

This was a surprise. Especially when I recalled the cool way Laila had told me that Hal was not her friend.

"Oh," I said. "I was sure Laila said she didn't know Hal well."

Nessa laughed. "Well, as to that, I don't know how well they really knew each other. Whatever they were doing was a secret. I saw them walking together late at night a few times. She never mentioned it to anyone else in our group that I know of, but I'm sure Sami knew. Sami and Laila are joined at the hip."

I certainly was getting a lot of interesting information from Nessa.

Perhaps it had not been a romance between Hal and Laila. In fact, I had a strong suspicion that it had not been. And, if that was the case, there was some other reason why Laila Maddox had been sneaking out to see Hal Jenkins.

CHAPTER SIXTEEN

I caught up with Sami the next morning. Truth be told, I was lying in wait for her.

Directly after a hurried breakfast, I had gone outside and wandered around the garden, waiting for her to appear. I wanted to see what she would have to say about her early morning visitor the previous day. I also hoped she might give me some information about the relationship between Laila and Hal Jenkins. And I needed to find a way to look at her identity card. I didn't want Sami to be guilty of anything, but I was here to do a job, and I intended to do it. I realized there was a fine line to tread when asking questions. After all, I was a stranger, an outsider in a group of longtime friends. They liked me well enough, but that didn't mean they would trust me with their secrets. What reason would they have?

All the same, I had to try.

"Good morning, Sami!" I called as she came out of the house.

She stopped when she saw me and waved, a smile on her face. "Good morning."

"Are you going to work?" I asked as I reached her.

"Yes. Another early shift today. I stopped by to see you

yesterday afternoon because Laila said you'd paid a visit. But Mrs. James said you were out with your young man again." She grinned broadly at me. "Are things going well?"

I tried to affect the hopeful look of a woman at the start of a new romance. "I think so."

"Walk with me and tell me all about it," she said. "Unless you've somewhere else to be?"

"No," I said. "I've been wanting to tell you about John."

We began walking together in the direction of the chemist.

"Have you kissed him?" Sami asked.

I laughed, and, because it was important to make my story realistic, I said, "We might have kissed a bit."

"Ah! Even better," she said, squeezing my arm. It was my scratched arm, and I winced slightly.

"Oh, I'm sorry. Did I hurt you?" she asked.

"I scraped my arm. In fact, I was going to buy fresh bandages at the chemist," I said lightly. "But, to answer your question, John and I are getting along very well, and I have high hopes."

She sighed dreamily. "How perfectly lovely."

"And what about you? As long as we're talking about romance: I thought I saw a young man in your yard quite early yesterday morning. Do you have an admirer?"

For just a moment, confusion flashed across her face. Then she realized who I meant, and all expression vanished from her lovely features. "Oh, no. That was just a fellow who came to my house by mistake."

"Oh, I see." I could tell now was not the time to press it. "What about Laila? She's not seeing anyone?"

"No," Sami said with a laugh. "She's very prim and proper, my sister. She doesn't believe in casual dating."

It seemed clear that Laila had not been involved romantically with Hal Jenkins. What had been their connection, then? Was it possible "prim and proper" Laila was involved with a proper spy ring somehow?

We reached the chemist, and I looked up to see that Carlotta was approaching. She smiled when she saw me, but I was certain I didn't imagine the wariness in her eyes.

"Morning, Lottie! Liz needs a bandage for her arm," Sami said as we all reached the door.

"How is it healing?" Carlotta asked me.

"Fairly well, I think," I replied. "I know the shop isn't open for ten minutes still. I'll wait outside."

"Just let us switch on the lights and things," Sami said.

She and Carlotta went inside. Stepping away from the window, I looked at Sami's identity card. It had been an easy enough thing to slip it from her handbag as we walked along. The squeezing of my bandaged arm had served as the perfect distraction.

I held my breath as I examined the front of Sami's identity card. The telltale flaw was not there. The card had not been printed at the illicit press. At least I could feel relief on that score—not that I had really expected Sami to be a German spy, especially not when Laila's card had not been forged. There was still the possibility that they were involved in some other way, of course.

Much to my chagrin, this thought was confirmed as I entered the shop. The girls had not closed the door all the way, so the bell didn't sound. I could hear their voices from somewhere inside.

"No," Carlotta said. "Of course, I didn't say anything."

"I just wanted to be sure. We have to be careful, you know."

"I know how to keep a secret," Carlotta replied tersely.

"I know you do. I only remind you because this is bigger than just you and me. There are people counting on us."

They said nothing more, so I pushed the door a bit harder so the bell jangled.

"Are you open for business?" I called out.

"There you are, Liz," Carlotta said brightly, coming from behind the shelf where she and Sami had been standing. "Let me rebandage your arm for you."

So Sami and Carlotta shared a secret. It was not necessarily a sign that they had killed Hal Jenkins, I reminded myself. But whatever they were involved in sounded dangerous. And a man was dead. How much of a coincidence could that be? At least both of their identity cards had appeared legitimate. And I managed to slip Sami's back into her handbag without detection.

I left the chemist and decided to walk to the post office to see if the letter Uncle Mick had forwarded me from Clarice Maynard had arrived.

The postmistress nodded when I gave her my name. "Yes, I believe there's a letter here. Wait just a moment."

My heart pounded as I waited, and once she handed me the letter, I opened it with trembling hands. It was strange how my hands were steady as a rock when I was removing locks illegally, but opening a letter that might relate to something that had happened a quarter of a century ago made my fingers fumble.

There was no sense in getting overly emotional about things. Whatever was in this letter could not change the past.

I slipped the piece of pale yellow stationery from the envelope. The writing was thin and loopy, and the scent of rose water came up from the paper.

My dear Ellie,

I must apologize for the delay in my reply. It surprised me to hear from you, and it took me some time to decide what I should say.

Let me say first that I am glad to hear you are well. I know your mother would have wished above all things that you had a happy life, and it is so good to know that your childhood home was a loving one.

I was your mother's dearest friend. She confided in me and entrusted me with information that she never told a living soul, information that may have cost her her freedom and, ultimately, her life.

There have been many times over the years when I've wondered if I did her a disservice by keeping her secrets. But what she told me was not mine to share, and I have kept it to myself all these years.

So you understand that I was conflicted upon receiving your letter. I've thought a great deal about it these past several days, however, and I have decided that I believe sharing her story with you is the right thing to do.

But some things are better not put on paper. Will you come and see me? It will be easier to talk in person.

Sincerely,
Clarice Maynard

The postscript contained her address and directions to her home from the Lincolnshire train station. And then a second postscript:

I am including a photograph that has been in my possession for many years. I thought it was time you had it.

The photograph was wrapped in a piece of folded yellow paper. I unfolded it and saw that there was writing on it. *Please keep this for me,* it said. *I don't want it to be found.*

Were they my mother's words?

I studied the photograph. It was of my mother and father.

They looked younger in it than in any of the ones I had seen of them, younger even than in their wedding photograph, which I still possessed. My mother was radiantly beautiful, my father tall and dark with bright eyes and a trim mustache. They stood close together, smiling happily, a wide vista of mountains behind them, a little cottage visible at the edge of the frame.

There was nothing particularly telling about the photograph, and I wondered why my mother had not wanted it found when she was arrested. It made no sense.

I reread the letter, once and then twice. I had hoped that she would reveal more, tell me something about my mother and her case or about what the photograph meant.

I supposed I ought to be glad that she was willing to talk to me, but the letter was frustratingly vague. What was more, there was something overly dramatic about it, as though Clarice Maynard was a woman who relished her secrets. I had known women like that in my time, women who placed exaggerated importance on what they had to say. Was it possible Mrs. Maynard's information would not be as crucial as she seemed to think?

There was only one way to find out. I would have to go and see her when all of this was over.

I returned to Mrs. James's then to see if there had been any word from the major. I was not surprised to hear there was not.

I went back to my room and sat down at the desk to think. So far I'd learned very little.

We knew that they were making false passports and documents in the defunct printer shop. But the major hadn't seemed to think that was information enough. If he had, he would have sent me back to London and swooped in to arrest the culprits.

No, there was more to this. The fact that they were printing documents for spies meant that there must be spies in Sunderland to collect them.

And there was the good possibility that one of them had killed Hal Jenkins. Surely it had been someone he knew who poisoned him, someone he trusted. So who among his acquaintances had turned on him?

I went down to dinner at Mrs. James's and was glad to see that Alfred Little was there. I hadn't seen him since that first night in the pub. I assumed he worked long hours in the mines.

Tonight, he looked tired, but his skin shone brightly and he smelled of soap. No doubt he'd just come in off a shift and had bathed before dinner.

I took a seat beside him at the dinner table.

"Good evening, Alfred," I said brightly.

He smiled, revealing a pretty set of very white teeth. He was handsome, I realized, when he wasn't shrinking into himself. "Good evening," he said.

"I haven't seen you about the place much. I suppose the mines keep you busy?"

"Yes, very busy," he said, taking a bite of his dinner and chewing it slowly.

"Do you like working in the mines?"

"It's a job," he said. "My father did it and his father before him. I don't suppose I ever considered anything else."

"It's very important work," I said. "Especially now."

"I would have liked to go to war," he said. "But I have a lung condition and was turned down."

"I have a very good friend who lost a leg, and he's taken up work at the hospital in London. It makes me feel good knowing there are some good men left at home to do the work that needs to be done."

He smiled politely, as though he knew I was laying it on a bit thick, and said nothing.

It was going to be difficult to make small talk with Alfred, I thought. He wasn't the sort of boy who would warm to too much attention. It would only make him retreat further into his shell. I would have to find another way to win him over.

And so I decided to press ahead with my most recent hobby. "I've taken up bird-watching lately."

"We don't get to see much of birds in the mines," he said with another small smile. This one was a bit melancholy, I thought. I found myself feeling sorry for the boy. It mustn't be the most cheerful of jobs, to spend all that time belowground.

"I don't know much about birds as of yet," I said. "But I intend to become an expert. Perhaps, once the war is over, I'll chase birds all over the world."

He smiled. "That sounds like fun."

"And what will you do when the war is over?"

Something like wistfulness crossed his face for just an instant before a shadow overtook it. "Suppose I'll keep working in the mines."

"Isn't there something else you'd like to do?"

He shrugged. "Maybe."

"Nessa told me today that life is short, and we must make the most of it. I think that's good advice, don't you?"

"Yes, I suppose," he said, but he had disengaged from the conversation now. He was very focused on his potatoes.

I studied him, a lock of his nearly colorless hair falling over his face as he ate his dinner. I couldn't easily imagine Alfred killing someone, but I knew better than to underestimate anyone.

"I've enjoyed meeting everyone. The Maddox girls and Nessa and Carlotta. Have you known them long?" I asked.

"Since I moved into the neighborhood a year or so ago. We're friendly enough."

"I suppose you and Ronald are chummy."

"He's more interested in girls, I think."

I smiled. "What about you, Alfred? Do you have a girl?"

He flushed. "No. I . . . I haven't met anyone yet, not anyone special, I mean."

"Oh, well. You're young. No sense in rushing things."

He said nothing. Was he really so painfully shy, or was it exaggerated for my benefit? He had been quiet when we'd all had dinner together, but surely he must have strong feelings and opinions about things. Of course, just because he wasn't willing to share them with a stranger didn't mean they weren't there.

Well, I was just going to have to press ahead and hope for the best.

"Were you good friends with Hal Jenkins?"

His face went white at this. The flush completely fell away, like a broken hourglass losing its sand.

"Not really."

"I was so sorry about his death. It was such a shocking thing. I'd only just arrived here when it happened."

"Yes. So sad," he said. "Hal was a nice fellow."

"I wonder what could have happened to him."

He ran a hand through his pale hair. "I don't know about that. That is, I heard he had a heart attack."

"Yes, I heard that, too," I said.

I could tell he wasn't going to answer any more questions, so I gave him a bit of a break and conversed with a few of the others at the table.

There was something distinctly strange about Alfred's behavior. He was so very uneasy, painfully so. Too much so to be the spy?

I wondered if I could sneak into his room and get a look at his papers. But it would be a fine thing indeed if he woke up to find me in his bedroom in the middle of the night. Poor Alfred would probably have a heart attack.

There had to be an easier way. I could pick his pocket, of

course. I was fairly adept at that, and I could likely do it without his noticing. The more I thought about it, the more it seemed like the best way to go about things.

As we rose from the table, I dropped my napkin. "Oh, how clumsy," I said, reaching slowly.

Alfred reached down and picked it up for me. As he did, I slipped my hand into his pocket and slid his wallet out. It was done almost too easily.

I slipped the wallet into my own pocket and took the napkin from him. "Thank you."

He walked from the room, and I hurried into the empty corridor. Opening his wallet, I looked at the contents. There wasn't much there. A few notes, his identity card to enter the mines, a book of matches.

I pulled out his National Registration Identity Card and looked at the cover. There wasn't the irregularity that signaled it was one of the forgeries. Not that I had expected it to be. Alfred wasn't the sort of young man who would make a good spy. I didn't think his deep shyness was an act. He was too clearly uncomfortable. I had the feeling he was always on edge, and the Germans, whatever else might be said about them, were too competent to send a man who so utterly failed to blend in.

Then I saw an almost-hidden pocket inside the wallet, and something was shoved deep down inside. What was that? Whatever it was, it was meant to be concealed.

I pushed my fingers into the flap and pulled out the object. It was the photo of a young man in an army uniform, with dark wavy hair and a dimple in his chin. Alfred's brother, perhaps? But no, their coloring was too dissimilar.

I flipped it over and looked at the back. There was a note scrawled: *All my love, Martin.*

I slipped the photo back into its slot. If that was Alfred's secret, then it was safe with me. It had no bearing on what we were doing here.

"Alfred," I called as I walked into the parlor. "You dropped your wallet."

He looked surprised, but only mumbled his thanks as I handed it to him.

Most of Mrs. James's lodgers were sitting in the parlor. A few of them were playing cards, and the rest were listening to the radio and chatting. I found I didn't feel like joining them.

"Have you got a match?" a young woman asked me as she came into the room.

"No, I . . ."

I suddenly remembered the matchbooks I had found in Hal Jenkins's pockets. Where were they? Where had I put them?

"Sorry. Perhaps one of the gentlemen has some," I said, moving past her and out of the room.

I had worn the same trousers to search his room that I had worn to the compound. Surely I'd emptied the pockets in between jobs. That was a cardinal rule of Uncle Mick's. No excess baggage. Nothing that could leave a clue behind. Those little axioms of his had become second nature to me over the years, so deeply ingrained that I didn't always realize I was following them.

I reached my room and found the trousers. The pockets were empty. Moving to the little desk, I pulled open the drawer. Sure enough, I'd set the two matchbooks inside.

I took them out and studied the covers. One was for a nightclub called Blue Breezes. There was, unsurprisingly enough, a rough illustration of blue waves on the cover.

The other was for a place called The Gale. The name seemed familiar to me somehow. Someone had mentioned it, I thought.

I flipped open the matchbook to see if it had been used. I

hadn't expected to see anything of interest, so I was startled to discover there was writing inside the cover.

It was a series of numbers. I studied it. It wasn't any recognizable configuration of numbers. Not a phone number or an address or anything of that sort. Nevertheless, there was some reason Hal Jenkins had written them down.

Or had he not written them? I thought how easily a matchbook might be passed from person to person. Had someone passed him this as a message?

I felt suddenly excited at the possibility. I wished the major were there so I could show him my discovery. He might have more insight into what the numbers could mean.

Turning the matchbook for Blue Breezes over in my hand, I flipped it open, too. There was nothing written inside that one. So The Gale would be the place to look.

I sat on my bed with a frustrated sigh. We were making a bit of progress, but I felt at every turn I was being thwarted. I was learning things, bits of information that might mean something, but I had no way to put them together into something meaningful.

I was sure the major was keeping something from me. That was no great surprise, as he never told me much. All the same, I felt rather as though I was fumbling about in the dark unnecessarily.

I put the matches away in the drawer and decided to walk down to the pub, to see if Ronald was there. He was the last of the group I needed to speak to.

I arrived at the pub to find it was crowded already, and the air was noisy and filled with cigarette smoke. I looked to the table in the corner. As luck would have it, Ronald was sitting there alone. If he was in his cups, I could perhaps even get a look at his identity card.

He had a half-empty glass before him and was staring at the

wall, whether in deep contemplation or more of a semi-stupor I couldn't quite tell. Well, there was only one way to find out.

I made my way over to his table. "Hello, Ronald."

He looked up. "Oh, hello, Liz."

He'd been drinking again. His eyes had taken on a glassy look, and his face was flushed. I hoped that he didn't have a job that was dangerous to do when inebriated. Of course, a lot of people were drinking more than usual these days. One couldn't blame a man for that.

"Hello, Ronald," I said. "Are you drinking alone?"

He shrugged. "I'm not particular about my drinking."

"Then do you mind if I join you?"

"I'd be delighted," he said, indicating that I should take a seat.

I slid into the booth next to him—I couldn't pick his pocket from across the table, after all—and he motioned the barmaid over. "What will you have?" he asked.

"A ginger ale, please," I said.

"Oh, come on, love. Have a bit of fun. Give her a pint."

"A ginger ale," I said to the barmaid, and she gave a nod and went back toward the bar.

I turned my attention back to Ronald. I smiled at him. "I'm already fun."

He grinned at this and raised his glass to me.

I didn't intend to give him the wrong impression, but I didn't suppose that a little bit of flirtation would hurt. After all, the group had seemed to enjoy light banter among them. I didn't think there was any danger of his misconstruing my friendliness.

"I thought you were stepping out with the RAF bloke," he said.

I shrugged. "We've been out a few times."

He leaned toward me, one broad arm on the table.

"The pilots like to swoop in and snatch up the girls, but the rest of us are doing a hard bit of work, too."

"Of course you are," I assured him.

He leaned even closer, and I tried not to flinch at the strength of his breath. He smelled like a distillery. "Where's your fellow now?"

I shrugged. "He's not really my fellow. I haven't known him long."

"You're a pretty girl, Liz," he said, his words slightly slurred.

"Thank you."

He slid an arm around me and I gently pushed it away. "Let's not get too friendly, shall we, Ronald?"

He flushed. "And why not? You can have a bit of fun with me like with the RAF lads, can't you?"

"Certainly," I answered. "But I don't want to give you the wrong impression."

The barmaid fortuitously arrived with my ginger ale then, and Ronald shifted away from me for just a moment as she set it on the table.

"None of your group is joining you here for dinner?" I asked Ronald when she had gone.

"What's the matter, Liz? You don't want to be alone with me?" He had slipped his arm along the back of the booth beside me again. I recognized that he was starting to get pushy. This wasn't an especially good situation to be in, but it did make it much easier to pick his pocket.

As he crowded me, I reached over and slid his wallet from his pocket.

"I don't mind being alone with you, but I think we'd better behave ourselves in public."

He snorted. "No one cares what we do in here. Come on, give us a kiss."

"If you'll excuse me for a moment," I said, his wallet safely in my own pocket.

"Aww, come on, love. You don't have to run away."

"I'll be right back," I said.

I got up and went to the toilet. Locking the door behind me, I took Ronald's wallet out of my pocket and opened it. It was crammed with the various detritus of a would-be man-about-town. Movie ticket stubs, a flattened cigarette, and a folded-up picture of a scantily clad pinup girl.

There was his identification card for the shipyard. It seemed he was who he said he was. I let out a sigh. So far, I was coming up with a losing hand.

I hoped the major was having more success than I was in whatever he was doing.

Just to be thorough, I pulled out his National Registration Identity Card.

Then I froze.

There, on the bottom corner, beneath the lion, was the tell-tale smudge.

CHAPTER SEVENTEEN

I hadn't expected to find anything. Ronald had seemed to me among the most unlikely of the suspects. Now that I had discovered that he might be a spy, I wasn't sure what I should do.

I needed to contact Major Ramsey. But how? He'd left me no indication of where he would be. If he didn't insist on being so secretive, I wouldn't be in this mess. I'd be certain to let him know what I thought of this when I saw him again. In the meantime, I would have to improvise.

I went back out into the pub and took my seat beside Ronald once again. Though I was loath to encourage his attentions, I leaned closer to him so I could slip the wallet back into his pocket. I'd had less practice replacing objects than I had lifting them, but Ronald was very drunk and was distracted by my leaning against him, and so I managed it easily enough.

"Have another pint with me?" he asked, apparently forgetting that I'd declined the first.

"No, I'm afraid I'd better be getting back. But thank you."

"Suit yourself, love. I'll just be shoving off myself."

He rose from the table. Where was he going? Somewhere related to his spying?

He moved a bit unsteadily through the crowd, and I watched him go, debating what I should do.

Then I followed him from the pub.

It took a moment for my eyes to adjust to the darkened street after the light inside the pub, but I spotted him soon enough. He was making his way down the street at a slow, deliberate pace. I wondered if the drunkenness had all been an act. It must have been; surely German spies didn't go about getting themselves blotto when there was more important work to be done.

But he definitely wasn't walking a straight line, and more than once he stopped to sag against a wall for a moment, seeming to catch his breath. He couldn't be faking for my benefit. I was certain he hadn't seen me slip out after him. What was all this about, then? I supposed it was possible he'd just had too much to drink tonight. Being a spy must be stressful work, after all.

He was easy to follow in his condition, and more than once I had to stand impatiently in the shadows while he took a rest.

Finally, he appeared to have reached his destination. He stopped in front of a door and, after hesitating for a moment, went inside.

After a suitable pause, I followed him to the door. It was unmarked, but I could hear the sound of music coming from within.

Taking a chance, I pushed the door open. I saw at once that I was in a small entryway that led into a wide-open space. There was music and dancing. It was a nightclub.

I looked and saw a sign above the bar. The Gale.

This was the nightclub where Hal Jenkins had acquired the matchbook with the code inside. It seemed this must be a popular place among spies. Or perhaps it was Ronald who had passed him the message. That seemed likely enough.

As these thoughts crossed my mind, it also occurred to me that perhaps this wasn't the safest thing I had ever done.

Major Ramsey would definitely not approve. All the same, it was a crowded nightspot. It was not as though I would be alone with the suspect.

I slipped inside. I wasn't exactly dressed for a nightclub, but I saw there were several couples in more casual clothes, no doubt having come directly from their jobs.

There was a good smattering of RAF men, soldiers, and a few sailors, and the place was loud with music and conversation and laughter. The dance floor was so packed that there was barely room to move, but no one seemed to notice. There was an air of strained gaiety, though I thought there was plenty of melancholy, too. It was a bittersweet thing to dance with your fellow, having the opportunity to feel his arms around you but not knowing when—or even if—you would feel them again.

"I beg your pardon," a voice said.

I looked up and was startled to see Rafe Beaumont.

"Yes, I thought it was you, Liz."

"Rafe," I said. "What are you doing here?"

"This is one of my favorite haunts," he said. "What brings you here?"

"Someone mentioned this place to me."

He grinned. "I believe that was me."

"Oh, was it?" I said airily. I remembered then that he had indeed recommended this place as one of the nightclubs he frequented. I wasn't sure whether I was glad he was here. It was nice to see a friendly face, but I was trying to follow Ronald and didn't have time for conversation. "I just happened to be passing and thought I would drop in to see what it was like."

"It's not much," he said, casting his eye around the place, as though trying to see it from an outsider's perspective. "But once you get used to a place, it starts to feel a bit like home."

"Yes, I suppose you're right."

"I've been eagerly looking forward to tomorrow," he said.

"Tomorrow?"

"Our date."

Truth be told, in all the excitement, I had forgotten about our agreement to meet. Now was not the most convenient of times in my life to be gallivanting around Sunderland with the handsome young pilot, but we had made the date, and I supposed I should keep it.

"You didn't forget?" he asked, his eyes searching my face.

"I forgot it was tomorrow," I admitted.

He put a hand to his heart. "You cut me to the quick, Liz. And here I thought you'd be counting the days."

I laughed. "I'm afraid I've been rather busy with my aunt's house."

"And how is that going?"

"It's rather more to sort through than I expected."

"You'll forgive me for saying I'm glad. That means you'll be in Sunderland longer."

I laughed at his flattery. If nothing else, a few hours with him tomorrow would prove an amusing diversion.

"I've borrowed a car for the occasion," he said. "I know you said you wanted to see Sunderland."

"That was sweet of you. And we won't waste too much petrol."

"I'm friends with the fellow who rations it at the base. It will be all right if we use a bit. He owes me a favor. What would you like to see? There's a monastery that dates back to the seventh century, though I'm afraid there's not much of the original building left. It's nothing compared to the Greeks, of course, but interesting enough."

"I'm game to see whatever you think is most interesting."

"I'm afraid I haven't seen much of the city yet to know," he said. "The RAF keeps me on rather a tight lead."

I smiled. "I imagine it's a big job, keeping you pilots in line."

His eyes flashed mischievously. "I'm not so very great a trouble-maker."

"I'm not sure if I should believe you, Captain Beaumont."

Even as I spoke with him, my eyes were moving around the room, trying to keep track of where Ronald Potter had gone.

"But I've been remiss in my duties. Let me get you something to drink," Rafe said.

"All right," I agreed. I didn't want a drink, but I didn't see any other way of getting rid of him for at least a moment. I had lost track of Ronald in the crowd, and I needed to find him before he disappeared.

"I'll be right back," he told me. "Don't let anyone steal you away."

He disappeared, and I made my way along the perimeter of the dance floor, trying to locate Ronald. I didn't want to be too conspicuous in my search. It would be much better if I saw him before he saw me. After all, even if he didn't know I was onto his illicit activities, he would, at the very least, think I had followed him here for some other reason.

"Care to dance?" a sailor asked.

"Not just now, thank you," I said, moving on.

"Liz!"

I turned, surprised to see Sami coming through the crowd. She was dressed in a gown of black satin, her hair and makeup artfully done. She looked like she had stepped from the pages of a magazine.

"What are you doing here?" she asked me, as she took my hands and squeezed them.

"Someone told me about this place, and I decided to see what it was like. What are you doing here?" I asked.

"I come here all the time," she said, smiling. "But don't tell Laila."

"I won't."

"Nessa is here somewhere, too. She's here more than I am. The girl is quiet, but I think there's a bit of a wild streak underneath." She winked. "Who were you talking to over there? That wasn't your Johnny from the pub." Her eyes followed the direction in which Rafe had disappeared.

"No," I said. "That was a different gentleman. Just a friend. I met him on the train on the way here."

Her dark brows lifted. "It's not exactly fair, your having two good-looking officers to yourself."

I laughed. "I don't suppose you have trouble attracting men, Sami."

She was beautiful enough to be a film star, after all. Even while she talked to me, I saw gentlemen hovering around, waiting for the opportunity to ask her to dance.

"Well, you might pass along whichever of them you decide you don't want," she said.

"I'll keep that in mind," I said with a laugh.

One of her admirers came to claim her then, and I slipped back into the crowd.

I made a circle of the room, but there was no sign of Ronald. Where had he gone off to?

"Here we are," Rafe said, returning to my side with the drinks. There was not much I could do but follow him to a table. He pulled a chair out for me, and we sat.

"I'm awfully glad I ran into you," he said with a smile. "I was afraid I was destined to spend a lonely evening."

I gave him a skeptical look. Rafe Beaumont was not the sort of man who'd ever lack for female company. "I think you would have managed all right."

He laughed.

"Liz, introduce me to your friend." I looked up to see Sami had appeared at our table. Rafe rose at once.

"Sami, this is Captain Rafe Beaumont. Rafe, this is my friend Sami."

"How do you do?" he said.

"Pleased to meet you." She held out a hand, and he took it and held on to it for a moment longer than was necessary while they smiled at each other.

I took a sip of my drink and watched the performance.

"I've told Liz she simply cannot keep all the pilots to herself," Sami said. "I hope you'll ask me to dance later, Captain Beaumont."

"Rafe. Please. And it would be an honor."

"Sami, this is my dance," said a gentleman, arriving at her side. He shot an annoyed look at Rafe.

"Coming, Lonnie," she told him. She smiled at me and Rafe in turn. "I'll see you later, then."

"I look forward to it," Rafe said.

Then Sami allowed herself to be led to the dance floor.

"Would you like to dance?" Rafe asked me.

I was going to refuse. I was tired. Furthermore, I'd never been particularly good at flirting as a means to an end, and I was annoyed at having to employ that particular strategy more than once tonight.

For all the good it had done me with Ronald. Now I'd lost him.

Then it occurred to me that a dance would be a good way to move unobtrusively around the room and look once more for Ronald.

"That would be nice. Thank you."

Rafe led me to the dance floor as a slow song started up. He pulled me toward him in a way that might have been romantic if I had any such feelings toward him. But there was something about Rafe Beaumont that kept me from being carried away by his charms. From the beginning, I'd had the sense that we'd both known there wouldn't be anything romantic between us. Though he flirted with me in a friendly way, there was nothing to indicate he wanted to pursue something more. I thought perhaps he had a girl somewhere.

We danced, and I kept my eyes peeled for Ronald. Had he slipped into some back room to confer with a group of shadowy associates? It was a bit dramatic, but I'd seen some strange things since I'd begun working with the major.

Then I thought I spotted Ronald standing near where we had been sitting. He leaned over our table and seemed to be collecting the glasses, so perhaps it was a barman. I squinted, trying to see through the dimness and cigarette smoke. Just at that moment, however, Rafe spun me around and I lost sight of him. When I looked again, the man at our table was gone.

Inwardly, I sighed. This had been a waste of time. It had been foolish of me to follow him anyway. In addition to the danger I might have put myself in, I didn't know what I had expected to accomplish. Had I thought he would lead me directly to the leader of the counterfeiting ring?

All I wanted to do now was get back to Mrs. James's and go to bed.

"I really need to be getting home after this drink," I told Rafe when he escorted me back to the table. I was, frankly, ready to leave that very minute, but I didn't want to appear suspicious to the captain. We were on friendly terms, and it would look strange if I acted in a hurry to get away from him.

So I took a few more sips of my drink, looking around for any other sight of Ronald. It was strange that he had disappeared so thoroughly. What had he been doing here? Was it possible that he had caught sight of me and abandoned his plans, whatever they had been?

"I'll walk you back to your lodging house," Rafe said as I rose to leave a few minutes later.

"It's not far."

"I know, but it would be remiss of me to let you go alone."

"Yes, well . . ." Perhaps it was a good idea, after all. Suddenly, I wasn't feeling all that well. I was very warm, and my head was swimming just a bit. It would be good to get out in the fresh night air.

"Is something wrong?" Rafe asked, his eyes on my face. He was frowning slightly, and I wondered if I looked as bad as I felt.

"No," I said, though my tongue felt thick. I had the sensation that I was well on my way to being drunk, though that was impossible. What was happening?

Rafe was watching me closely now, and I squinted at him. He had gone a bit blurry around the edges.

"I'm fi . . ." The words slurred away from me, and I didn't have the energy to catch them.

"Liz?" The captain's words sounded far away, as though I were underwater. I could feel myself slumping slightly toward him, but I observed it almost from a distance, as though it were happening to someone else.

"I think . . . need some . . . air," I said. At least, I think I said it. It was getting harder to differentiate between what was going on inside my head and what was happening outside of it.

I tried to take a step, and I stumbled. My drink, I realized. Ronald had put something in my drink when I'd seen him leaning over the table. Was it the poison that had killed Hal Jenkins? I knew I should be panicked at this thought, but, somehow, I couldn't seem to make myself grasp the possibility well enough to care much about it.

Rafe caught my arm with one hand and slid the other arm around my waist, but I barely felt him touch me. It was surreal, the sudden sense of detachment from my body.

I shook my head to try to clear it, but it was as though I was doing it in slow motion. I was vaguely alarmed, but there was also a strange lethargy that kept me from being utterly terrified.

"I'm going to take you out of here," he said from very, very far away.

There was no chance to make a reply before I slumped and my vision gave way to a warm, soft blanket of blackness.

CHAPTER EIGHTEEN

I woke up with a groan. Or perhaps it was the groan that had awakened me. Either way, I turned my head and gave a second groan as my head swam and the blood pounded in my ears.

"It's all right, Miss McDonnell. You're safe."

I squeezed my eyes shut tight against the steady thumping inside my brain. It was Major Ramsey. But what he was doing here and where exactly here was, I didn't know. At the moment, I didn't particularly care. I was preoccupied with trying to keep from being sick.

"How do you feel?" In contrast to the distant sound of the voices I remembered last, his voice sounded almost unnaturally loud. The pain in my head was merciless.

"Wretched," I managed to mumble. "What happened?"

"You were drugged."

I lifted my head ever so gently and squinted at him from eyes that felt dry and puffy. He was sitting in a chair beside the bed I was lying in. He had discarded his jacket and tie and was in shirtsleeves.

"Yes . . . Ronald Potter . . ." I began. But the rest of the question didn't want to form, and I fought down another wave of nausea. Thankfully, the sick feeling gradually abated, though my thoughts were still muddled.

"Here," he said, rising from his chair and picking up a glass from the bedside table. "Drink this."

He slid a hand beneath my head to help me lift it and pressed the glass to my lips. Water.

I swallowed a small sip, testing the endurance of my stomach. There was no feeling of sickness, and the cool liquid was a balm to my dry mouth.

"Drink a bit more if you can."

He didn't have to press me. I was suddenly as thirsty as if I'd walked the desert, my mouth completely dry. I tried to take the glass but found my hand was unsteady.

"It's all right," he said. "Let me."

I dropped my hand and let him hold the glass to my lips. I drank the entire contents without stopping and then lay back weakly against the pillow. Soon I would feel very embarrassed about all of this, I was sure, but at the moment, I was just trying to get my bearings.

"Thank you," I said.

"You're welcome," the major said, setting the glass down and taking his seat again. "If you can drink another glass in a bit, it will help. And I'll make some coffee for you if you like."

I grimaced at the mention of coffee, but it would probably help to clear my head. If nothing else, the ghastly taste of it would pull me further from my stupor.

"Where are we?" I asked, looking around groggily. It was a small bedroom, sparsely decorated, with wooden walls and exposed wooden beams on the ceiling above me. There was one small painting on the wall behind the major's head, a ship sailing on blue seas.

"We're at my cottage," he said. "It was the only place where I could carry in an unconscious woman without undue attention."

I managed as much of a smile as my splitting head would allow. "Yes, I suppose I was a sight. I'm sorry to put you to such trouble."

"No trouble," he replied. "I'm only glad I was there."

"So am I," I answered. "But how did you happen to be at The Gale?" I wondered if he'd also discovered something that had led him there.

He seemed to be debating something with himself, and then he admitted: "I saw you leave the pub and followed you."

"I wish I had known," I said, too glad of his help to be annoyed at the moment. "I didn't know how to get in touch with you. It's Ronald. He's a spy, I mean. There's a smudge on his identity card. He isn't who he says . . ."

"Wait a moment," he said calmly. "Slow down. What are you talking about?"

I marshaled my sluggish thoughts into the most concise explanation I could manage.

"You remember the imperfection I pointed out on the identity card plate? Well, I've been checking the cards of everyone in the group for the smudge it would create. Ronald's is a forgery."

"You shouldn't have taken that risk," he said. I was surprised at the gentleness in his tone. Normally, he would have chided me in that irritated tone of his. Perhaps he was feeling sorry for me since I'd been drugged.

"I only noticed that Ronald's was false last night. Or . . . is it still night?"

"It will be dawn soon."

Then I had been out for a long time.

"I followed him to the nightclub. I saw him near my table while I was dancing. He must have . . . put something in my drink. But we need to find him. Perhaps if you go . . ."

"Don't worry about that now," he said. "You need to rest."

"He might have poisoned me," I said, remembering that I could easily have had the same fate as Hal Jenkins. The thought made me feel sick all over again.

"Try to sleep," the major said. "We'll talk about it some more in the morning."

"I should get back . . ." I said, though I was having a hard time keeping my eyes open.

"There's no sense in going back right now. Rest, and I'll bring you back when it's light."

I was much too tired to argue with him, and the bed I was lying in was so comfortable. I meant to say that I supposed it would be all right to stay a little longer, but I fell back to sleep before I could mutter a word.

I felt sick the next morning when I woke up, like the time as a fifteen-year-old I'd sneaked an unattended glass of Uncle Mick's ale, and it took me a moment to remember where I was and what had happened.

Ronald Potter had drugged me. But why? He could easily have killed me, as I assumed he had done to Hal Jenkins. Had it been meant as a warning? Why had I been spared?

I sat up gingerly. Aside from a head that felt a bit woozy, there didn't seem to be any permanent damage.

I looked around the room. By daylight I could see it was a small, spartan bedroom with one window looking out toward the sea. The floors, like the walls and ceiling, were of rough planked wood, overlaid with a pale blue woven rug. There was a lamp on a table at the bedside, and the chair where Major Ramsey had been sitting when I awakened earlier.

This was his bedroom, no doubt. What would Nacy say if she found I'd spent the night in Major Ramsey's bed? I wondered mischievously.

Then my thoughts sobered. I was sorry that I'd inconvenienced him, but I was glad he had been there. What might have happened to me if he hadn't been?

What became of Rafe Beaumont? The thought came suddenly. I wasn't sure why it had taken so long to occur to me, but now I wondered where the captain had gone after I'd blacked out. I had so many questions.

I got out of bed slowly. I was a bit stiff but none the worse for wear. I walked across the small room on my stockinged feet— had the major removed my shoes?—and opened the only door. It was my first chance to look at the cottage where the major was staying. The bedroom opened up into a little sitting room with a fireplace. On the other side, there was a table with two chairs and a door that I assumed led to the kitchen. The cottage was small and rustic but tidy, almost cozy.

I heard a door to my left, one I hadn't yet noticed, open, and the major emerged. Apparently, this was the bathroom, because he was shirtless, wiping the remnants of shaving soap from his face. Having only ever seen him formally attired, this display of casual morning routine caught me off guard. As did the rather impressive musculature his uniforms had been concealing. Annoyingly, I could feel a blush creeping up my face.

"Oh. I beg your pardon," he said. "I didn't know you were awake."

"Good morning," I said stupidly.

He walked past me to where his uniform shirt rested over the back of a chair and then turned back toward the bathroom. "If you'll excuse me for a moment?"

"Of course."

I moved to the little sofa. It was a bit worn, but it was very comfortable. I sank into the cushions as I sat.

A short time later, Major Ramsey came back into the room, his jaw clean, his shirt neatly buttoned.

"Pardon my informality, Miss McDonnell," he said. "I thought you'd sleep later."

I waved a hand, doing my best to be breezily dismissive. "I grew up with boys, Major."

Although, Colm and Toby, athletic as they were, did not look quite like *that* without their shirts on.

"How do you feel?" he asked, his eyes on my face.

"I've felt better," I admitted. I reached up to my aching head and encountered a wayward mass of curls. No doubt my hair looked worse than my head felt.

"You need to drink more water."

"I'd love some tea," I said hopefully.

He nodded. "I'll put the kettle on. Do you want something to eat?"

I grimaced. "No. I couldn't eat a thing at the moment."

Thankfully, he didn't argue with me.

"Just tea for now, then. I'll start the tea, if you'd like to wash up," he said, nodding toward the bathroom.

"Thank you." He went to the kitchen, and I went into the bathroom and closed the door. The lingering scent of his shaving soap was the only evidence he'd been there. Even the sink was dry.

There was a small mirror above the sink, and it confirmed my suspicions. My hair could have been mistaken for a greenfinch nest.

I turned the tap and splashed cold water on my face and then ran my wet hands through my hair, trying to tame it. As usual, it did very little good.

When I had finished a few moments later, I came back out into the sitting room and walked toward the kitchen. "Can I help with something?" I called.

"No. You're pale this morning. Sit down."

I was in no condition to argue, so I went back to the sofa.

"I'm sorry to have inconvenienced you," I said, glad he was still in the kitchen as I made my apologies. "It's very embarrassing."

"You have no reason to be embarrassed, and I haven't been inconvenienced."

"But I . . . I took your bed."

He came out of the kitchen then with a steaming tin mug. "I've slept much worse places than a sofa, Miss McDonnell."

"Thank you," I said, as he handed me the mug.

"Now," he said. "Why don't we start at the beginning. Tell me again what you know about Potter."

I related the story to him as clearly as I could. The tea made it much easier to think. It was strong and sweet, and I had never tasted anything so wonderful.

"Did you talk to an RAF captain last night?" I asked, remembering it was Rafe Beaumont who had caught me when I began to get dizzy. "I mean, was he with me when you arrived? I was talking to him when I began to feel ill."

"I spoke to him," he said, and there was nothing in his tone to indicate what had passed between him and Rafe. Had Rafe argued with him about taking charge of me? I wanted to ask, but something about the set of Major Ramsey's face made me think he wasn't going to reveal much.

"What happened to him?" I asked. "He might have more information."

"I told him I would contact him, if necessary," Major Ramsey said. "By the by, how do you know him?"

"He's just a fellow I met on the train. We've been spending a bit of time together."

"And you thought it wise to make friends on this mission?" he asked mildly.

"I can't help who strikes up a conversation with me, can I?" I replied, bristling slightly.

"I suppose not. All things considered, a less attractive woman would have been more ideal, but we must work with what we have."

I looked up at him, surprised and unsure whether to be flattered or insulted. In the end, I decided to just ignore the comment.

"So what are we going to do about Ronald?" I asked.

"You're not going to do anything," Major Ramsey said.

"But I'm the one who discovered . . ."

"Yes," he said, cutting me off. "After I distinctly told you that you were not to act on your own."

"It was just a bit of pickpocketing," I said.

"And following a dangerous man alone through the city streets at night," he pointed out. "When you were told to play things safe."

"That's your fault for leaving me unsupervised, then, isn't it?" The retort came naturally, but there was no heat in it. I wasn't really up to arguing with him this morning.

"Yes, I suppose it is," he said, and there was something in his tone I couldn't quite interpret.

"I do thank you for your help, Major Ramsey, but I should get back. I'm sure Mrs. James is wondering where I went, and Sami . . ."

"Yes, I know," he said. "But they will keep for a bit longer. I have something I need to check up on. I need you to wait here. I won't be long."

"All right." I couldn't force him to take me back, after all. And, really, a part of me was enjoying the feeling of comfort and safety after everything that had happened.

"There's food in the kitchen," he said. "Help yourself."

"Thank you."

He left without further ado, and I was alone in the little cottage. I finished my tea and went to the kitchen to wash and put away the mug.

It was a very small kitchen with an ancient oven, but it was extremely clean. I opened two wrong cupboards before finding where the tin mug went, and I saw that the major had the place well stocked with provisions, though there was nothing much of interest.

This was my chance to snoop a bit, to possibly learn a bit more about the major, but somehow I found I didn't want to. In any event, I doubted Major Ramsey would have left any clue to his personal life in this temporary lodging. He certainly wouldn't have left anything he didn't want me to see.

I decided to go for a walk on the beach. I was feeling better after the tea, though still not ready to eat anything, and I thought the fresh sea breeze would help to further clear my head.

Stepping outside the cottage, I was instantly greeted with a bracing wind off the sea. The sky was gray and looked like rain, but I breathed deeply of the salty air and felt instantly cheered. This walk would be good in more ways than one. Perhaps, in addition to the exercise banishing the remnants of whatever drug I had been given, I would be able to make some sense of recent events.

I walked on the dunes above the beach, and, without conscious thought, I moved in the direction of Sheridan Hall's manor.

It honestly didn't occur to me until a few minutes later when I spotted his thin silhouette in the distance. I wavered on whether I should make contact with him, but then he saw me and waved, and the decision was made.

"Good morning, Mr. Hall!" I called when I was within earshot.

He smiled as I approached, squinting at me through his glasses. "Good morning, Mrs. Grey. I thought that must be you when I saw a figure walking there. How are you, my dear?"

"I'm very well, thank you," I said. "I'm just giving John a bit of quiet and time to work on his book."

"Creativity is very demanding," he said gravely. "I know that well."

"Do you write?" I asked him.

"I have dabbled a bit in my day," he said. "I am very fond of books. Once upon a time, I owned a small publishing company. Perhaps when the war is over, I will open it back up again."

"How wonderful," I said brightly. "What sort of books did you publish?"

"Birding books, mainly."

"Oh, of course. That sounds very interesting. Was it located in London?"

"No, no," he said absently. "It was very nearby. Just a mile or so up the beach. I'd show it to you, but there's nothing of interest happening there now."

I wondered. Was it at all possible he didn't know about the guards that were on the premises? It seemed unlikely.

"You visit it often, I suppose," I said. "To keep things ready for when you can open again?"

If he noticed that I was fishing for information, he gave no sign of it. He seemed happy enough to talk. "No, I haven't been there in several months. There's no need. I have someone managing things for me."

"That's good," I said, hoping he would tell me more. "It's nice that you have someone you trust to keep an eye on things for you."

He nodded. I wished that he would reveal the name of the person he had left in charge. Had it been Hal Jenkins? That would make sense. After all, the major had mentioned that he had worked at the printer before the war. I tried to think of a way that I might bring the topic up, but the thought was startled from my head as Mr. Hall gave an exclamation and grabbed my arm.

"Look! Look there," he said, pointing excitedly. "*Accipiter gentilis*. The northern goshawk. I haven't seen one in quite some time."

I looked at the bird soaring overhead and tried to feign some enthusiasm.

"I have a very interesting monograph on them, published in Edinburgh. It was owned by Darwin himself and has a few of his handwritten notes in it."

"Oh, really?" I was beginning to fear a long conversation about birds was forthcoming, and I hoped I could fake my way through it.

Providentially, a large raindrop landed with a splatter on my cheek in that moment. I looked up, and another hit me on the tip of the nose.

Though he had been watching the skies for birds only moments before, Mr. Hall looked up, confusedly, as though taken aback by the sudden change in weather. I supposed he was one of those men who lost himself so deeply in his interests that the details of the world were mere shadowy outlines. I'd teased Uncle Mick that he wasn't to be in his workroom anytime an air raid might be imminent for fear he'd be so lost in his work he wouldn't hear the sirens.

"I'm afraid it looks like rain," I said, stating the obvious, ready to be on my way. "I'd better hurry back. I'll be soaked by the time I get back to the cottage."

"Nonsense, my girl. Come up to the house with me. It isn't far. Just over that ridge there. We can have a nice cup of tea, and I can show you the *Accipiter gentilis* monograph, along with a few of my other treasures."

I hesitated. Major Ramsey would not be pleased if he returned and found me missing. Besides that, he'd specifically told me that I was not to approach Sheridan Hall on my own.

All the same, I hadn't done it on purpose, and I didn't know if I could resist the opportunity when it had fallen in my lap.

"Come along," Mr. Hall said, taking my arm. "Your husband won't mind. It will give him more time to write."

I could hold out no longer. "If you're sure I won't be intruding?"

"Not at all. Not at all. Now, come along," he said.

So as the rain started to patter in the marram grass around us, I followed him toward Vangidae.

CHAPTER NINETEEN

We walked quickly, but my hair was still rather damp by the time we reached the front door. I could feel by instinct that it had taken to flying in all directions once again, and I did my best to smooth it down as I took in my surroundings.

The entrance hall was enormous, with flagstone floors covered with a huge, ancient, but clearly expensive rug that led to the wide wooden staircase. The high wainscoting was of gleaming wood, and the walls above were covered in dark mauve wallpaper. Golden light spilled from evenly spaced glass sconces, and there were several framed paintings that were, unsurprisingly, of birds. It was, despite its grandeur, a strangely warm and comfortable place.

We were greeted by a grim-looking man in a dark suit, but Mr. Hall waved him away. "Bring us some tea to the library, Bevins," he said. "And then leave us alone."

"Yes, sir."

"If you'll follow me, my dear, we can have a chat in my study. Bevins is my valet, though he really does a bit of everything. He's been with me ages and tends to fuss, so I have to be stern with him. I'm so glad you've come; it's been some time since I've had someone new to admire my collection."

I smiled at his enthusiasm. It was very possible he was linked to German spies, but he certainly wasn't feigning his love of birds.

We went to his study, and I couldn't help the little catch in my breath that came as we entered it. It was a lovely room, with high windows facing out to the sea. There had been no noticeable incline as we'd walked to the house, but we had nevertheless risen gradually until we had a very good view of the water, choppy now that the rain was coming down in earnest.

"It's a lovely view," I said, taking in the gray swells crashing against the shore.

He smiled at me. "I'm glad you think so. I've a niece about your age who refuses to visit when I'm here. Says the place is gloomy."

"I think it's a very comfortable room," I said honestly. In addition to the windows, there was a cozy arrangement of leather furniture before the fireplace and a large, untidy desk. Shelves ran from floor to ceiling along the walls adjacent to and opposite the windows. Some of them were filled with books, and others held an assortment of bird carvings and figurines of different styles, no doubt collected from around the world. I would say one thing for Sheridan Hall: he was committed to the theme.

"Do you keep bird nests and eggs and things?" I asked, caught up in his enthusiasm, despite myself.

"Not unless I am certain the nests or eggs have been abandoned. I have always been against collecting merely for sport," he said. "No good can come of interfering with the natural habitats. I have, however, come across abandoned nests and those that have been prey to other creatures. In such cases, I have often taken them here for closer study."

"I see."

"No," he said, turning away from the bookcase. "The monograph isn't here. It's one of the rarer ones, so I've probably put it with the collection in my vault. I keep all my most important objects there."

Naturally, this caught my attention. "Your vault?"

"That's what I call it. I had a large safe, but then I decided I needed more space, and I had it converted into an entire room. I keep most of my precious collector's objects there."

"Oh?" I asked, trying to sound interested, but not suspiciously so. "What sort of objects?"

His eyes sparkled with enthusiasm, and he went on eagerly. "Oh, all manner of things. The rarest and most valuable of my specimens, some delicate nests, and several very old books on birding. All the things I would most hate to lose in case of theft or fire."

"It's an excellent idea," I said.

"Yes," he agreed. "I've been told it was too extravagant, but every true collector knows how irreplaceable rare objects are, and I'm glad I did it."

I wondered if Major Ramsey had known about this safe and, if so, if that was one of the reasons he had brought me here. I had come to realize that Major Ramsey often had ulterior motives, and he didn't reveal them until he thought it necessary. Well, if that was the case, it was a good thing I had found my way into Sheridan Hall's house and into his good graces.

He looked at me with what could only be described as suppressed excitement. "Would you like to see it?"

I smiled. "There is nothing I would like more."

He led me through a door and into a smaller room, a library filled with leather-bound books. Rain pattered against the windows, and a fire was crackling at the grate. It was warm and homely, and I almost wished I could choose a book from the shelf and sit down to read.

I remembered why I was here, however, as he led me to a little green door on the other side of the library. I recognized it at once as a safe door.

"Eventually, I would like to have it concealed behind a wall of books," he said. "But I've spent enough money on this contraption at present."

He twisted the combination, and, though I tried to look over his shoulder, he was positioned in such a way that I couldn't see what it was.

The door gave, and he pulled it open. There was a locked collapsible gate behind it, I realized. He was taking extraordinary precautions with his collector's objects.

He took a small gold key from his pocket and fit it into the gate's lock. It clicked open, and he pushed it to one side.

I considered slipping my hand into his pocket to retrieve the key, but he would no doubt notice it was missing and might link its disappearance to me. If it came down to it, I could pick the lock easily enough.

He flipped on a switch, and a bright light came on above us. I looked around and was instantly reminded of a small, well-tended museum. Everything was in pristine condition, lovingly preserved. There was not a speck of dust to be seen.

The entire room was walled with shelves, and there was a small table with two chairs in the center of the safe, which Mr. Hall apparently used to study his objects.

On the shelves closest to me sat bird's nests of every size and shape. Beyond those, there was a collection of bird art. I saw statues of bronze, jade, and even gold. Another full shelf held rolls of compartmentalized trays with eggs of all descriptions carefully displayed and labeled.

"This is magnificent," I said. And I meant it. There was so much to look at that my eyes couldn't quite decide where to land. I'd never seen anything like it.

I also took in the state of the room. Though the shelves and the objects inside gave it a somewhat inviting feel, there was no mistaking the steel of the walls behind the shelves. We were very much in a vault.

There were no windows, and the air was cool and dry. It was clear that he had spared no expense on this room. It would definitely preserve his objects for as long as he lived and much longer.

"Why don't you keep these things on display where others can see them?" I asked, genuinely curious. "You could start a museum."

"Perhaps one day I will," he said. "It's just that each of these items is so precious to me, I worry about something happening to them. I suppose I'm a miser of these objects, in my way. I find enjoyment in simply being near them."

We walked a bit farther into the room, and I stopped short, momentarily startled. Near the back was a display of two huge, dark brown taxidermied birds with white heads. They were suspended from the ceiling, posed as if in flight, wings and talons extended, beaks open and glass eyes glaring at each other.

"Gruesome things, aren't they?" he said cheerily. "*Haliaeetus leucocephalus*. The American bald eagle. Their national bird, you know. These are rare specimens. I don't, of course, agree with killing birds for specimen collection, but these two were found just after they killed each other, and I was able to purchase them. I had them posed in their final fight."

"Fascinating," I said, and it was. Everything about this room, and this gentleman, was unusual.

"They're protected now in the United States, you know," he said. I didn't know, but I had a feeling I was about to learn more.

"As of June, collectors may no longer gather specimens such as these—or even feathers, nests, or eggs." He smiled. "While we fight the Germans, they are protecting their eagles. Not that I blame them, of course. They are indeed majestic birds. But you can see why I keep them in this safe at present. They're contraband." He cackled delightedly to himself and then turned away from the eagles.

"The books are over here," he said, leading me to a shelf in one corner.

It was stacked with a variety of books, folders, weathered folios, and sheets of yellowed and crumbling pages. I smelled old paper and leather.

"Most of my books are in the library, of course," he said. "But I keep the rarest books here. Some of them are actually quite valuable among collectors. I have, throughout my career as a collector, been robbed more than once of valuable items."

"How dreadful," I sympathized. But I wondered if Mr. Hall wasn't a bit dotty. Surely no one would want to steal any of the items in this room? Then again, I had known a few collectors in my time who would go to great lengths to get their prized possessions.

"I only just acquired these," he said, sifting through a small pile. "I haven't yet had time to ascertain their value."

He set those aside and rifled through another shelf for a moment. "Ah! Here it is! Come and see."

So I moved to his side and for a good ten minutes dutifully admired the faded etchings of the *Accipiter gentilis* and the spidery notes Darwin had scratched in the margins.

"Well, Bevins should have our tea ready by now," Mr. Hall said at last.

We left the safe room, and he closed the gate behind me, locking it again with a simple click of the latch. And then he closed the safe door and gave the combination dial a spin. He was thorough in his methods.

"Thank you for showing me your collection," I said when we were back in the library that adjoined the study. "I enjoyed it so much."

"I'm so glad, my dear. Now, come back into my study, and we'll have tea."

We walked through into the adjoining room.

"Ah. Here you are, Elizabeth."

I could not say I was entirely surprised to see the major standing there. What was surprising was that his usual grim demeanor and the expression of anger I would have expected at his having to come and search for me was supplanted with one of obvious relief.

"John!" I said, as though I was delighted to see him.

"I've been looking everywhere for you, darling," he said. "I'm so glad to have found you here, safe and sound. I was rather worried when the rain started and you didn't return home."

Yes, I'd be in for a scolding, all right. All the same, he was doing a rather nice job of pretending to have been concerned about my well-being. And, anyway, it would be beneficial for him to see the inside of the house as well.

"I'm so sorry," I said. "It started raining when I was talking to Mr. Hall, and he was kind enough to invite me in for tea and to see his collection."

I was proud of myself for not sounding the least bit awkward, nor appearing so, as I went to the major and took his arm in mine. "Come sit down and have tea with us."

He didn't move, his arm rigid beneath my hand, and I realized he wasn't just cross with me; he was angry. It still wasn't visible in his expression, however, and Mr. Hall didn't seem to notice.

"I apologize for alarming you," Mr. Hall said, moving toward the tea tray. "I, too, would be worried about missing so pretty a wife. We only thought to stop here until the rain had let up, but I'm afraid we got rather distracted."

"You'll never believe it, Johnny," I said. "Mr. Hall has the most delightful collection. You should see it."

"Perhaps another time," the major said. "We should head back while there's a break in the rain."

Mr. Hall chuckled. "Not much on the topic of birds, eh? Well, that's all right. My late wife didn't care for birds at all. She thought them dirty creatures. It was the one thing we didn't agree on."

"I plan to bring him round," I said stoutly.

"You do that, my dear. When you have, you may bring him here, and I'd be happy to show him the collection. And do come back for tea one afternoon when your husband is writing. I'd enjoy your company."

"Thank you. I'd like that very much."

He tugged the bellpull, and in seconds Bevins appeared in the doorway. No doubt he had been lurking since he'd shown the major in, waiting to see if there would be instructions.

"Show Captain and Mrs. Grey out, Bevins, and bring me a fresh pot of tea. This one's gone cold."

"Very good, sir," Bevins said. He rivaled the major in terms of grimness, and I wondered how Bevins felt being cooped up—to use a pun—in a house with so many birds.

We said our goodbyes to Sheridan Hall, and I continued to hold the major's arm as Bevins led us back through the house to the front door.

"Are you a birding enthusiast, Bevins?" I asked him as we walked across the entry hall.

"Not to speak of, madam," he replied.

"I suppose you've learned rather a lot about them, working for Mr. Hall."

"Yes, madam. A great deal."

He opened the front door for us, and we stepped out. Then he gave us a stiff little bow and shut the door behind us.

"Friendly fellow," I remarked. Major Ramsey did not reply.

We began walking down the driveway.

"Major, did you know about the . . ."

"Not now," he said shortly.

He really was angry with me. I could feel the tension in his arm as I continued to hold it in case Mr. Hall was looking out those large windows. His posture was stiff, and there was a set to his jaw that didn't bode well.

When we were out of sight of the house, I let go of his arm.

I decided not to speak to him until we got back to the cottage, where we wouldn't be observed. If there was an argument coming, it would best be done in private.

CHAPTER TWENTY

It was a long walk. He said nothing and was clearly brooding.

We reached the cottage, and he pulled open the door. I preceded him, and he shut the door behind us slightly harder than necessary.

I turned to face him. We might as well get on with it. "We're going to have a row, aren't we?" I said.

He narrowed his eyes. "We are not. I am going to talk, and you are going to listen."

I bristled, but my finely tuned sense of self-preservation had gotten me this far in life, and something told me that I shouldn't push him at this moment.

It wasn't that I was afraid of him. He was curt and imposing, it was true. But somewhere, deep in my gut, I trusted him. I trusted him as I'd trusted very few people outside my family.

This was something I had known instinctually, but to put it in those words in my mind was something of a revelation. Perhaps that was the root of my attraction to him, the knowledge that I could rely on him.

There was Felix, of course, but he was very nearly a member of the family. I had known him for years. Unexpectedly, I felt the strange mixture of conflicting feelings at the thought. *Felix is like family.* How far did that familial feeling go?

I was attracted to him, certainly; he was a handsome, charming man. It occurred to me for the first time, however, that my feelings for him might be rooted more in a sense of comfort and familiarity than in something more romantic. It was not an easy thought, and I pushed it away for the time being. Besides, there was nothing wrong with being comfortable with someone. Birds of a feather flocked together for a reason, after all.

Major Ramsey, on the other hand, was from an entirely different world than Felix and me. A different class, a different background—and a different moral center, if we were being honest. And, though I hated to admit it, there was something in that steadiness I was drawn to. Something in his firmly rooted sense of right.

It also made me a little envious, when I reflected deeply on it.

I realized my thoughts had wandered right in the middle of the major's reprimand.

"You gave me your word that you wouldn't go to visit Sheridan Hall alone," he said.

"I didn't visit him intentionally," I said, annoyed at my desire to explain to him. "I went for a walk to clear my head, and I happened upon him."

"Do not lie to me." His voice was tight, and it was clear to me that he was dangerously close to losing his temper.

"I'm not lying!"

"As if last night was not enough, you throw yourself back into danger the moment my back is turned. I don't know when it will finally permeate that stubborn head of yours that you cannot do whatever you please without consequence."

"It was me who got drugged, Major. I don't know why you should be so upset by it."

"Enough," he said, his voice once again cold and controlled, though his eyes were still blazing. "We're not getting anywhere with this, so there's no sense in discussing it any further. If I have to send you back to London, I will. Perhaps that will be for the best."

That was the comment that got to me. Because I believed he was ruthless enough to do it, even after everything I'd done to help.

There had been so much death and destruction the past few months, the constant weight of fear and anxiety. The nagging doubts that we would make it through another day, let alone the war. And in that moment, all of it seemed to come crashing down on me. I'm rather ashamed to admit it, but I started to cry.

I wiped at my face quickly with the sleeve of my jumper. *Stop it, Ellie,* I commanded myself. *Stop it at once.*

But it was no good. The tears were coming too fast, and my nose was beginning to run.

I refused to look at him, but I heard him come toward me. A moment later, his warm hand pressed a handkerchief into mine. "Here."

"It's not because you're cross with me," I said stubbornly.

"No. It's a perfectly natural reaction to accumulated stress." He let out a short breath that was almost a sigh. "I need to remember that you haven't been trained for this."

I had expected derision, so I was surprised by the gentleness in his voice. Annoyingly, unexpected kindness made it harder to quell my tears. I dashed them away with a furious stroke of the handkerchief. It smelled like Major Ramsey's shaving soap.

"He invited me back for tea. I didn't want to miss the opportunity to see inside his house. He has a safe where he keeps his valuables, and . . ."

"I understand the impulse," he said, cutting me off. "But we had an agreement. I need to be able to trust that you will keep your word, Miss McDonnell."

I nodded, sniffed. While it always made me angry when he scolded me, I knew that, to a certain extent, he was right about this. If Sheridan Hall had been a villain, he could easily have killed me, and no one would have been the wiser. It seemed I had still not learned my lesson.

"You need something to eat," Major Ramsey said.

"I'm not hungry."

"That doesn't change the fact. When did you last eat?"

I tried to think back. Had it been dinner yesterday? It wasn't like me to forgo meals, but everything had happened so quickly yesterday.

"If you have to think that hard, it's been much too long."

This sort of pronouncement from him would usually have annoyed me, but I didn't seem to have the energy to be annoyed.

I was exhausted and upset, and the last thing I felt like doing was eating. All the same, I knew he was probably right. If there was one thing Nacy had drilled into me over the years, it was the importance of keeping up one's strength.

"Sit down," he said, nodding toward the sofa. I obeyed, glad for the chance to get my emotions in check. I wasn't prone to crying. Being raised with boys had cured me of that habit early in life. All the same, I felt I had earned the right to a few tears. And, if nothing else, it had stopped Major Ramsey's lecture.

He went into the little kitchen and a moment later brought out a tray with a sandwich, a glass of water, and a mug. I could smell the coffee from where I sat. I wrinkled my nose.

He set the tray on the table and held out the coffee cup. "This will help."

"No, thank you."

He took my hand and pressed the cup into it. "Drink it."

The tin mug was hot, and I pulled my sleeve over my hand to keep the metal from burning my skin.

I detested coffee, but I didn't feel up to arguing with him. I took a sip and was surprised to find that it was cloyingly sweet. The major knew I had an affinity for very sweet tea, so I supposed he figured the same would be applicable to my coffee. It was thoughtful of him, I had to admit. And, as much as I hated the stuff, the sweetness did make it a tiny bit more palatable.

"Now," he said, taking a seat across from me. "Tell me what you saw at Mr. Hall's house."

"You might have seen it yourself if you hadn't been in a fury," I said before I thought better of it. I didn't want to start the row back up again, but I did think his temper had been detrimental in this case.

"I didn't need to see it," he replied. "I'm not the one who would need to open it."

"So you did know about the safe," I said. "It's the reason you called me here in the first place, isn't it? You assumed we would need to get in."

"Eat your sandwich."

I glowered my disapproval at him, but I took a small bite. I'd expected to have to choke it down, but as soon as I began to chew, my body jumped back to life, and I was immediately ravenously hungry. I took a second, larger bite, and the major gave a nod of approval.

"We had heard about the safe," he admitted. "Although, we didn't know for certain that it would be necessary to get into it. At this point, we have seen nothing to connect us back to Sheridan Hall."

"Nothing besides the fact it's his press being used to create the documents," I said around a mouthful.

"Yes. It's still possible he's involved."

"I don't think he's spying for the Germans," I said.

"No?"

"No."

"Why not?" I was a bit surprised at the question. I was accustomed to the major's terse replies to most of my input, but it seemed as though he genuinely wanted to know the answer.

"You'll think I'm oversimplifying it," I said. "But I had a long conversation with him. That man cares about nothing but birds. I cannot see him investing his energies in anything else."

"Good spies excel at concealing their identities." There was no derision in the comment, only the suggestion that I might have been fooled.

"You forget that I come from a background steeped in deception, Major," I answered lightly.

"I do not forget it, Miss McDonnell," he replied.

I wasn't sure what that meant, so I took another bite of the sandwich.

"Once you've finished that, I'm going to take you back to Mrs. James's establishment so you can pack your bag."

I looked up at him. Was he going to make good on his threat to send me back to London? "Why?"

"You're going to stay here again tonight."

This was not what I had expected, and I was momentarily speechless. It was clear enough why, however. He didn't trust me on my own anymore.

"You'll tell her and anyone else who asks that you're staying at your aunt's house for a few days to clear through some things," he went on.

I felt both contrary and petulant, but letting him see it would only feel like an admission of defeat.

"Everyone will think it odd if I disappear," I said logically.

"It's no longer safe for you there."

I knew what he wasn't saying: he wanted to keep an eye on me.

Well, perhaps he was right, in a way. I'd done a foolish thing or two since I'd been in Sunderland. Of course, when men did foolish things, they were called brave. But that was a conversation for another time.

As much as my natural streak of independence chafed at being told what to do, I felt a certain sense of relief that the major was making this decision for me.

I finished my sandwich and drank half of the wretched coffee before he said my color had improved and he would take me back to collect my things.

He dropped me off a little way down the street from Mrs. James's. I thought it would look too scandalous if he were to drop me off at the doorstep early in the morning.

"My reputation's going to be in tatters by the time all this is over," I said lightly.

"Consider it another casualty of war." Major Ramsey had apparently used up his allotment of sympathy for the day.

We agreed to meet up in an hour.

I walked up to the house and found myself a bit nervous to encounter Mrs. James. No doubt she was wondering where I had been, and I was going to have to make my excuses convincing.

Sure enough, she greeted me when I came in with a worried frown. "There you are, dear. I was awfully concerned when you didn't return home last night."

"I'm so sorry I didn't let you know, Mrs. James. It was un-expected. I went to my aunt's house, and there was so much to do that I lost track of time. I didn't like to come home after dark, so I stayed there for the evening. And there was no telephone for me to call."

I don't think she believed me. She no doubt thought I'd spent a night of passion in the arms of my RAF captain. I felt myself flush at the thought.

Then I remembered the dizziness and nausea, and the flush faded. It was not as though I'd had an enjoyable evening.

"Well, I'm glad you're all right."

"Yes, I'm very well. Thank you, Mrs. James. But I believe I will spend a day or two at my aunt's while I'm sorting through things. I just came back to gather my bag. I'll still pay for the room, of course. And you'll keep it for me at least through the end of the week?"

"Of course, dear, if that's what you want," Mrs. James said. "By the way, there was a letter for you that came in the morning post. I slipped it under the door to your room."

"Oh, thank you!" I could think of only one person who would be writing to me here: Felix.

I hurried up the stairs and into my room and went inside. I needed very badly to bathe and change my clothes, but that could wait for the moment.

I snatched up the envelope that lay on the floor and broke the seal, quickly pulling out the letter. I felt a jolt of nostalgia at the sight of Felix's familiar handwriting.

Then I had to laugh—familiar for Felix was a relative term, after all. Expert forger that he was, his handwriting could be anything he wanted it to be. But this was the hand he always used when he wrote to me, and I was surprised at how comforting it was to see it now. There was also the faintest scent of his cologne and tobacco on the pages.

I sat on my bed and began to read.

Hello my lovely Liz,

What are you up to now? I know you won't tell me, but you do ask me the most dashed strange things. I've been over the rubbing that you sent me. It's a complicated task you've set before me, but you know I love a challenge. Since you haven't told me what I'm looking for, it was a bit like a needle in a haystack. But there are a few scraps that I thought might be relevant, given what I do know. These are the phrases that most stood out to me that were penned in the same hand, and possibly more recently than the other words, as they were imprinted over the other letters.

VAN . . . STOP . . . THESE PEOPLE WILL KILL

YOU MAY BE INT . . . YOUR . . . LECTION

I'm sorry I haven't more to give you, but I hope this can be of help. Be good, sweet. I live on the memory of your kisses.

Yours,
Felix xx

P.S. The memories aren't nearly as good as the real thing. Looking forward to making up for lost time.

I reread the letter twice. Felix had written *VAN,* not *VON* as I'd originally assumed. So was it possible that line referred to Vangidae, Sheridan Hall's manor? Had he been writing to Mr. Hall to warn him of something? Hal Jenkins had been tragically correct about these people being willing to kill.

The *YOUR . . . LECTION* part was not mysterious. I thought it likely it had been written to Sheridan Hall. After all, Hal Jenkins had worked for him at one point. No doubt he had been sending him a specimen or some other item for his collection.

I tucked Felix's letter back into my handbag and hurried to throw a few things into my valise as the major had instructed. I wanted to talk to him as soon as possible, but I realized I would feel better after a bath and a change of clothes.

I accomplished this as quickly as possible, pinned up my curls, and brought my valise down the stairs with me.

I had reached the front porch when I saw Sami approaching.

"Liz! There you are. I was worried about you!"

"I'm so sorry, Sami," I said. "I didn't mean to give everyone a fright. I was going to tell you, but something came up at my aunt's house and I had to go, and then I ended up staying the entire night. I'm going to go back for a day or two. John has said he'll bring me."

She smiled. "When you disappeared last night, I assumed it had something to do with John. Did you have a good time? I assume he . . . helped you at your aunt's house?"

I was secretive by nature. It had come with the territory of a life of crime. So my instinct was to be evasive. But there was really no reason to pretend I hadn't been spending time with my faux suitor.

"He drove me there and then picked me up this morning," I said.

Her eyes sparked with mischief. "You don't have to make excuses to me. I hope you two had a nice time."

"You needn't worry," I said. "John's a perfect gentleman."

She laughed. "How very disappointing. Anyway, I've been waiting for you. I wanted to talk to you about something."

"Oh? What is it?"

She glanced around, though it was perfectly obvious that we were the only ones standing here on the porch. "It's about Laila. I wanted to ask if she'd said anything to you about . . ."

"Sami! Liz!" A voice, filled with panic, reached us.

I looked up to see Nessa. She rushed toward us, and I could see that she was sobbing.

"Nessa!" Sami said, hurrying off the porch toward her with me close on her heels. "What is it?"

She looked up at us, her face streaked with tears. "Carlotta's dead."

CHAPTER TWENTY-ONE

Sami let out a little shriek.

I felt a rush of shock, and then I realized, somehow, that I wasn't entirely surprised. She had known something, and she had tried to warn me. Had that been what had cost her her life, or was there some other reason she had been silenced?

I felt sick to my stomach, almost dizzy with the force of the emotions that hit me all at once: shock, sorrow, guilt. And, I was not too proud to admit, just a bit of fear. Absurdly, I wished the major were there.

"What happened?" Sami was asking, her voice shaking.

"I don't know," Nessa said. "I only just heard. I came right here to talk to you. Oh, poor Carlotta."

The two of them cried and hugged each other, and I stood numbly, wishing that I had done something differently. I should have confronted her sooner. We might have protected her.

But there would be time enough to deal with the guilt later.

Someone was killing members of this group, someone who was not afraid to do it brazenly. Because, though Nessa didn't know the details, I had no doubt that Carlotta had been murdered. There was no chance that it was a coincidence.

Had it been Ronald who had done it? Perhaps he had seen me

following him last night and had drugged me as a warning. But why had he killed Carlotta? It didn't make sense. None of it was making sense, and my head was swimming.

I needed to get back to the major. He was waiting for me in his car. I could only hope that he would know how to proceed from here.

There were so many questions and so few answers.

Somehow, I felt that the noose was tightening around our necks, but the maddening thing was that I couldn't see the executioner.

I accompanied Sami and Nessa through the garden behind my rooming house and back to Sami's house, where Laila awaited them. She'd paled at the news, but she'd gone to make tea, and the girls had calmed a bit in her presence.

"I . . . I'm supposed to meet John," I said at last. "I'll go and tell him what happened."

Sami nodded, and I excused myself.

Hurrying down the street to the major's waiting car, I saw that he was standing outside of it. I was probably late, though I had no idea at the moment how long had passed since he had dropped me off. It suddenly seemed ages ago.

"Where's your bag?" he asked as I approached. Then he saw the look on my face. "What's happened?"

"Carlotta's dead," I said. "I . . . she told me I should stop asking questions and now . . ."

He reached out and took my arm, squeezing it ever so slightly. I knew, after the tears I'd already shed this morning, he probably worried I would go to pieces. I wasn't altogether sure he was wrong. "Tell me what happened."

I related how Nessa had just come to share the news of Carlotta's death with us.

"She doesn't know how . . . how it happened yet."

"All right. Did you pack your bag?"

"Yes. I . . . I think I left it on the porch."

"Get in. We'll go get it."

I nodded. He led me around the car and opened the door. He drove back to the house, collected my bag, and then turned the car around and drove back toward the seashore.

"I should tell Sami where I'm going," I said vaguely.

"She'll know you're with me," he said.

I didn't feel like arguing. I was suddenly exhausted, heavy with the weight of all that had happened. We McDonnells weren't the sort of people to crack under pressure, and I knew I would shake off the shock soon enough. All the same, I was glad of Major Ramsey's solid presence beside me as we drove away.

"I should have asked her what she meant," I said. "Some customers came in, so I couldn't press her then. But I should have waited, or . . ."

"Don't play that game," he said. "There's no sense in debating what might have been."

Uncle Mick would have said the same thing. It was easier to say than to do, however.

We rode in silence most of the way back to his cottage. I was lost in my thoughts, and it seemed the major was lost in his as well. I wished I knew what he was thinking about everything.

As he parked the car, I remembered that I needed to tell him about the letter from Felix, what had been written on the blotter.

"There's something else," I said.

He looked at me, and I felt the teensiest bit of dread. He wasn't going to like that I had shared the blotter with Felix or shared my location with him. But there was no helping that now, not when Felix's letter might be important.

I took the letter out of my pocket. "I took a rubbing of the blotter on Hal Jenkins's desk that night we broke in."

He said nothing. He knew there was more.

I plunged ahead, the words coming out in a rush. "I sent it to Felix. I didn't tell him anything about the case, only asked if he could make out any of the words in the scramble of writing. You know Felix is rather a handwriting expert, and . . ."

Major Ramsey held out his hand.

I realized I was clutching the letter, crumpling it. I held it out to him.

He opened it, his eyes scanning the words, his features expressionless. I had forgotten the rather personal postscript, but if Major Ramsey was shocked, he didn't show it.

"This might be of use to us," he said when he'd finished. He returned the note to me, and I shoved it back into my pocket. "We've had some intelligence that fits with a portion of this."

I was surprised he wasn't going to shout at me, but I wasn't going to look a gift horse in the mouth.

"What sort of intelligence? Which portion?"

"I'll explain it to you later. There's one more piece we need."

Somehow, I had the impression that the *we* did not mean him and me. There was someone else he intended to bring in, then?

"Is there someone else in on this?" I asked.

He studied me for a moment. "There are other players in this game, yes. I have someone meeting us back here this afternoon."

I nodded. It wasn't a surprise that he would have brought someone in. After all, in London we'd always worked with his operative Kimble, a colorless, emotionless ice sculpture of a man who didn't blink an eye at theft or murder or anything in between.

We went inside the cottage, the major carrying my valise into the bedroom.

I sank onto the nearest wooden chair, pulling Felix's letter out of my pocket once again. Did the major know to whom Hal Jenkins had been writing the warning? It wasn't a surprise that he was keeping things from me, but we'd reached the stage where we were going to have to lay our cards on the table.

"I think this must be Sheridan Hall's collection he was writing about," I said as he came back into the room. "It's possible it isn't even related to the case. But he does refer, presumably, to Vangidae in the warning line. I had thought it was *VON*, possibly referring to Pavonine Press, but Felix has it as *VAN*, and I'd trust his judgment over mine on this. So perhaps Mr. Hall is in on it after all."

He took a seat across from me. "Let me tell you about recent developments."

I nodded, eager to connect the missing pieces.

"We've only just intercepted radio communications that point to the reason Hal Jenkins may have been killed," he said. "The counterfeiting ring was operating at Pavonine Press, as you know. The operation there was making false identity cards and presenting them to spies when they came into this country."

I nodded again.

"At some point, Hal Jenkins became aware of what was happening. Whether he was in on it from the beginning or merely stumbled across it, I don't yet know. Whatever the case, he got greedy and decided to go into business for himself."

I frowned. "How so?"

"He stole the plate used to print the identity cards and, from what we can tell, the most recent batch of cards they had printed, and he was blackmailing them to get it back."

"'We know you have it,'" I said. "That's what the note in his hand said when I found him."

He nodded. "Someone discovered it was he who had stolen the plate."

"But why murder him? Had they already recovered the plate?"

He shook his head. "From what we can tell, they still don't have it. I believe he may have had an accomplice who betrayed him to the counterfeiters. His accomplice may have thought to deliver the plate and take the compensation for himself. It seems, however, that Jenkins took precautions and hid the plate and blank identity cards."

"Well, we know Ronald Potter is involved. Perhaps he is the accomplice who poisoned Hal Jenkins. And perhaps Carlotta learned something about it and had to be silenced. Though I still don't understand why he didn't just kill me outright if he'd done that to both of them. Why drug me instead? What did he hope to accomplish?"

Major Ramsey's gaze settled on mine. There was the briefest pause, and he said, "Ronald Potter didn't drug you."

I frowned. "Of course, he did. You saw the state I was in. It must have been him."

"No," the major said. "It was Beaumont."

That didn't make sense. "What . . . what do you mean?"

"Captain Beaumont saw you following Potter and drugged you to get you out of the way."

I stared at him, incredulous. There had been something about Rafe that hadn't seemed quite right to me, but I had not expected this. Several emotions coursed through me all at once, and I wasn't certain which of them had precedence. "He's working with them?"

"No," the major said. "He's working for me."

It took a moment for the words to sink in, but when they did, it was rage that butted its way to the forefront. "He's what?"

"Captain Beaumont was under orders to make your acquaintance and keep an eye on you while you were in Sunderland. He's been following you."

My entire body went cold and then hot. It was almost beyond belief, but, somehow, it was not. Somehow, I felt I ought to have known, and I felt incredibly stupid for not having seen it. The book of Greek myths in Rafe Beaumont's pocket had been a nice touch. Major Ramsey knew my love of mythology.

"Did you tell him to drug me?" I whispered. I was so angry that I almost couldn't speak.

"No. That he did on his own, and he has been reprimanded for it."

"Oh," I said, through clenched teeth. "I'm so glad you didn't approve of that bit of it. Only his following me, lying to me."

"I had my reasons."

"I know perfectly well what your reasons are, Major," I shot back. "You don't trust me. You never have."

"Miss McDonnell . . ."

"You didn't think the little thief from Hendon would do your bidding, and so you sent along your lackey to keep an eye on me. When he couldn't keep up, he resorted to drugging me."

"Miss McDonnell, you must realize that I cannot have everyone running around mucking things up. This is a war we're fighting."

I'd struggled with my temper for as long as I could remember, but I don't think I'd ever been as angry as I was in that moment. I was incandescent with rage. I could feel it shooting through to my fingertips, every bit of me charged with it.

"I am not *everyone,* Major," I said, rising to my feet. "I'm the woman who has repeatedly risked her life to help you when your prim and proper group of soldiers couldn't get the job done. Well, you don't have to worry about my mucking things up from now on."

I called him a name that would have mortified Nacy, and then, without thinking about what I was doing, I hurled the empty ashtray from the table beside me at his head.

My aim was good, but he dodged the ashtray easily, barely moving, just tilting his head slightly to one side, and then he shot to his feet.

I didn't know what he meant to do, and I didn't care. I made for the door. I would walk straight back to Sunderland and get on a train. I never wanted to see him again, and I didn't care what happened to his mission.

I had a head start, and the wooden chair I'd been sitting in was between us, but he tossed it aside like so much kindling, sending it crashing to the floor.

I was turning the knob when his hand hit the door above my head, preventing me from opening it.

"Let me out of here," I said, pulling on the door with all my strength. It was useless, of course; he was much too strong.

"Electra, listen to me. I was trying to keep you safe."

Whirling to face him, I shoved his chest. "I haven't asked you to protect me."

My shove didn't move him, but when I looked up at him, I froze with my hands still on his chest, the look in his eyes raising the gooseflesh on my arms.

There was anger there, but it was overridden by something else entirely. I felt the awareness of it, crackling like electricity in the space between us.

His hand dropped from the door, and I knew I could leave. I could walk out, and he wouldn't stop me. But I felt powerless to move.

We stared at each other for what seemed like an eternity, and, despite everything, I willed him to do it.

And, finally, he did.

He gave an almost imperceptible shake of his head, and then his hands grasped my face and he kissed me.

There was no finesse to it, no leisurely, coaxing seduction. His mouth captured mine in a fierce kiss that sent a bolt of heat clear through me. No slow fire, this kiss. It was like an explosion.

I slid my arms around his neck and kissed him back.

His hands had moved from my face, sliding around me to pull me tighter against him, but I could feel the tension in him and sense the restraint he was exercising. He was being careful not to overpower me, not to make me feel as though I couldn't stop him.

But I didn't want to stop him.

I'd never been kissed like this, never with the same sense of reckless passion that drove me to forget everything else. I pushed closer, my fingers gripping the wool shoulders of his uniform. I was aware of him as I had never been before. The smell of shaving soap and starch. The slight bristle of stubble on his jaw. The heat of his hands through my clothes.

There was absolutely no thought in my head of what might happen in the next moment. There was only this moment, now.

And then, dimly, I realized someone was knocking on the door. We stilled, broke our kiss.

"Major?" a voice called. It was Rafe Beaumont. "I'm here."

His eyes met mine. He was still pressed against me. I could feel him make the effort to control his breathing.

"In a minute, Beaumont," he called at last.

I was amazed at the steadiness of his voice. In that moment, I didn't feel as though I could have managed a word.

Everything went silent. We were still holding on to each other, but the spell had been broken.

He released me suddenly and stepped back. I was glad I had the door for support, because my legs had gone to jelly. For a long moment we looked at each other, both of us still breathless.

"I'm sorry," he said at last.

"Don't say that," I whispered.

His eyes held mine, and I could see that he wanted to kiss me again. I wanted it, too. The contact between us had been broken so suddenly that I felt cold and unsteady on my feet. I wanted his arms around me again.

But I could also tell from his face, from the regret already in his expression, that it wasn't going to happen.

"Please move away from the door, Electra."

Wordlessly, I stepped aside on slightly unsteady legs. Then he strode forward and pulled the door open. He passed through it without another word, closing the door firmly behind him.

CHAPTER TWENTY-TWO

Well, we'd done it now, hadn't we?

We'd crossed into territory it was going to be difficult to come back from. I knew he regretted it. That had been very apparent from almost the moment it was over.

And he had reason to. Because we obviously didn't belong together. We both knew that. We were too different in every way that mattered. We came from different worlds, and our views on most things were vastly divergent.

That kiss had been a momentary lapse, the friction and suppressed attraction that had simmered between us finally erupting in the heat of our argument.

It was that temper of his that was the chink in his armor, I realized. He'd let the anger come to the surface, and something else had overflowed with it. What exactly my excuse was, I wasn't sure.

We were fortunate, I supposed, that Rafe Beaumont had appeared when he did. It would be easy to have a torrid affair with no thought to the consequences. I'd never considered myself a woman who would fall easily into such an arrangement, but now I could see how passion made one willing to make concessions. I'd certainly been in no hurry to put a stop to things.

But neither of us was the sort of person who could throw caution to the wind. We both looked too far ahead, were too focused on the future to be cavalier with the present.

So we would just have to find some way to undo what we had done.

Perhaps an hour later, the door opened, and Major Ramsey came back in, followed by Captain Beaumont. I'd had time to clean up the glass from the shattered ashtray and right the chair the major had flung aside, so the room was once again in order.

The same could not be said of my thoughts. I still didn't feel ready to talk to either of them.

My gaze flickered of its own accord to the major. He was looking at me, and I felt a hot flush spread through me as our eyes met.

I looked to Captain Beaumont next. He was giving me a contrite expression. "I owe you an apology, Liz—or, Electra, is it?"

"Ellie," I said. "And you owe me more than one, Captain Beaumont. Or is that your real name? Perhaps that was a lie, too?"

He was polite enough to look chagrined. "No, it's my name. And you're right. I'm very sorry I deceived you. I was assigned to keep you safe, and I overplayed my hand."

"You drugged me," I said coldly.

"I was afraid you were going to get hurt and acted impulsively. It was an error in judgment."

A sneaking suspicion occurred to me then as I thought of dangerous things done in the name of "protecting" me. "Was it you who bumped me in front of the lorry the day I arrived in Sunderland?" I demanded.

He winced. "I followed you when you thought we'd parted ways. I was hoping to come to your rescue and further cement our friendship, but Hal Jenkins beat me to it. I realized you would probably be suspicious if you saw me there, so I disappeared into the crowd."

I felt my ire rising again at his machinations, but I remembered where losing my temper had gotten me last time.

"You might have got me killed!"

"You were in no real danger, I swear to you. I was right there, but Hal Jenkins reached out and grabbed your arm first."

"You're quite diabolical, Captain Beaumont."

The man had the nerve to look hurt. "I only wanted to protect you. Everything I've done has been aimed to that end, and I would never have allowed anything to happen to you. Please believe I was not feigning my regard for you. You'll forgive me, won't you?"

It was a pretty speech and very nicely delivered. Rafe Beaumont had no doubt had great success in life getting women to do what he wanted. Against my better judgment, I felt inclined to waver.

"I'll consider it," I said.

He put a hand over his heart. "You have my word I will never do anything like that again."

"Now that we have that taken care of," Major Ramsey said brusquely, "we have another matter to discuss."

I looked over at him. Our eyes caught for just a moment, and then he looked back at Rafe.

"Miss McDonnell is up to speed on the missing plate."

Rafe nodded. "We've decoded some of the messages between the Germans and the counterfeiters. There has been a great to-do about all this because it seems a new group of enemy agents will be arriving soon and need identification, and the plates are apparently not easy to replicate."

"They're not," I said. "It takes a good deal of time and skill to make plates. Counterfeiters usually work for years perfecting the art of replicating plates. Banknotes, for example, are very difficult to forge because of the talent required to make exact plate copies."

I realized that Rafe was looking at me strangely. I wondered if Major Ramsey had told him of my background and the sort of people my family associated with. Probably not. Major Ramsey never volunteered information that wasn't relevant to the case.

"So who is the mastermind behind all of this?" I asked. "Ronald?"

Rafe looked at Major Ramsey. The major's eyes didn't so much as flicker. He was hiding something, then.

"We think Ronald is probably not involved in this at all," Rafe said.

"But he had the false identity card," I said. "I saw it myself."

"We'll get to the bottom of that," Major Ramsey said dismissively.

I had an uneasy feeling about all of this. There was something they weren't telling me. Then again, there were a lot of things they hadn't seen fit to tell me.

I felt a fresh wave of anger at the fact that Rafe had drugged me to get me out of the way rather than revealing himself to me. It was infuriating.

"What's going on?" I asked. "There's something you aren't telling me."

"I had a chat with Ronald Potter last night," Rafe said. He spoke casually, but there was something in the words that gave me a little chill. "I'm fairly confident he knows nothing about the counterfeiting operation."

"But his identification card was printed with that plate," I said. "I'm sure of it."

"That may be so," Rafe agreed. "But we didn't know that last night."

"No," I agreed. "Because no one saw fit to share things with me. It was better to get me out of the way instead."

Rafe grimaced apologetically.

"Can't you ask him where he got his card?" I asked.

"He's . . . unavailable for more questions," Rafe said.

"Did you kill him?" I demanded.

"No," he said, though he didn't seem the least bit affronted that I'd assumed him capable of it. "I let him go when I was sure he wasn't a spy, but it seems I frightened him. He's left Sunderland."

"What about Carlotta?" I asked. "Who killed her, and why?"

"We don't know, as of yet," Rafe said.

"Do you . . . know how she was killed?"

"Cyanide. The same as Hal Jenkins," Major Ramsey answered. "Only her dose appears to have been injected. There was a small puncture wound in her arm."

I shuddered. Poor Carlotta. I wished there was some way I might have helped her, some way I could have prevented what happened.

"I overheard a conversation between her and Sami Maddox," I said carefully. "They were involved in something together. Sami said that people were relying on them. You don't think . . . surely they couldn't both be working for the Germans." I didn't say the rest of what I was thinking. That it was possible Sami had thought Carlotta was a liability and eliminated her.

"We can't rule out their involvement," Rafe said. "Maybe once we locate Potter and find out the provenance of his identity card, we'll know more."

"We've sent someone to find him," Major Ramsey said. "But that doesn't solve our most immediate problem."

"Which is?" I asked.

"As Beaumont mentioned, there is a new group of spies being ferried across the North Sea very soon."

"Then why not go and capture the lot of them?" I asked. "Surely you can rouse the troops for that."

"Certainly," Major Ramsey agreed. "However, it would be best if the spies do not know that we're onto them, not yet."

"You mean you're just going to let them into England?"

There was another pause, and again Rafe Beaumont glanced to the major, waiting to see what he wanted to reveal.

At last, the major spoke. "We believe that these spies are part of a group of saboteurs that are being deployed locally. They will make contact with others in their individual groups once they arrive here in Sunderland. Therefore, we would rather that they believe themselves to have made it safely to English shores rather than taking them into custody when they arrive."

I was gratified that they had explained this much of the matter to me. Of course, it would have made things much easier if they had done it from the start. Kiss or no, I was still angry with Major Ramsey for having kept these things from me.

"So you need the plate and the missing identity cards back."

"Yes," Major Ramsey said. "We need to find the plate and deliver it back to the counterfeiters, without their being aware that they've been compromised. Once we've traced the spies to their local group leaders, we will be able to shut down the operation."

I sometimes forgot that's how this game was played: that it was better to let the Germans go on causing a small amount of harm rather than showing them that their sources were compromised.

"It seems Ronald Potter is your best lead," I said. "We need to find out where he got that identification card."

Rafe Beaumont looked at the major. "You have your radio, sir?"

"In the bedroom," the major said, nodding his head in that direction. "In the wardrobe."

"I'm going to radio my man. See if there's any sign of Potter."

The major nodded, and Rafe went into the bedroom, closing the door behind him.

Major Ramsey turned to me. "We need to talk, Miss Mc-Donnell."

So I was Miss McDonnell again. An hour ago, he'd had his arms around me.

I nodded. I knew what he was going to say. There was really no need to talk about anything. I also knew, however, that he was not a man to let things rest. We were going to have to discuss what happened, sooner or later.

"There are no excuses for my behavior, so I will make none," he said. "I can only assure you that it won't happen again."

I tried not to feel disappointment at this assurance.

"Are you talking about deceiving me, or about . . . what happened after?" I asked.

"You know what I'm talking about," he said, his eyes on mine. I felt that frisson of heat again and blinked against it.

"There's no need to apologize," I said, as lightly as I could manage. "After all, I had a part in it as well."

"We cannot do this, Electra."

Why not? It was what I wanted to say, even though I knew the answer. I had known it as soon as my head had cleared a bit.

"I know," I said instead.

He was studying my face, as though trying to determine what my feelings in the matter might be. He would have a difficult time of it, as I didn't know what they were myself. I hadn't had enough time to process what had happened. I knew, however, that my feelings didn't matter, not really. He had made up his mind. But perhaps he was assuring himself that I hadn't tumbled into love with him.

"It would be . . . ill-advised to pursue anything along personal lines," he said. "Not to mention unethical. I am, for all intents and purposes, your commanding officer, and my behavior was an unpardonable breach."

"I understand," I said, wanting to cut him off before he went on listing excuses.

"It should not have happened."

I shrugged, trying to maintain an air of nonchalance. "It was only a kiss. If we were a little attracted to each other, perhaps that kiss . . . doused the spark, so to speak."

"That is not, as a general rule, how it works," he said in a low voice.

I forced myself to look up at him and managed a tight smile. "Well, it will have to work this time, won't it?"

He looked, for a moment, as though he was going to say something else, but then the bedroom door opened, and Rafe came out.

"They still haven't found Potter," he said. "But they have intercepted another message from the Germans. They're expecting the drop tonight. Their contact is expected to deliver the identity cards for the incoming spies and return the plate."

"Tonight?" I asked. "That puts rather a crimp in things."

Rafe nodded. "We need to find the plate and identity cards, and fast."

"We tossed Hal Jenkins's room," I said. "Even though I didn't know what I was looking for, I made a thorough search. I think I would have found it."

"Then he must have hidden it somewhere else," Rafe said. "But where? The plate would not be very large, correct?"

I nodded. "Not much larger than a small book cover, and thin."

As I said the words, my mind turned. I thought about what had been written on the blotter: YOU MAY BE INT . . . YOUR . . . LECTION.

And suddenly, it clicked. "I know where the plate is."

They turned to look at me.

"It's in Sheridan Hall's safe room."

Rafe looked skeptical. "We have yet to find any link to Sheridan Hall. He doesn't seem to be involved in this."

"He doesn't know he is," I said.

"Explain," the major said. He was never overly polite when he was in commanding officer mode, and I supposed that's what was happening now. I decided to ignore his terseness and continue.

"There were books in Hal Jenkins's room," I said. "Several books on birding. I didn't see anything special about them. But when I was talking to Sheridan Hall, he told me that he'd recently been sent a collection of antique birding books."

Major Ramsey watched me expectantly.

"I think Hal Jenkins hid the plate inside one of the books and sent them to Sheridan Hall. There was a paper knife and glue in his desk drawer. Perhaps he hid the plate and identity cards inside one or more of the books. Sheridan Hall's safe would be somewhere Hal knew was absolutely secure until he needed to retrieve it. Then he would only have to visit Mr. Hall on some simple pretext in order to get it back. Those are the books Mr. Hall told me he was storing in his safe room until he'd had time to appraise them."

"Then you think they're locked in that vault," Rafe said.

I nodded. "It's the surest bet we have."

Major Ramsey let out a short breath. "Then we'll have to get it back."

"But couldn't we just ask him for it?" Rafe said. "Or Liz—I'm sorry, Ellie—could ask to be let back into the vault to look around?"

"We don't have time," the major said. "We need that plate tonight. Besides, we can't be certain Sheridan Hall is not involved, and we don't want to rouse any more suspicion than we already have."

"Well, it's a good thing you have me along now, then, isn't it," I said, feeling not a little triumphant.

CHAPTER TWENTY-THREE

We made our way in the direction of Vangidae under cover of darkness. We had done this before, at Pavonine Press, but somehow the darkness around us felt heavier now. Or perhaps it was simply that I was investing it with meanings of my own.

The night was cool and clear, a steady breeze blowing in off the sea. I looked out at the dark water, wondering if the next group of spies was even now approaching our shores.

I hoped we could get the plate back in time. I hoped I was right about what Hal Jenkins had done with it.

The house was dark as we approached. There were blackout curtains in place, of course, so that didn't tell us much. I knew Mr. Hall liked his morning walks, so I had to hope he was an "early to bed, early to rise" sort of gentleman.

We crept through the back garden and up toward the house. The door leading to the small kitchen garden was not locked, and once inside, we were shielded from the outside world.

We'd decided on the kitchen door for the best means of ingress. The staff was not live-in. The major and Rafe had determined that Mr. Hall had a cook and a maid who came during the day, but they went home after dinner. There was Bevins, of course, the valet and all-around manservant who stayed in the house, but I surmised his room would be close to Mr. Hall's, as he was his valet, butler, and nurse rolled into one.

We moved up to the back door, and I took out my tool kit. This wasn't difficult work. Major Ramsey could likely have done this himself, though perhaps not without leaving marks. That was the advantage of my experience as a thief: I was able to get in and out without leaving a trace.

I inserted my pick into the lock and felt for the give in the mechanism. Though I made very little noise, one benefit of a seaside manor was that the sound of the waves and wind gave us a bit of cover for what we needed to do.

The major kept his back to me as I worked, his eyes scanning the perimeter. We were fairly shielded here by trees and by the high stone wall of the kitchen garden, so I didn't think we were likely to be seen.

The kitchen lock gave easily, and I pulled the door open slowly. I looked at Major Ramsey for instruction, and he gave a short nod.

I stepped inside the house. It was dark and very quiet. Major Ramsey came in after me and closed the door softly. We were still for several moments, just listening.

The major, as he was wont to do, stood very close beside me in the darkness, and I fought down my awareness of him to pay attention to my surroundings. *Don't get distracted.* That was one of Uncle Mick's cardinal rules. And here I was, every bit of my body trying to attune itself to the man with me. That would never do.

This was another good reason we could not get romantically involved. When focus was a matter of life and death, distraction was dangerous.

Mustering all my attention and training in these matters, I stood still and listened to the sounds of the house. There were the waves outside and the occasional rattle of the windowpanes in the wind. Farther inside, the tick of a clock somewhere in the darkness.

We didn't know the layout of the house as well as we would have liked, since I'd only been through the front door and into the study and library. Nevertheless, I had a decent sense of direction, and I thought I could find my way back there easily enough.

When we were certain that nothing moved within the house, I quietly began to make my way in the direction of the library with the major following behind me.

We didn't dare use a torch at this point, and the house was very dark, but not entirely devoid of light. Besides, I was used to the darkness. It had long been my ally.

I found the door to the library with little trouble and tried the handle. It was open.

I stepped quickly inside. The major came in behind me and closed the door.

Wordlessly, I moved toward the safe room.

The door concealing the safe had slid open easily, that I remembered. I noticed the way that doors moved. It was a by-product of my training. If there were creaking hinges or the scrape of wood, I was instantly aware of them. And I recalled the smooth way the door had opened when he had turned the combination.

"You're going to have to give me some space," I whispered to the major.

He nodded and moved closer to the library door, presumably to keep an eye on things.

Then I turned my focus to the combination.

I hadn't opened a safe since our first foray with Major Ramsey's merry band of outlaws, and I was worried that I might be a bit rusty. But opening a safe is like riding a bicycle, Uncle Mick always claimed. Once you knew how to do it, it was a skill that didn't leave you.

That was easy for him to say, of course. He could do the

maths in his head. I required a pencil and a paper to graph out the points in the combination. I had brought them with me, and I set them on the floor as I knelt before the safe and placed my hand on the dial. I steadied my breathing, cleared my mind, and began to work.

It did come back easily enough as I started feeling for the slight differences in give that indicated a correct combination number. As I worked, I graphed the points on the sheet of paper on the floor. The only sound in the room for a long time was the occasional, almost indiscernible scrape of my pencil against paper.

Major Ramsey, to his credit, gave me space and silence. He stood in the background, not making a sound, as I worked. After a while, I almost forgot that he was there. It was just me and the combination, a battle of wills between us. And I'd always had a very stubborn will.

Finally, the combination gave itself up, and I felt the rush of triumph that comes with solving a complicated puzzle. I turned the combination to the numbers I'd graphed, the final steps in the dance. There was a little click as the lock gave, and I pulled the safe door open.

Almost before I had finished opening the door, Major Ramsey was beside me. "Well done," he whispered.

I nodded and turned back to the safe.

There was still the little metal gate behind the door. I had never seen someone invest so much in protecting personal property, especially not bird-related memorabilia. To each their own.

The gate wasn't exceptionally difficult to open after cracking the combination. It only required a bit of pressure from my pick at the right point before it gave.

I pushed it aside with the slightest creak of metal. And then the safe room was open to us.

I went inside and Major Ramsey followed, pulling the safe door mostly closed and then switching on his torch.

He shone it around the room, taking in the impressive display I had been able to enjoy perusing. I wished I could have seen his face to know what he thought about it all. Of course, his face never gave much away.

I would have liked to get his opinion on the collection, but I knew he would only tersely remind me why we had come and that time was of the essence, so I refrained from questions.

I moved along, past the nests and eggs and statues, past the eagles locked in their final, fatal flight. And there at the back was a bookshelf filled with the rare books.

Mr. Hall had spoken of a few that he had acquired only recently, a small stack of them at the corner of one shelf. I moved closer. If I was right, one of these held the missing printer's plate that the spies were waiting for.

If I was wrong . . . well, we wouldn't think about that at the moment.

I moved over to the books. There were several that looked so old they might fall apart if I touched them. I didn't have time to handle them with kid gloves. We needed to get out of the house as soon as possible.

There were a few that looked a bit newer, and I checked them first, picking them up and flipping through the pages while Major Ramsey held the torch.

I flipped through one, then another. Nothing.

I picked up the next, and a piece of paper fluttered out. I unfolded it and read.

Dear sir:

I know that you have always had a keen eye for valuable books on birding. Here are some I have recently come across that I think you may be interested in adding to your collection. The illustrated edition in

particular is quite rare, I believe, and the artwork is
exquisite.

Please accept them with my compliments and best
wishes.

Yours sincerely,
Henry Jenkins

"It's the note he wrote at his desk," I whispered. The words
were the same that Felix had made out on the blotter.

Major Ramsey gave only a curt nod in reply, and I knew he
meant for me to get on with it.

I looked down at the book in my hand. It was the right size to
conceal the plate. Many of the other books in this stack seemed as
though they would be too small. This was the illustrated edition,
too, the one Hal Jenkins had casually mentioned might be worth
keeping safe. It seemed the plate must be here.

I flipped the book open, though I could tell from the way the
pages lay that there probably wasn't anything thick enough to be
the plate stuck inside the pages.

I gave it a quick flip through, the vibrant illustrations moving
quickly past, almost like birds in flight. But there was nothing
hidden within the pages, no metal plate tucked between the star-
tlingly lifelike paintings of doves, pheasants, and nightjars.

I felt a rush of disappointment. I had been so sure.

I looked at the book again. There was something a bit off in
the way it felt in my hand. I passed it from one hand to the other,
assessing what felt wrong.

Then I realized what it was. The back cover was heavier than
the front.

"Do you have a knife?" I asked Major Ramsey.

He hesitated only a moment before reaching into his boot
and pulling out a sharp-looking blade. I ought not to have been

surprised that he had weapons hidden all about his person, but it was a bit startling nonetheless.

I took the knife from him and set the book on the table. Flipping to the back cover, I felt along the endsheet. There was something hard beneath it. I felt a surge of excitement, but I tamped it down.

I placed the blade of the knife against the seam and cut. It sliced open neatly to reveal the space between the endsheet and the back cover. There was a thin piece of metal inside.

"I've got it!" I whispered, feeling the same thrill of victory I imagined must come with the unearthing of buried treasure. I slipped my fingers into the space and was able to grab hold of the side of the plate. I slipped it from its hiding place.

I was sorry I'd had to slit the book cover, but, really, Hal Jenkins was responsible for that. And it could be mended.

I looked down at the plate. It was difficult to believe that all of this trouble—two people's lives—had been the cost of this little sheet of metal. I studied it. Sure enough, it was the engraving of the National Registration Identity Card. In the metal, just beneath the right-hand lion, was a small irregularity, just as I had seen on the printed cards.

I looked up at the major.

"Well done," he said. "Are the identity cards here, too?"

"Let me check the other books." I handed the plate to him, and he slipped it into his pocket.

I flipped through a few of the other books and found nothing. Then I saw the book at the bottom of the stack. It looked slightly more contemporary than the others, clearly not an antique. It seemed out of place and something that Sheridan Hall would not have been much interested in. I opened it, or tried to. The pages were stuck together.

I slipped the edge of the major's knife between the cover and the first page, slicing neatly through the glued-together portion.

Opening the cover, I saw that the inside of the book had been hollowed out, and there lay a neat stack of identity cards.

I pulled them out. They were blank, ready to be filled out with the false identities of the spies who would shortly be arriving on our shores.

"Let's go," he said.

I nodded.

He turned back toward the front of the safe room, and I looked at the book I had cut open to find the plate. With a glance to be sure the major wasn't looking, I slid the book into the large pocket inside my jacket. Then I followed him toward the door.

We had just reached the entrance to the safe, the major's hand on it to push it open, when there was a sudden creak from somewhere nearby.

I looked up at Major Ramsey. He was looking though the small opening we had left, and then he turned to me and gave a sharp shake of his head. What the blazes was that supposed to mean?

"There's a light in the hall. I see it beneath the library door. Someone's coming," he whispered into my ear.

Sure enough, I could hear then the soft, shambling footsteps of what was no doubt Mr. Hall. He was muttering, to himself I assumed, and it seemed he was coming in the direction of the library.

There was no time to think, and there definitely wasn't time to get out of the safe and hide. Without hesitation, I pulled the safe door closed, locking us inside.

CHAPTER TWENTY-FOUR

For good measure, I pushed closed the metal gate. I felt it snap into place. It had a locking mechanism. I hadn't really considered that it might. But no matter. I would get it open when the time came.

Major Ramsey had switched off his torch when we'd heard the noise, but he switched it back on now that we were alone in the pitch-dark safe.

"This isn't ideal," he said with typically masterful understatement.

"No," I agreed. "But hopefully he won't need to come into the safe for anything. With any luck, he's just come to the library for some late-night reading material. We can get out once he's gone back to bed."

"You can open the safe from the inside?"

"All of these large safes have an inside release lever so that people don't get trapped inside. Let me see your torch a moment."

He handed it to me without comment, and I flashed it around until I saw what I was looking for.

"There," I said, shining the light at a spot near the door. The release lever was right where it should be, thank God. "That will open it for us."

"And the gate?" he asked.

I hesitated.

"You locked it, too, I think?"

"Yes," I admitted.

"Can you unlock it?" He asked this casually, as though we weren't sealed together in a vault.

It was a good question.

Normally, the answer would be a simple yes. It's generally easier to get out of a place than to get into it, but the lock was on the outside of the gate. I was going to have to stick my hands through and do it backward, so to speak.

Well, I'd always enjoyed a good challenge.

"It won't be a problem," I assured him without meeting his gaze.

He said nothing.

"How long do you suppose we'll need to wait?" I asked after a moment.

"It's a gamble," he said. "Perhaps he came in only to get a book or to write a letter. Or perhaps he'll settle down to read until morning."

"And we have no way of knowing if he's out there until we open the door."

"Precisely."

That thought was depressing. I hoped Sheridan Hall had only meant to fetch a book and bring it to the comfort of his bedroom. But we had better wait for a while, all the same.

In the meantime, we were locked inside a safe together.

Not ideal, indeed.

It felt different now, being alone with him. We had agreed that nothing could happen between us, but I still couldn't help feeling that possibility hung in the air. One couldn't rid oneself of attraction just by refusing to acknowledge it, and I knew that, for both of us, it was still there.

I had to imagine that Major Ramsey didn't like it any more than I did—probably a great deal less so, if we were being honest—but that didn't change the fact that it was still hovering between us.

It was natural enough, after all. A great many people thrown together by circumstance developed an attraction to each other. And it certainly wasn't the first time a woman had been drawn to a man who was entirely unsuitable for her. Truth be told, that was often just the sort of man a woman preferred. There was something alluring about the forbidden, wasn't there? It had been so since Eve and the apple.

That pull of doing what was prohibited had been a part of my life since I'd first put my hand to a safe's handle. It was not entirely surprising, then, that I might find myself drawn to a man I had absolutely no business fancying.

The fact that it was not unusual, though, did nothing to make me feel better about it. It had been bad enough when I had been struggling with my own unwanted attraction to him. Now that I knew he felt the same way about me, it would be twice as bad.

I wondered if it would be like this from now on, or if it would die out in time. I had to believe it would fade into the background. Especially once I was back home, surrounded by my family and Felix.

Felix. I felt a hot flush creep up my face. What was I going to tell Felix?

Did I have to tell him anything?

I was no stranger to keeping secrets, of course. It was something I'd always excelled at. But it was different with Felix. I had always shared so much with him, and I didn't know if I could keep this from him.

Whether I was obligated to tell him was a different matter. We weren't technically dating exclusively. There had been no parameters set on our relationship. And what, precisely, did I feel for Felix? I was still working that out.

I had never had any patience for girls in this sort of situation, girls who wouldn't seem to make up their mind which of two gentlemen they most favored. But I couldn't help but feel conflicted about my feelings toward Felix and the major. It wasn't just about them, it was about who I wanted to be, what my future might hold.

Not that it was really a matter of choice. After all, Major Ramsey had made it very clear where we stood.

And anyway, now was not the time to be thinking about this. We were locked in a safe when time was of the essence. We had the plate, and we needed to get it back, needed to see if we could make contact with whomever was running the operation and hand it over.

I glanced over at Major Ramsey. He wasn't looking at me, and I noticed he had put a bit of distance between us. Was it because he was worried that he might not behave himself? Somehow, the thought cheered me a bit. I liked to think that he still wanted to kiss me, even if we both knew that he shouldn't.

"I'm going to switch off the torch in case we need it later," he said.

"All right." So we would stand there together in the dark. Wonderful.

"There's a light in here," I told him. "Sheridan Hall turned it on when we came inside. The switch is by the door."

"I don't think we'd better turn it on."

"I'll just make myself comfortable, then," I said, settling myself on the floor.

He nodded and switched off the light.

It was pitch dark inside the safe, naturally. They'd done a good job with it, not a pinprick of light shining in from anywhere.

We sat in silence for a full ten minutes.

"All right?" the major asked me at last.

I nodded and then realized that, of course, he couldn't see me. "Yes," I said.

It would be a good opportunity for discussion, but what was there to discuss?

All the same, I was beginning to feel stifled, sitting in the darkness with him like this. Something needed to be done, and so I reverted back to the games my cousins and I had played at bedtime, when we'd been forced to quit our rowdy play.

"If you could eat anything in the world right now, what would it be?" I asked.

There was a brief pause. "What?"

"Anything at all," I said. "What's your very favorite thing to eat?"

"Ful medames," he said at last. "A traditional Egyptian dish, a sort of stew of spiced fava beans. I ate it constantly in North Africa and haven't had it since I returned. What's yours?"

"Nacy's bread pudding," I answered promptly.

"Of all the things in the world?"

"Of all the things in the world."

"Not surprising, I suppose, given your sweet tooth."

I sighed. "It's become something of a burden in wartime."

We lapsed back into silence, but the levity of the conversation had taken some of the weight out of the air.

We waited for perhaps another hour. Then the inside of the safe began to grow warm. I realized there probably wasn't very good ventilation inside, and, while there was likely enough air to last us several hours, I didn't relish the idea of being trapped in here any longer than necessary.

As I was thinking this, Major Ramsey spoke. "Miss Mc-Donnell . . ."

"Don't you suppose you can call me Electra now?" I asked.

"I think it's best if we maintain some semblance of . . . formality."

I sighed, as I always did when he became priggish. "It's a bit late for that, isn't it?"

He ignored me, as he always did when I became sarcastic. "Are you ready to open the gate?"

"Yes."

The major switched on his torch, and we moved toward the gate.

I examined it. The lock was on the outside, and the space between the grates was very small. I wasn't sure I would be able to fit my hand through.

"Major, will you come and shine your torch here?" I asked.

He came to my side and shone the torch where I indicated. For the briefest of moments, I allowed myself to be aware of his nearness, of the faint scent of his aftershave in the warmth of the enclosed space.

And then I focused my attention on the lock.

Pick and tension tool at the ready, I slipped my hands through and found they just fit, with a bit of wiggle room for my wrists. I felt for the lock and used my tools to begin working. It was silent in the room except for the light scrape of metal and the sound of the major's breathing. I'd noticed that his breathing was only audible when he was impatient.

"How long . . ." the major began at last.

"If you think you can pick a lock backward without being able to see it faster than I can, you're welcome to have a crack at it."

He didn't reply.

It was not exactly an easy task when I couldn't see the lock and I had only so much space to move my wrists. But, eventually, I found the right angle of the pick and tension tool. Then it was just a matter of applying pressure, and . . .

There was a little click, and then the lock gave, and the release clicked open. Breathing a sigh of relief, I pulled my pick free and pushed open the gate.

Now we had only to open the safe door and hope Sheridan Hall was not sitting on the other side of it. Taking a deep breath, I pushed the lever. The safe door slid open without a sound.

Cool air rushed to greet me as I stepped back into the darkened library. I breathed a sigh of relief that Mr. Hall wasn't there. We had only to make our escape.

The major came out after me, closing the gate behind him. I slid the door back into place and spun the combination dial so that it wouldn't be set where I'd left it.

Then we began to creep from the house. There was no sound, only the wind off the sea and the distant crash of the waves.

We reached the kitchen door, where we had entered. I locked it on our way out, and then we were off across the garden.

I moved quickly, not looking back. I knew the major was there behind me, even though I couldn't hear him. I could sense him somehow, though he moved as silently as a wraith in the darkness.

I had just gone through the door in the stone wall surrounding the kitchen garden when there was a clunk in the wall beside me, as though someone had thrown a rock. I turned to see a deep chip in the stone.

I moved closer, pressing my fingers to the chip. It looked like a bullet hole.

I shrank quickly into the hedge and nearly jumped when the major appeared beside me.

"I think someone is shooting at us."

"Go quickly. Stay low."

I did as he said, and we darted along in the darkness. When we reached a small wooded area, he took hold of my arm and hustled me through the foliage ahead of him. I had the impression he was keeping his body between me and the direction from which the bullet had come. His innate sense of chivalry again, no doubt.

We reached a fallen log, and he pushed me behind it, dropping down beside me.

I saw he had his gun in his hand again. He was like a magician pulling a rabbit from a hat with that weapon.

"Are you all right?" he asked.

"Yes," I said breathlessly. "But who was it? It didn't come from the direction of the house."

"Someone may have been following us," he said. "Or perhaps someone was staking out Vangidae for reasons of their own."

"What do we do now?"

"We wait."

And so we did, for perhaps twenty minutes. There were no more shots, nor sounds of anyone following us.

At last, the major motioned for me to move, and we went in the direction of the cabin.

"Once we hit open ground, run," he told me in a low voice.

It wasn't exactly a comforting command, but I had learned not to expect such things from Major Ramsey.

Once we were out of the trees, I did as he said. I took off at a full run in the direction of the cottage. It was dark, but light enough to see where I was going.

We reached the cabin a few moments later, and Major Ramsey pulled the door open for me.

Once we were inside, he shut it again, and we both stood there, catching our breath. That had been quite a run we'd been on.

"I was about to come searching for you." I had almost forgotten Rafe was here, waiting for us.

He had shed his uniform jacket and tie, and the sleeves of his shirt were rolled up to the elbows. He looked casually dashing in contrast to Major Ramsey's habitual formality, and I wondered how often the two of them worked together and if their personalities clashed.

"It's a good thing you didn't," Major Ramsey answered. "You wouldn't have found us."

"We . . . were locked inside a safe for a bit," I told him.

His brows rose. "But all is well, I take it?"

Major Ramsey reached into his pocket and took out the plate, holding it up.

"Well done," Rafe said with a smile. "I wish I'd been there to see you work, Ellie."

"We may have been shot at," the major said.

Rafe's brows went up. "Then someone's onto us."

"At the very least, someone saw us leaving the back garden at Vangidae."

"There was no sound of a shot," I said, wondering if I could have been mistaken. But something had hit the stone wall beside me, and that deep gash in the stone had not been caused by something harmless.

"They might have used a silencer," Rafe said. "In that case, we're talking a professional, not some common bystander with a gun."

"We weren't followed back," the major said.

Rafe nodded. "I've been busy myself while you were away. My men picked up Ronald Potter."

"And?"

"He says he lost his identity card and bought a replacement from a friend. Said it was easier than admitting to the authorities he'd been careless with his own."

"And the friend?" Major Ramsey asked.

"He claims it was a woman called Nessa Simpson."

I started. "Nessa? But she . . . surely she isn't . . . The *VAN* in the note. Could it have been part of the name Vanessa?" Had

Hal Jenkins been writing to her? *THESE PEOPLE WILL KILL,* he had written. Was it possible they were in on this together and he had been warning her?

It all fit, and yet I hated to believe it.

"She must have been Hal's accomplice," I said. I remembered how Nessa's scream had alerted us that Hal Jenkins had been killed. Was she the one who had poisoned him? She had been the one to tell us Carlotta was dead, as well. Had she also killed Carlotta? The possibility was horrifying.

"We confirmed the drop for oh one hundred, but they mentioned a prearranged location, and we don't have it."

"Go and pick up Nessa Simpson," Major Ramsey said. "She'll be able to tell us."

Rafe nodded and turned toward the door.

And that was the moment we heard the sound of approaching aircraft and the distant whine of Sunderland's air-raid sirens.

CHAPTER TWENTY-FIVE

Major Ramsey and Rafe swore in unison, though they chose different words.

As one, we all turned toward the door and hurried outside. Above us, we could see the glint of metal in the moonlight as planes roared overhead in the direction of the city.

Then there was that familiar shrieking sound of bombs falling through the air, followed by the distant sound of explosions and brilliant flashes of light as they hit their target.

It was London all over again.

"What do we do now?" I asked.

"Nothing, if we don't know the location of the drop," Major Ramsey said darkly.

"Can we change the meeting time?" I asked. "You could send an encoded message."

"Not without arousing suspicion."

"I'll go and look for Simpson," Rafe said.

"We don't have time. We don't even know where she may be sheltering," Major Ramsey said. "Think, Beaumont, was there any hint of where they may be bringing the spies ashore?"

"They mentioned something about the usual coordinates," he said. "I assume it was the place Hal Jenkins previously made the drops of false documents, before he decided to go into business for himself and stole the plate."

Coordinates. I gasped. "The matchbook I found in Hal Jenkins's coat pocket in his room had a series of numbers scribbled inside of it. Could those be them?"

"When did you intend to tell me about that?" Major Ramsey asked, his voice just hovering on accusation.

"I forgot about it," I said.

"Give me the matchbook," he snapped.

"I don't have it, but I remember the numbers." I recited them aloud.

Rafe looked at the major. "Those are coordinates, all right."

Major Ramsey looked at me. "You're fairly certain of the numbers?"

I nodded. I had a mind for numbers. It came with safecracking.

The two men looked at each other and then, as one, moved back inside the cottage. I followed with a sigh.

The major was spreading a map on the table as I entered, and the two of them made some calculations that they had no doubt learned in the military.

"Here," Rafe said, pointing to a spot on the map near the coast. "Is there anything there?"

"It's coastline," the major said.

I looked at the spot on the map. "We're here, correct?" I said, pointing to a place a little way off.

Major Ramsey nodded.

"Then I know what that spot is. There are some old smuggler's caves there. Sheridan Hall mentioned them to me."

"The caves would be an ideal place for spies to make a landing," Rafe said. "Secluded and out of sight from anyone watching along the coast."

"And the bombing tonight is the ideal distraction for them to come ashore," the major added.

"Then we'll be able to pull it off," I said. "With any luck, we can deliver the identity cards to the spies and turn over the plate, and they won't know we're onto them."

"As to that, there's just a bit of a complication," Rafe said.

I heard the major let out a short breath of annoyance. "What is it?"

"The Germans know Hal Jenkins was eliminated by his confederate, Nessa Simpson. They're expecting a woman."

I knew as soon as he said it what it meant, and I didn't hesitate.

"All right. Then I'll deliver it."

"Absolutely not," Major Ramsey said, as predictable as clockwork.

"You heard what Rafe said. They're expecting a woman."

"I don't care."

"Major, you've got to listen to reason. I'm the only one who can do this. With any luck, none of them will have met Nessa Simpson in person. They were dealing with Hal before she killed him. Besides, it'll be dark. I can pull this off."

"You will not be going there alone," he said. "And that is my final word on the matter."

"Of all the . . ."

"He's right," Rafe put in. "It's too dangerous."

I might have known they would gang up on me. That's usually the way it went. Whenever things came down to brass tacks, the men decided I had to be protected. I resisted the urge to stamp my foot in frustration.

I turned on Rafe. "Why don't you mind your own business?"

He was unruffled by my ire. "I simply point out that the matter is too dangerous for a civilian to attempt alone. We're trying to protect you."

The protecting bit again. I wanted to scream.

"Oh, is that what you're trying to do?" I asked. "I would have thought you would have avoided pushing me in front of lorries and giving me dangerous drugs without my knowledge, then."

"The drugs weren't dangerous," he protested.

I ignored him and turned to Major Ramsey. "And as for you, you brought me into this to do a job. So let me do it. I told you: I don't need to be protected."

His eyes met mine, and there was something unsaid in his gaze. "I understand your point of view, Miss McDonnell," he said. "But the point stands. You're not trained for this sort of mission, and I can't allow you to do it alone."

"Would you let me do it if I were a man?" I demanded.

"You are clearly not a man, Miss McDonnell."

"I should say not," Beaumont murmured, and Major Ramsey shot him a look that could have frozen water. Rafe smiled.

"Thankfully not," I said. "Because, as previously mentioned, *they're expecting a woman.*"

His eyes met mine, but it was Rafe to whom he spoke. "Give us a minute, Beaumont."

With one last look between us, Rafe went out and closed the door behind him.

I decided to beat Major Ramsey to the punch. "You cannot make this personal," I said in a low voice, in case Rafe was listening. "You know as well as I do that we can't afford it."

"I can't guarantee your safety in this, and I did not bring you to Sunderland to take these kinds of risks."

I stepped a bit closer. "I know the risks. And it's my decision to take them. You have to let me do this."

He looked into my eyes, and I felt that prickle of awareness move through me again. He wanted to kiss me, and I wanted him to. But it wasn't going to happen. And so we both just stood there, wishing we could do more.

Finally, the major tensed his jaw.

"Beaumont!"

Rafe opened the door. I saw the speculation as his gaze moved between us, but he said nothing except, "Well?"

There was a brief moment of silence, and then Major Ramsey answered. "Miss McDonnell is going to make the delivery."

It would be a lie to say I wasn't a bit nervous about walking into the lion's den. I'd done plenty of dangerous jobs before this, but I'd done them under cover of darkness and with my family around me. This was something else altogether.

I tried not to think too much about it as I hurried in the direction of the caves, the plate and identity cards tucked into my pocket. It was something that had to be done, that was all. With any luck, I would hand over the plate, receive the compensation Nessa Simpson had anticipated, and be on my way.

Of course, I knew things were rarely as simple as we hoped. There was always the chance that the counterfeiters would be willing to rid themselves of Nessa as well.

That was why Major Ramsey had insisted on following me. He had taken another route to the caves and would be there in case of trouble.

After some discussion, Rafe Beaumont had decided to return to Sunderland and find Nessa Simpson. There was the possibility she would come to the caves to explain why she had failed to get the plate back, but, if so, the major would intercept her. And I rather expected she would not want to show her face when she had failed in her mission.

There were still the distant roar of plane engines and the flash and crash of the bombs over Sunderland, and I hoped that Rafe Beaumont would make it through in one piece. I had mixed feelings about the man after what he had done to me, but I didn't want any harm to come to him.

I slowed my pace as I got closer to the caves. I wasn't worried about being overheard with the crashing of the waves and the wind blowing. However, I didn't want to be seen before I saw who was there.

I slid down the sandy dune and made my way along the dark beach toward the mouth of the cave. I could see nothing inside. If the counterfeiter was indeed inside, they were not using a light.

Moving silently to the entrance, I slid inside, pressing myself against the wall in case anyone decided to shoot first and ask questions later. The tide was coming in, and waves washed into the mouth of the cave. There was a pit near the entrance, water falling into it, and I skirted it carefully.

"Hello?" I whispered.

Then suddenly someone caught me roughly by the arm and pulled me toward him, shining his torch into my face.

"I have what you're looking for," I said, trying to sound irritated rather than alarmed.

The man said nothing but led me deeper into the cave.

He was no longer shining his light into my eyes, so I could see where we were going. The cave wasn't extremely deep, and I could see that there were four men inside. One looked familiar, and I thought perhaps he was one of the men who had been guarding the printer the night the major and I had broken in.

Three other men were standing around a rowboat. The German spies.

My heart rate increased.

"I have your identity cards, gentlemen," I said, my voice steady.

One of the spies stepped forward. He was of average height, with a pleasant but nondescript face. When he spoke, he sounded as British as I did. "Thank you. We were concerned you wouldn't be able to deliver."

I smiled. "Glad I could be of service."

From a shadowed corner of the cave came the voice of a fifth man I hadn't noticed. "There's only one problem. You aren't the right girl."

Well, that sent a cold chill right through me, but I'd had enough experience playing poker with cousins not to let my face slip.

"The plate and identity cards in my pocket say differently," I said.

The man holding on to my arm reached into my pocket, taking an unnecessary grab or two while he did so, and pulled the items out. He held them up.

The man in the shadows stepped forward then, and there was enough light from the torch my captor held to see his face.

It was Bevins. Sheridan Hall's valet.

"Hello, Bevins," I said, concealing my surprise.

"Good evening, madam. Or should I say 'miss.' You are, after all, unmarried, are you not?" I noticed that he was holding a gun in his hand. No doubt it was he who had shot at us as we left Vangidae.

I shrugged. "Does it matter that I'm not married?"

"Not particularly," he said. "What matters is that you are not Nessa Simpson."

"I'm working with Nessa," I said.

He shook his head. "Nessa was working with Hal Jenkins. We were, however, able to persuade her to see our point of view, and she eliminated him."

"Yes, but she couldn't find the plates," I said. "So she asked me to help."

Bevins smiled coldly. "I admire your fortitude, miss, but I know that is not the case . . ."

I heard movement at the front of the cave, and one of the German spies pulled a gun from his pocket and moved forward.

A moment later, I was both relieved and vexed to see Major Ramsey standing at the entrance. I had hoped he would stay out of sight, but I couldn't help but be glad to see him. It was nice not to be alone here.

Now only one question remained: Could we brazen this out?

Major Ramsey and the spy began conversing in German, and I turned back to Bevins, putting the pieces together. "You were taking care of Pavonine Press for Mr. Hall while it's shut down, and you realized it could be lucrative for you."

"No sense in wasting resources," he replied.

"And Mr. Hall has been none the wiser."

Another cool smile. "You have seen, I think, that Mr. Hall is rather preoccupied with his interests."

"But then Hal Jenkins stole the plate and shut down operations."

"It was most inconvenient. He sent word that he would return the plate, for a fee. Fortunately, he was acquainted with Nessa Simpson, an associate of ours. She passed him a note, letting him know that we were aware of his treachery. She hoped, I think, to bring him around, but he remained determined to work against us. And so she was willing to eliminate him. They met at the pub one last time, ostensibly to talk things over, and she put the cyanide in his drink." No doubt Hal had realized what was happening to him as he neared the rooming house and had clutched the note to point to his killer.

"And what about Carlotta Hogan?" I asked.

"She began asking too many questions. Unfortunately, Nessa Simpson had a lapse in judgment and provided Ronald Potter with a counterfeit identity card when he misplaced his own. I believe he mentioned it to Miss Hogan. She was cleverer than she appeared. It became clear that we could not take the chance of her revealing what she knew."

"And so Nessa poisoned her, too."

He gave a little nod. "A quick injection when she wasn't looking, I believe. Miss Simpson seems quite adept at administering cyanide without being detected."

I felt sick to my stomach at the thought of Nessa poisoning

her friends, subjecting them to gruesome deaths to further her aims, but I didn't let my distaste show on my face.

The major and the spy came farther into the cave. So far so good.

The major wasn't looking at me. No doubt he wanted to appear indifferent to me, but I wished he would at least glance my way, send me some sort of signal.

"Ah. Captain Grey. So good of you to join us, sir," Bevins said.

"As I was explaining to your friend here, Elizabeth and I are sympathetic to your cause."

Bevins shook his head. "I thank you for retrieving the plates. You have done a great service to us, but now . . ."

He raised his gun.

"Get down, Electra," Ramsey ordered, drawing his own gun, and I wrenched myself free from my captor's grasp and threw myself to the floor of the cave as the air exploded around me.

CHAPTER TWENTY-SIX

Several shots rang out loudly in the cavernous space, echoing in my ears, and the air filled with smoke.

The man who had been holding me fell to the ground beside me, the torch rolling across the ground, light skittering wildly over the rocky interior of the cave. I turned to scramble toward the entrance, toward the major, and it was as I looked in his direction that I saw him stagger backward as the force of a bullet hit him.

"Major!" Without thinking, I rose to a crouch and rushed toward him. Then I saw another bullet strike him, a dark red stain spreading across the front of his uniform.

With a horrified cry, I lunged in his direction, but I was suddenly grabbed from behind by my hair and jerked backward. Then an arm clamped around me. I struggled violently, but whoever held me was much too strong.

The smoke began to clear, and I saw that one of the German spies and the man who had held me both lay unmoving on the ground.

My eyes were still on Ramsey. I thought I could see the slow rise and fall of his chest, but I didn't know if it was wishful thinking.

What if he was dead? I didn't want to think about that. I couldn't think about it now. I had to keep a cool head and try to find a way out of this situation. He would expect it of me.

Bevins and the guard emerged then from behind a small rocky outcropping. They'd avoided injury, it seemed. The guard stooped to pick up the plate that lay on the ground and handed it to Bevins.

"I have what I've come for," Bevins said to the spies. "And you have your identity cards. Our transaction is complete."

"What do we do with her?" one of the spies asked.

"Whatever you like," Bevins replied. Then he walked past me, past Ramsey's unmoving form, and disappeared from the cave.

The guard moved along behind him. When he reached the major, he paused. His gun was still in his hand, and, as casually as flipping a switch, he fired another bullet into Ramsey.

I screamed and struggled, and the man holding me grabbed a handful of my hair again, jerking my head back so that I couldn't move. Hot tears ran down my face, and my entire body felt numb. My mind was numb, too, but I forced myself to try to stay alert. *Focus, Ellie girl. Don't give up.* That's what Uncle Mick would say. I had to try to survive this, for him. For my family. I could not die here.

The spies were conferring heatedly in German, but I could tell they were talking about me from the way my captor jerked me every so often. They were trying to decide if they should shoot me, too, I supposed. Or worse.

Finally, one of them went to the boat and removed a length of rope. He came to me and roughly jerked my hands behind my back and secured them. Then the two of them led me toward the pit that I had noticed toward the mouth of the cave. Did they mean to throw me down?

They pulled me toward the edge, and I struggled mightily, but it was no good. There were two of them, and my hands were still tied behind my back.

We got to the edge of the pit, and I was relieved to see that it wasn't as deep as I had feared. What wasn't a relief, however, was the sight of water from the rising tide washing into it.

They looked into the pit and conferred a bit more in German.

Then one of my captors dropped in, and the other shoved me down toward him. The water at the bottom was icy cold and halfway to my knees. It was dark in the cave and even darker in the pit, but I saw then that there were metal rings bored into the wall of the pit, and from them hung a length of rusted chain. This had no doubt been used by smugglers or other brigands in centuries past for some nefarious purpose.

"We'd rather not shoot a woman," the man in the pit with me explained, as though this was a point in his favor.

"I'll drown," I said.

He shrugged.

Another of the spies tossed something down to him, and I heard the click as he secured a padlock to the ancient chain.

Then he climbed out and left me. I heard them talking a bit more and then the sound of receding footsteps. Then silence.

"Ramsey?" I called after a moment. "Ramsey, can you hear me?"

There was no answer.

A wave washed over the side of the pit, soaking me with frigid water, and I gasped. The pool around my calves grew deeper.

For just a moment, I fought down a rush of panic. *Breathe, Ellie,* I told myself. *Breathe and focus.*

It's no good losing your head when you need it the most. That was something Uncle Mick had always told me.

And so I tried to think. The chains weren't exactly up to modern prison standards, and I thought perhaps I could reach one of the pins in my hair if I twisted my head back far enough.

I leaned my head back and brought my arm up as far as I could. There was wrenching pain, but I ignored it. I could work out sore muscles later.

I had just pulled the pin from my hair when a wave crashed over the edge, followed swiftly by a second, and I lost my hold on the pin. It was swept from my fingers.

I cursed loudly, and it echoed in the space around me. *Sorry, Nacy.*

Then I went about trying to find another. Thankfully, it took an arsenal of pins to keep my hair in place, so I soon found another and pulled it out carefully.

Now to get to work on the padlock.

Another wave crashed in, and the water in the little pit was now above my knees. It was coming in faster than I expected, and I was not entirely sure how deep the pit would fill. I was going to have to hurry.

With numb fingers, I did my best to flatten the pin to make a pick of it. These old locks were sturdy, but they weren't exceptionally complex. If I could find the right angle, I thought I just might be able to get it to give.

It took me a few minutes to get the pin fitted in right. My hands were tied with rope beneath the chains, and between the pressure of the rope and the temperature of the water, I could barely feel my fingers.

By this time the water was up to my waist. It was a diabolical way to kill someone, letting them drown in a pit like this. They could have just shot me and been done with it. I was glad, of course, that they hadn't.

It was going to be their undoing.

I redoubled my efforts, pushing the edge of the pin against the pressure point inside the old lock. If it wasn't too rusted to lock, I hoped it wouldn't be too rusted to open.

The water was up to my chest now, cold and salty as it

splashed against my face. My body was shaking with the cold, and I tried to keep a tight hold on the pin in violently trembling hands.

I mustered all my focus as Uncle Mick had taught me. I blocked out the icy water splashing over the edge of the pit and the gritty wash of the sand against my skin. I blocked out my fear that Major Ramsey was dead. There was only the lock and the pin.

Finally, it gave.

I let out a little cry of triumph just as another wave crashed over the edge of the pit, and I sputtered water as I shook free of the chains.

Now the rope. That posed less of a problem, as there were several sharp rocks jutting out from the wall of the pit. I turned my back to one and began to rub the rope hard against it. It was an exhausting effort, but fear and fury gave me strength, and it was only a few moments before I felt the snap of the rope threads. I was free.

The pit wasn't deep, so I thought I could manage to climb out all right. I hadn't counted on the slippery surface of the rocks, however, and it took several attempts to pull my numb and shaking body over the edge.

I looked out at the cave entrance, making sure that there wasn't any sign of the Germans. It didn't appear they had left anyone to guard us. After all, why would they? They'd intended to let us die. They could come back and throw our bodies in the sea later.

Bodies. The word carved a cold gash in my middle. I wanted to lie on the edge of the pit for a moment and catch my breath, but there wasn't time for that. I could see the still form of the major a bit farther into the cave. Was he dead? What would I do if he was?

My entire body was numb, and not just from the cold against my wet clothes, as I moved slowly toward him. I knew I should hurry to his side, but I was afraid of what I would find.

When I got closer, however, I could see that he was no longer in the same place they had left him. A trail of blood on the stone floor of the cave showed he had moved a few feet before collapsing onto his back. He had been dragging himself toward the pit.

I knelt beside him. His uniform jacket was soaked with blood, but I saw it move ever so slightly. He was still alive!

"Gabriel?" I choked out, reaching to touch his face. His skin was cold.

His eyes fluttered open.

"You . . . all right?" His voice was rough, but it sounded like angels singing to me.

"Never mind me, how bad is it?" I asked, knowing already that it was very bad indeed.

"Certainly . . . not good." His breathing was ragged, and I clenched my teeth against a wave of panic-induced dizziness.

"Let's get your shirt off," I said. My voice was shaking, but I couldn't stop it.

"Knife . . ." he rasped.

I remembered the knife in his boot. I pulled it out and set to work cutting his jacket and shirt away. Both were thick with blood, and my hands were slick with it.

"We'll get this bleeding stopped," I said in as calm a voice as I could manage. I wondered how much blood he could possibly have left.

"Get . . . Beaumont," he said.

"We'll tend to you first."

He didn't argue. I pulled back the bloody shirt and just barely managed to keep from gasping in dismay. There were four holes in him that I could see. Two in the left shoulder, one in the right side of his chest, and another in his right side.

The shoulder wounds seemed to be clotting, but the one in his chest was still welling with blood, and the wound in his side was bleeding freely. Not knowing what else to do, I pulled my jumper over my head and cut it in half. Balling one part of it up, I pressed it against the wound in his side. Then I tied a knot in the two sides of his shredded shirt to hold it in place and pulled it tight. He gave a grunt of pain, but he seemed to be slipping out of consciousness.

"Gabriel, stay awake," I commanded. "Do you hear me? Stay awake."

I quickly did my best to stanch the wound in his chest, too, and then I looked up into his face. He was watching me through half-open eyes. They were cloudy with pain and probably shock at all the blood he had lost. His face had gone gray.

"Electra . . ." he murmured.

"I'm going for help," I told him, though the thought of leaving him made me sick. For the first time I allowed myself to admit the possibility that he might die here alone.

"Try . . . try to stay awake," I said, touching his face and leaving streaks of his own blood there.

"Hurry," he whispered.

I nodded, unable to speak. There was so much I wanted to say, but there wasn't time. And so I leaned down and brushed a kiss across his cold lips.

Then I turned and ran from the cave as fast as I could.

I scrambled up the bluff and ran in the direction of the cottage. I only hoped that I could get there in time.

Suddenly, I saw the light of a torch. I dropped to the ground, wondering if it was the Germans. Surely not. Surely things could not end this way.

But then I saw the figure hurrying in my direction, and my body sagged in relief. It was Rafe Beaumont.

Help had arrived.

CHAPTER TWENTY-SEVEN

The night passed in a blur, like something from a nightmare.

Rafe had been unsuccessful in reaching Sunderland and had returned to back us up. He'd heard the shots and had decided to investigate, he said. I'd led him back to the cave, where he'd done his best to tend to the major, and I'd run back to the cottage to get the car.

After driving the major's car at reckless speeds across rugged terrain, I'd reached the bluff. Between the two of us, we'd managed to get him into the car and back to Sunderland.

The city was chaos after the bombings, but one look at the major's unconscious form and the doctors had rushed him into surgery. I had wanted to stay and wait for word on his condition, but the hospital was overcrowded, more civilians injured in the bombing coming in every minute, and Rafe had convinced me we'd only be in the way. Reluctantly, I'd agreed to go and return in the morning.

Rafe drove me back to the cottage, where I'd washed the major's blood away with shaking hands and changed into fresh clothes.

"You should try to get some sleep," he said.

But I knew I wouldn't be able to sleep. Not now. Not until I heard how the major was.

"Did you find Nessa Simpson?" I asked.

"No. I couldn't find her, so I came back, and that's when I heard the gunshots."

A few hours later, we received word. The major had survived the surgery. Miraculously, nothing vital had been injured, but the blood loss had been severe, and the doctors had said that it had been a very close thing.

I felt weak with relief.

Overwhelmed with all that had happened, I had fallen into a deep sleep for several hours.

Rafe called the hospital in the morning and was informed I'd be able to visit at ten o'clock. In the meantime, there were a few other loose ends to tie up.

I went first to Mrs. James's lodging house and was relieved to see it had been spared in the bombing. I quickly packed the rest of my things and found Mrs. James to settle my account.

"It was nice having you, dear. I wish you well, wherever you're off to next," she said in that vague way landladies have of saying goodbye to the people who briefly lived within their walls.

Then I went to say goodbye to Samira and Laila.

I knocked on the back door, and it was opened by Sami, her face a mask of grief.

"Sami, what is it?" I asked, alarmed. Their house seemed to have escaped damage, but I knew at once something terrible had happened.

"Nessa is dead," she whispered, fresh tears streaking down her face.

I gasped, though, somehow, I felt I shouldn't be surprised.

"Come inside," Laila said from behind her sister, and we all went into the parlor, where Laila and I had shared tea and light conversation only days ago. It was another grim reminder of how quickly things changed in wartime.

"What happened?" I asked when we were all seated.

"It's dreadful," Sami said, pressing her lips tightly together.

Laila took up the story, her face pale but composed. "Apparently, a window exploded, and a shard of glass managed to somehow slice her throat. Nothing else in the house was damaged, just the window when she happened to be near it. Such a horrible accident."

"Yes," I agreed, though I wondered. Had it been the explosion, a piece of glass, or had that been the work of the charming, affable Rafe Beaumont? I wasn't sure I wanted to know.

"So many of my friends gone, in just this week," Sami whispered. "I almost can't believe it."

"What happened to Carlotta?" I asked, wondering what story they had been told.

"It seems she took the wrong sort of medicine by mistake," Sami said. "Something mixed up at the chemist . . ."

"You two were close, weren't you?" I asked. I met her gaze, letting her know that I knew there was more she still hadn't told me.

She hesitated, opened her mouth to speak, and then shut it again. She looked over at Laila, and her sister nodded.

"Carlotta and I were . . . well, we'd been stealing supplies from the chemist and selling them to local organizations in need. Orphanages, mental institutions, the home for soldiers of the Great War. Things are difficult to get in wartime, and we had access."

"A black-market operation, you mean," I said.

Sami flushed. "It wasn't like that. We were trying to help. And we didn't take much, just things that we thought could be spared. We used to exchange the things in crowded places, like the pub or The Gale. The bottles are small, so it's easy enough to do. The man you saw at my door that morning was one of our . . . customers, so to speak. He was angry that I hadn't got the supplies he asked for, but with Hal dead and suspicions high, we had to be careful. And you were asking questions."

"I thought there was something strange going on," I admitted.

"I warned her against it," Laila said. "It was not the right thing to do, but her heart was in the right place."

"You won't tell anyone?" Sami asked me.

"No," I said. "I won't tell."

I looked from her to Laila as they sat with their hands clasped. "I'm glad you have each other. Family is so important in times like these."

"What about you?" Laila asked. "Are you all right?"

"Yes," I said. "I'm fine." Though I wasn't, not really. I had a feeling the impact of these events would be long lasting.

It was strange how there was so much going on that most people would never know. Regular citizens, fighting for their lives in all the little ways wars force upon them, would never know that the major and I had encountered spies in a cave on the beaches of Sunderland. That our efforts would probably save lives. That we had nearly lost our own.

And that was the way it had to be. The work I was used to had always been secret. But because we were protecting ourselves, not because we were protecting others. This was a new sort of secrecy, a kind that felt satisfying deep down in my bones.

"I suppose I'd better go," I said. "But I've brought something for you."

I reached into my bag and pulled out the book I had taken from Sheridan Hall's safe, holding it out to Laila. I didn't suppose he would notice it had gone missing. And, really, it rightfully belonged to the Maddox girls.

Laila took it and looked down at it for a long moment, then she looked up at me. "Where did you get this?"

"Hal Jenkins meant to get it to you," I said.

She looked down at the book again, her eyes glittering. "I knew he acquired things for his former employer, and I had paid him to get it for me. I thought . . . I thought he had simply taken my money."

"He misplaced the book for a while, I believe. But I found it."

"What is it?" Sami asked.

"It's a book of birds illustrated by Mother," Laila said. Her voice was tight, and I could see that she was having a hard time suppressing her tears.

She and Sami flipped through several of the pages.

"It's beautiful," Sami whispered, reaching out to touch one of the illustrations. "She was marvelous."

Laila looked up at me. "Thank you, Liz."

"I'm glad I could help. As I said, family is important."

She nodded, her eyes on mine. "We all must find a way to incorporate the legacy of the past into our present."

The words touched me. She was right. I could not change my past. I couldn't change what had happened to my mother. But I could find out the truth and bring that truth with me into the future.

"You'll write to me?" Sami asked.

"Yes," I agreed. I wished I could tell her my real name and that I'd had no dead aunt. That I was a locksmith who had gotten involved with the government. But my secrets were the cost of what we were doing, and I would have to accept it. And so, for years to come, I would write letters to Sami Maddox and sign them "Liz."

I allowed Rafe Beaumont to give me a ride to the hospital. I had forgiven him, for the most part, for drugging me. After all, he had been instrumental in saving Major Ramsey's life, and he had been a shoulder to lean on in those grim hours while we waited for news on whether the major would survive. All the same, I was wary of him, especially given Nessa's convenient death. I thought there was probably something ruthless hidden behind that handsome face, and I would never be as comfortable with him as I had once been.

Apparently, he didn't feel the same way.

"I'd like to see you in London," he told me as we drove. "But I don't think Ramsey would approve."

"No, I don't suppose he would. I'm sure he would say that it's a breach of protocol since you and I work together." Besides, I didn't want to see Rafe Beaumont socially, not when I wouldn't feel safe accepting a drink from him.

Rafe glanced at me. "That's not what I meant."

"No?"

He gave me a knowing smile. "It's a secret, then. All right. My lips are sealed."

"What are you talking about?" I knew, of course, what he was getting at, but I didn't intend to acknowledge it if I didn't have to.

"You and Ramsey. I've known that all along. You'll pardon the expression, but I was told 'hands off' from the beginning in no uncertain terms."

"There is no 'me and Ramsey,'" I said firmly.

He looked at me again. "You're serious, aren't you?"

"Of course, I am."

"So it's one-sided on his part."

It seemed he was going to press the issue. Well, I didn't want to have this conversation. I needed to find a way to put an end to it.

"Major Ramsey's feelings for me are strictly professional," I said. It wasn't entirely true, but it was the way things were going to be from now on, so it was true enough.

"You're wrong about that. When he found out I'd drugged you, he nearly tore my head off. I think he would have happily shot me if he could have gotten away with it."

I smiled. "He does have a bit of a temper."

"It's none of my business, of course," Rafe said, his eyes on the road. "But Ramsey is a good chap if you're looking for one."

"I'm not his sort of woman," I said.

He laughed. "You're smart, you're spirited, and you're beautiful. You're exactly his type of woman."

Despite myself, I flushed a bit at the compliment. "You're too kind, Captain," I said stiffly.

"Fine. I'll mind my own business. I know when I'm intruding, but you should know that he does care. I've never seen him so angry as he was about my endangering you—and I've seen him very angry."

"Thank you, Captain," I said. "I'll keep that in mind."

He said nothing else about it as we neared the hospital.

He'd judged things correctly, of course. There had been something simmering between the major and me. We'd stirred up feelings that would probably be hard to put to rest. And those moments when I'd thought him dead or dying had roused emotions that I was still grappling with. All the same, I knew that we had to let it settle somehow. Everything that had happened here in Sunderland would have to fade into the past when we returned to London.

Rafe hung back in the waiting room, letting me have a private word with the major first, which I appreciated.

Major Ramsey was lying in a hospital bed, one arm in a sling. I was so used to seeing him hale and hearty that it was a jolt to see him pale with dark circles around his eyes.

"So you are human, after all," I said from the doorway, affecting a light tone. "Put holes in you and you bleed just like any other man."

He looked up when he saw me, his mouth tipping up slightly at the corners. "Miss McDonnell. You'll excuse me for not getting up."

I gave a little laugh as I walked to his bedside. He would be formal to the death.

"How are you feeling?" I asked, though it was clear he was still in pain.

"Not bad, all things considered."

He felt wretched, but he would be the last one to admit it.

I hesitated, unsure of what to say next. I had come to say goodbye. I'd wanted to stay in Sunderland to look after him, but I'd had a telephone call from the ever-efficient Constance. She had told me orders were that I return home. When I'd tried to argue, she'd explained that the major was being transported to the military hospital later in the day and then back to London himself when he was well enough to be moved. So that was that.

But I hadn't been able to leave without seeing him.

"I . . . I came to check up on you," I said. "I'm going back to London this afternoon. Unless . . ."

I wasn't sure what I expected him to say. We'd had this conversation already, and I didn't think what we had experienced together had changed it in any significant way, at least not on his part.

"Yes," he said. "You'll be safer at home. Are you traveling alone?"

I looked up at him. "No . . . Felix is coming up to bring me back to London," I admitted. Felix was arriving on an afternoon train. When I'd called Nacy and Uncle Mick to let them know I was coming back, Felix had been there and had insisted on coming up to escort me home.

"Good," Major Ramsey said.

I looked into his twilight-blue eyes, trying to tell what he was thinking. Whatever it was, it was concealed behind that impenetrable shield he kept up, with the added haze of pain and morphine.

He held out his uninjured hand, and I stepped forward to

take it. His fingers were warm around my cold ones. "Thank you for saving my life, Electra."

"You saved my life, too," I said softly. "I suppose that makes us even."

Again, the faintest smile. "Take care of yourself."

"Will . . . will I see you back in London?" I asked. I hated the uncertainty in my voice, but I had to know.

He looked down at my hand, rubbing his thumb across my knuckles, and then he looked back up at me, his expression impassive. "If another job arises."

I blinked, nodded. That was clear enough.

He squeezed my hand and then released it.

"Take care, Major," I said softly. Then I turned and left.

We found the house on a small side street in Lincolnshire.

Felix and I had taken a detour on the way back to London, stopping to visit Clarice Maynard.

Initially, I was torn over whether I wanted him to accompany me, but, while there were some parts of this that I had wanted to do alone, Felix had supported me since the beginning on this journey to learn about my mother, and it felt right that he should come with me now.

Our reunion had been a happy one. I was always glad to see Felix, always felt a sense of comfort and reassurance when he was by my side. I couldn't help but feel something in our relationship had shifted, however. Though I knew Major Ramsey had no intention of pursuing a romantic relationship with me, I could no longer deny that there were feelings there that would need to be dealt with before I could form any sort of lasting attachment to Felix. I wasn't exactly sure how I would resolve these emotions, but I reminded myself of Uncle Mick's old adage: *You needn't solve all the problems of the world in a single day. One at a time is sufficient.*

And the visit to Mrs. Maynard had priority.

"It's all rather mysterious, isn't it?" Felix said when I showed him her letter. "Sounds like something from a melodrama."

"Yes," I agreed. "I don't know whether to put any stock in it."

"Well, it certainly can't hurt to hear what she has to say."

We were shown into a small, dark parlor by a silent maid. A fire was burning, making the room overly warm, and the curtains were drawn against outside light.

I took a seat on the velvet sofa, and Felix chose a chair nearby. I looked over at him as we waited, and he smiled reassuringly.

Clarice Maynard came into the room a moment later, and we rose from our seats.

She stopped in the doorway with a gasp, a hand to her chest. "Forgive me, dear," she said after a moment. "But you look just like her."

Clarice Maynard was tall and thin, and her dark hair had gone mostly gray. But her face was smooth and unlined, and her pale blue eyes were bright as she looked at me.

"It's nice to meet you, Mrs. Maynard," I said. "This is my friend Felix Lacey. He has been helping me learn about my mother."

She nodded. "It's nice to meet you, young man."

We all sat, and Mrs. Maynard took another long look at me. "It's like seeing her all over again," she muttered.

"Thank you."

"You said in your letter that you wanted to know more about your mother," she said. "What do you want to know?"

Where to start? There were so many things I wanted to know, so many things only this woman, my mother's closest friend, might be able to tell me. But there was one thing above all that had started me on this journey, and that was where I would begin.

"I . . . I have reason to believe she was innocent," I said. "I'm trying to prove it."

She looked at me, and it was difficult to tell what the emotion was that played across her face.

I glanced at Felix. Mrs. Maynard was acting so strangely. What was it that she felt she had to hide, after all these years?

"Are you sure you want to open this door, dear?" Mrs. Maynard asked me. "Sometimes, it's best to let the past lie."

"I need to know," I said simply.

She studied me for a long moment, and then she nodded. There was something like resignation on her face.

"Your mother was innocent," she said. "And she had her suspicions about who killed your father, though she wouldn't give me a name."

I felt a rush of disappointment. I had been hoping that if Clarice Maynard knew anything, it might be the identity of the person who had really caused my father's death.

"What did she tell you?" I asked.

"She told me your father was killed because of what he was involved in."

I frowned. "You mean, something related to safecracking?" My father and Uncle Mick had worked together as safecrackers before my father's death. But surely Uncle Mick would have known if that had contributed in some way to my father's murder. And, if he had, he wouldn't have let my mother be convicted for it.

"No, dear," she said. "Not that."

She looked at me, her face very grave. Though we were alone in her parlor, the curtains drawn, she leaned closer as though she might be overheard.

What she said next was the last thing I expected.

"During the last war, your father was spying for the Germans."

ACKNOWLEDGMENTS

At the close of every novel, I'm reminded how thankful I am for the help and support of so many wonderful people.

My deepest thanks to Ann Collette, my agent and friend; Catherine Richards, editor extraordinaire; the fabulous Nettie Finn; and the fantastic team at Minotaur. This book quite literally would not exist without you, so it is impossible to overstate how grateful I am for all you do!

All my love and gratitude to my family, the greatest people I know. I'm a lucky woman to belong to such a marvelous group.

I must give a shout-out to the members of Book Club 2.0 (name still TBA)—Christian Gaudet, Amber Weidner, Clark Weidner, and Dan Weaver—for their encouragement, enthusiasm, and many, many weird conversations.

My appreciation also goes out to Amanda Caudill for hosting me and brainstorming with me on a long-awaited getaway, and, most of all, for more than two decades of steadfast friendship.

And, finally, I'm indebted to the usual suspects, my friends through thick and thin: Amanda Phillips, Courtney LeBoeuf, Ty Cedars, Angela Larson, Kallyn Lagro, Sabrina Street, Stephanie Shultz, Becky Farmer, Denise Edmondson, and Victoria Cienfuegos.

From the bottom of my heart, thank you!